THE HEYDAY OF THE INSENSITIVE BASTARDS

THE HEYDAY OF
THE INSENSITIVE
BASTARDS

ROBERT BOSWELL

Stories

Graywolf Press

This publication is made possible by funding provided in part by a grant from the Minnesota State Arts Board, through an appropriation by the Minnesota State Legislature, a grant from the National Endowment for the Arts, and private funders. Significant support has also been provided by Target; the McKnight Foundation; and other generous contributions from foundations, corporations, and individuals. To these organizations and individuals we offer our heartfelt thanks.

Published by Graywolf Press
250 Third Avenue North, Suite 600
Minneapolis, Minnesota 55401
All rights reserved.

www.graywolfpress.org

Published in the United States of America

Cloth ISBN 978-1-55597-524-1
Paper ISBN 978-1-55597-566-1

2 4 6 8 9 7 5 3 1

Library of Congress Control Number: 2010922919

Cover design: Kyle G. Hunter

Cover photograph: Eye Candy Images

*This book is dedicated to Antonya Nelson
and the next twenty-five years.*

CONTENTS

THE HEYDAY OF THE INSENSITIVE BASTARDS

NO RIVER WIDE

Both things first: Greta Steno is two places at once and walking. She is in a Chicago neighborhood in the early fall on a sidewalk made ramshackle by tree roots, and she is barefoot in Florida on a warm winter evening, the broad leaves of a banana tree swiping at her hair. She is thirty-nine and forty-two years old.

In Chicago, she wears paint-spattered clothes and walks with her husband to the house of Ellen Riley, who is her closest friend and who is about to move to Florida. In Florida, she is in a tight black dress and walks beside Ellen, whose last name is no longer Riley, and they are on their way to a party. In Chicago, the late-morning air still conjures the façade of summer, and Greta's husband stumbles on the ragged sidewalk, falling to his knees. In Florida, Greta and Ellen drink scotch from transparent disposable cups, the winter dusk as warm as spring, Greta's husband two years in the ground.

"A good thing we're wearing our nasties," her husband says, examining the tear in the knee of his slacks. Duncan is slow finding his feet. The weight of middle age has settled in his trunk and limbs. He's been awkward lately, wooden in his expressions. He'd been a lanky boy in a rock band when Greta met him in college. Now their son has the gangly build, while Duncan's body has become thick and ponderous. Their daughter, thankfully, looks like Greta.

"It feels like they're doing this to *us*," he says, getting up. "I know that's silly." He's talking about the move. Ellen's husband, Theo, has accepted a transfer. He has gone to Florida this weekend to look for a house.

At the intersection, they can see the top of the great white oak, a landmark tree in a Chicago burg known for its trees. Ellen and Theo's house was built in the 1920s, and the architect designed a notch in one corner to accommodate the oak, which even then was enormous. Today, its upper limbs tremble, and though neither Greta nor Duncan mentions it, they understand the destruction has begun.

In Florida, Greta talks about Duncan's quick decline and death. Either she's drunk or acting drunk to hold Ellen's attention. Ellen's neighborhood is the kind of leafy habitat that encourages intoxication—tropical trees leaking oxygen like bad tires, houses rising out of the green abundance like pastel mushrooms. The banana tree that flounces its wide leaves over the sidewalk forces Greta to step to the curb. In one hand she holds her shoes—black mules with outrageous heels—and in the other, her plastic cup of scotch.

"I got through it," Greta is saying. She thinks perhaps she has gone on too long. "The kids got through it."

They're not young women, Greta and Ellen, and neither are they old, beyond the childbearing pale but clinging bravely to the sheen of ripe sexuality. Ellen has changed her appearance since moving to Florida. Except for her long midwestern gait, everything about her has changed. She's severely tan and so thin as to teeter on that precipice of chic that overlooks serious illness. Her short hair stands in pointy reptilian barbs and is the blond of taco chips. She doesn't look her age. She doesn't look any age.

Greta's appearance has changed less. A wardrobe update and a smart new do that snakes about her head. She has dyed her hair but only a lighter shade of the same brown. She's prettier than Ellen, something that's always been a factor in their friendship. Now that they're single, it plays a larger part: it is her job tonight to get a specific man to Ellen's house.

Would she do such a thing for anyone but Ellen? She can't quite believe she's doing it at all, but Ellen wants them to be conspirators again, as they'd once been when they had to wedge their husbands from the golf course or convince the children to visit a museum. They're substituting men—single, sexual males—for their families, but their roles are the same: conspirators, intimates, sisters. Greta is willing to do anything to get past this awkwardness. She mentions again the class she took.

"The Greeks put friendship ahead of romantic love. They thought it a worthier topic." She wants them to talk as they used to, and she's pressing. "Whatever happened to those guys? When was the last time somebody brought up Plato or Sophocles?"

"There's a rapper in Miami who calls himself Euripides," Ellen replies. "He spells it with a capital U. U-Rippa-Deese."

"You can't possibly listen to rap."

"You're reading the Greeks, of all things. Why can't I listen to rap?"

"I took a class."

It was actually Duncan who signed up for the course. Greta was there to operate the wheelchair and tape recorder. He hadn't finished the semester, which meant she'd had to quit, too. But she has kept the tapes.

"I only read an article about that singer," Ellen confesses.

It's finally dark, but a weightless sort of dark, as if they're walking in the shadow of a transparency. Their destination is a house with a huge picture window. The room is brightly lit and people skulk about in the light, drinking and displaying their clothes. A flagstone path warms Greta's feet, even though the sun has set and it's supposed to be winter. Her feet like Florida. The remainder of her has qualms. Nothing about the landscape seems consequential: anorectic palm trees, golf carts driven on city streets, grown men in shorts and Pooh shirts. It's hard for her to imagine anyone taking the place seriously. When Ellen met her at the airport, she whisked her off to a squat pink building where they rode stationary bicycles and performed aerobics before an unrelenting wall of mirrors. The trip to the gym irked Greta and left her with sore legs. She sips the last of her scotch considering this window of well-dressed strangers.

She says, "You know all these people?"

"Put your shoes on," Ellen replies. "I have lip liner." She pats her purse. "Your mouth could use some definition."

"It's that big hole in the middle of my face," Greta says. "What more definition could it need?"

She sets the mules on the walk and steps into them. A couple of houses away, a sexy kind of fog—pleasant and billowy like a giant's gentle exhale—makes moving shapes on the lawn.

"There's the hostess." Ellen points. "She's the consummate *bitch*."

A woman in a black dress spins away from a dark little man, a velvet V cutting her backside. She crosses the room with careful strides, as if she's stepping on bodies.

"I used to love drive-in movies," Ellen goes on, indicating the window with her chin. "Hard to believe they're gone. Half the women I know lost their virginity at the drive-in."

"The kids still seem to manage," Greta says.

Unlike everything else she has seen in Florida, this show on the glass screen seems to have substance: adults dressed to the nines and drinking liquor from crystal tumblers, smoke churning from their mouths like the exhaust of internal combustion.

"People here call me Elle," Ellen says. "You don't have to."

"You changed your name?"

Ellen snatches the plastic cup from Greta's hand. "New last name, new first name." She tosses the cups in the shrubs. "She's got a gardener. We're not littering."

She doesn't knock on the door but throws it open.

The crane extends its black frame far above the great oak. Greta will not openly question Ellen's character, but secretly she wonders whether this had to happen. The destruction of the tree has about it the feeling of expedience. Ellen is practical, and old trees have root systems that burrow into sewer lines and rupture foundations. A tree specialist found a crack in the vast trunk, and the buyer withdrew his offer. The connection to the sale of the house troubles Greta. One crack hardly seems reason enough to fell this tree. The crane takes up most of the street and a good portion of the sky.

"Wait here for me," she says.

"I know what you're doing," Duncan tells her. "They wouldn't cut it down if they didn't have to."

"I just want a minute."

The young man standing at the base of the tree sees her coming. He's blond, thin, and vaguely unsettled. He's a boy who never liked school but had relied on its routine. Without it, he's at loose ends, restless and lethargic at the same time. Today he'll trim small limbs from the tree's highest branches. "Watch for snakes," his boss told him. The boy thought he was kidding. Snakes in Chicago? They were only a few blocks beyond the city's margin. "Believe it," his boss said. "They go after bird nests and they sun on the limbs." What would his boss say about this woman approaching him? *Watch out for older women.* She's decades older than he is, but she's pretty and he likes the way she dresses—old clothes that don't go together, in an interesting way. He decides he'll have sex with her, given the chance, even if it costs him his job. This thought pleases him. He has now this decision, this solid thing around which to build his adult life.

"Are you one of the tree men?" she asks.

The boy nods. He likes being called a man. He lifts a chainsaw to add to his manliness. He's had the job all of three days and he overslept this morning. He can't imagine doing something like this (*work,* he means) for the rest of his life.

"Does it really have to come down?" she asks. "I know what they're saying, but is it dangerous or is that just an excuse?"

"I don't in reality know trees." He offers an uncommitted shrug. "I'm not afraid of heights or a chainsaw. That's how I got this job."

"I'm not trying to interfere," she assures him. Her hand touches his arm, a reassuring and flirtatious pressure. "I'm just curious."

The touch makes him bold. "You don't look old enough to own a tree like this."

She smiles at him, the hand on his arm suddenly warmer. "No one is old enough to own this tree," she says. "That's my point. But I'm *plenty* old."

"A person wouldn't think so," he says. "I'm Aaron Jack. Friends call me AJ."

"I'm Greta." She starts to say more but his boss calls for him.

7

Actually he yells, *Where's that jackass kid?*

"I've got to go," AJ says. He tips the chainsaw as a gesture of farewell.

Where her hand held his arm remains warm, as if she's passed on a fever. Once he's strapped into the harness and among the high branches, he considers unbuttoning his shirt to examine the spot, see if it's swollen. He's clumsy in the harness, which is like a child's swing with a seat belt. Just lifting the chainsaw makes him twist in the air. Every time he thrusts the blade against a branch, he's pushed backward. His tools, tethered by cords to the harness, knock against his feet. Hours pass, yet he's still near the top of the tree when he spots Greta on the street. He wants to see where she goes. "A little higher," he calls to the crane operator. She turns on Roosevelt Avenue and disappears, but he feels he can track her right through the obstructing houses. He's wrong, of course, but he does find her the next block over. The house she enters has a red tile roof.

Greta, he repeats in his head. *Red tile roof.*

Over the summer, AJ went with his father to Disney World. The trip was sponsored by his father's employer in recognition of twenty years of custodial work. AJ and his father flew to Florida together. When they went to pick up the rental car, the agent asked for a credit card. His father did not have one and reminded her that the car was covered by the firm. But the agency required a damage deposit: five hundred dollars. His father counted out the cash. The hotel room was paid for, as were the passes for the amusement park, but they were left with little money for food and no money for anything else. They stuffed rolls from the complimentary breakfast into their pockets and snacked on them in Fantasyland.

A few days after they returned, a breezy afternoon when his parents were away at work, AJ came across his mother's sleeping pills and swallowed a handful. He went to the back porch and waited to die. Instead of perishing, he threw up in his father's rose bushes.

Dangling from a wire on another breezy afternoon—this one filled with the noise of the chainsaw—AJ doesn't know why he'd felt he had to die. Something about the huge heads of the cartoon figures that had walked among them at Disney World, something about the crumbs he could not get out of his pockets, the way his father nodded to the woman at the car rental as if he could dole out hundreds of dollars without thinking about it.

AJ is wondering about his feeble stab at suicide when he encounters the snake. By this time he has worked halfway down one side of the tree, clearing the branches for the more experienced men. He is aware of his fatigue, but only feels it when he sits still in his harness. The snake makes him still. The chainsaw idles in his hand. The snake is as thick as his arm. Its body doesn't wrap around the limb but curlicues over it. Its head is close to the trunk, and it twists back to stare at him. Its eyes are black and seem to be made of metal.

He has the idea that the snake knows things he doesn't, and that frightens him. Yet there are things he knows that a snake can't. Such as the purpose of a chainsaw. He revs it and takes a swipe at the snake's body. It leaps at him. It seems to fly right off the branch. Only the circulating blades of the saw keep it from reaching him. A part of the snake falls, smacking into the branches below. AJ doesn't think to yell, and the men on the ground make noises.

He is splattered with blood and doesn't know what he ought to do. On the branch, the severed half of the snake lies crookedly. The ruptured end lifts and pauses in midair, as if considering him. It screams. It seems to be screaming. He hears a scream. Then it peels off the branch and falls through the network of limbs.

Entering the party house, Greta thinks, *Now I'm one of the characters on the big screen.* She is "the wild friend from out of town." This is the role she and Ellen settled on. Greta's mother is watching her daughter for the weekend, her son is safely off to college, and Greta is a thousand miles from home—she may as well cut a wide swath.

"My friend from the old country," Ellen says, introducing her.

The Temptations flare up in the next room: "Can't Get Next to You." Hidden among the glamorous throng are a few unattached middle-aged men. One by one they make their way across the floor to Greta. These are men who have been without women too long.

Loneliness rounds their shoulders. Their shoes make swamp noises. Men without women wear ugly shoes, she has noticed. They are the opposite of the Temptations—the Repellents, the Resistibles. They're like towels too often laundered: dull and soft, transparent in places, of no use but to buff a car. Little wonder women are so often attracted to the husbands of friends.

The Supremes take over the stereo, arguing that love's a game of give and take. Greta uses it in her chat. "Aren't you sick of these oldies?" She touches the bulging shirt of the man she's talking to, the soft expansion of his gut. "Diana Ross has a sweet voice, but she isn't Sylvia Plath or Zora Hurston or, I don't know . . . *Euripides.*" She laughs. The man follows her lead—his laughter a gurgling chortle, as if he's choking. She keeps going. "Her *work* doesn't hold up to forty years of listening, do you think?"

The man's head wobbles, unable to consider the question for the feminine hand pressing against his fabric. She moves her fingers over his belly to heighten the effect. What she likes about dating as an adult is the same thing she liked as a girl: it's pleasing to have power over someone.

Ellen signals with a jerk of her head. Andrew Holzman, the man she has targeted, has emerged from the adjoining room to get a drink at a bar set up in the corner. A young woman with a ponytail— hired help, evidently—cocks an ear in his direction.

Andrew Holzman does not impress from a distance. Ordinary face, graying hair, pale eyes that might be made of ash. He's missed a loop with his belt. But his shoes are presentable. That means something, Greta supposes. He has a cast over his wrist and thumb and up to the elbow of his right arm. It's her task to invite him to Ellen's house on one pretext or another. She can provoke a group to skinny-dip in Ellen's pool. She can see if a handful want to smoke pot. Ellen simply wishes for him to visit. Nothing has to happen. The cast, she realizes, rules out a swim.

Greta met Ellen years ago at a neighborhood playground when they were both lugging small children. One invited the other to dinner, and they all—spouses and children included—hit it off. Their husbands jogged and golfed together. Their children held hands in preschool. Greta saw Ellen every day. They made excuses to go off together, to a spa, a cabin in the Upper Peninsula, even a hike in the Rockies. Greta had never had such a friend. Ellen taught her bridge, made her wear short dresses, drove her to the hospital when her daughter fell from a swing and went into convulsions. They cooked elaborate meals together—pheasant under glass, beef Wellington, souvlaki with homemade pita—and went door-to-door together, handing out pamphlets for a local candidate. From the beginning, each participated in the other's thoughts. Once, after they'd gone downtown with their husbands to see a Tennessee Williams play, Greta had tried to explain her disappointment with the production. "It's like they weren't really *acting,* just talking," she said, and only Ellen had understood her. "They performed as if their characters were merely *people,*" she'd replied. How terribly surprising and addictive it was to be understood.

Then Theo accepted a transfer and Ellen was gone. Within a year of the move Theo and Ellen's marriage fell apart. Greta followed the deterioration by phone. Theo slept with a company receptionist. Ellen had anxiety attacks. She went to bed with a man she met in a self-help class. Greta can't remember the man's name, but the class was called "How to Take Charge of Your Life."

Duncan's deterioration was going on during that same time. Greta's stories were duller. "He can't tie his shoes," she would say. "He can't button his shirt." Duncan had his own ideas about Ellen and Theo's move, but he refused to divulge them. The disease made him stubborn.

"Here she is," Ellen says, tapping the shoulder of Andrew Holzman, "the one I've told you about."

He turns as if to shake Greta's hand, but he holds a drink in the hand with the cast and a cracker smeared with cheese in the other. Greta bends down and takes a bite of the cracker. She raises her head at the same moment the girl with the ponytail passes along a drink. Liquor splashes over the front of Greta's dress.

"My fault," Greta says before the bartender can apologize.

Andrew Holzman runs a finger over the damp spot on her dress, sticks the finger in his mouth.

"My," he says. "You're delicious."

Duncan finds his wife in the study standing next to Ellen. They're staring out the window, watching the tree men. He has spent the past few hours carrying dusty boxes down a narrow attic staircase. Even though he has washed his face, it's pink from exertion. Sweat darkens his shirt. His back aches. The tear in his pants is rimmed with blood, like lipstick, and the wound bites at him with each step he takes.

The window is too close to the oak's massive trunk to provide any perspective on what the men are doing. Leaves and small branches tumble down and settle among the roots. From the attic window, Duncan was able to watch a young man—a boy, really—suspended on a swing, trimming small limbs with a chainsaw. The kid did not inspire confidence, the saw jumping and growling in his hands like a dangerous pet. Down here, the noise is not as loud but it's fierce. Like being inside a hive and hearing all the worker bees.

The room—the whole house—has an air of injury about it: furniture swathed in plastic wrap, rugs rolled and bound, bookcases gaping morosely. *I'm missing them in advance,* he thinks. Darkened spots mark the walls, as if the photos that had hung there left bruises. He has fetched bottles of beer from the refrigerator. He needs to rest, and the beer will give him an excuse later for his fatigue.

"Beverage break?" he says.

The women turn to him. "It's not even noon." Greta taps her watch. "If we start drinking now, we'll never finish."

He shrugs. "We need to empty the fridge, don't we?"

Ellen offers her hand. "We've just been admiring the butts these young men possess," she says, accepting a bottle.

"I've got one of those, too." Duncan turns to display his evidence. The divide of his slacks is marked with sweat. "I've been watching the trimming from above."

"You can't call it *trimming*." His wife takes a bottle. "It's wholesale destruction."

"That tree would have crushed us," Ellen says. "Don't forget that. We've been living quite literally in death's shadow."

"That's quite a feeling," Duncan says, "isn't it?"

"I can't help thinking about the tree itself," Greta says. "If there's a tragedy, it's that oak coming down."

"The tragedy would've been not finding out," Ellen insists. "Even if it hadn't crushed us when it fell, it would have made a mess of our lives."

"All right," Greta concedes, "but felling the tree is a tragedy, too."

"I know it is." Ellen puts her arm around Greta. "Once it's cut, I want you to come over and count the rings with me."

Greta softens immediately. "What am I going to do without you?"

The embracing women send a small erotic charge through Duncan's weary body. He is the most familiar and least celebrated of romantic heroes—the man who loves his wife.

"You finish the attic?" Greta asks him. She wants him to walk home and fetch their station wagon. "Ellen's giving us all these books," she begins, but she reads his reaction accurately. "Or I can get the car. You look pooped."

"I wouldn't mind resting."

"I'll go." Greta sets the bottle on the window ledge. "Only take a minute. The beer won't even get warm."

She vanishes. The closing door creates an echo. Duncan decides to use the time with Ellen. He has something to tell her and something to ask.

"I need to talk to you," he says, "while we have some privacy."

"About anything in particular?"

"Something very particular."

"Cigarette?"

The back stoop is made of concrete and has a distinct slope. Duncan leans against its metal rail. The tree men have hauled in a trailer with wire mesh sides and are filling it with twigs, leaves, and limbs. In the shade of the house, the afternoon air is surprisingly cool. Duncan understands that autumn is really beginning. In the Midwest, seasons often change hands during a single day. It is the last day of summer and it will be the first evening of autumn, warm in the sunlight and cold in the shade. He lights two Merits, passes one to Ellen.

"I've been to the doctor," he says, "and a specialist." He reveals his diagnosis. The symptoms are just starting to show. "Greta doesn't know. I've tried to tell her, but it's harder than you might think. I don't know what I should do."

"Take her dancing while you can," Ellen says. She quickly adds, "Sorry, I shouldn't have put it that way."

The cold makes him shiver, and he thinks perhaps Ellen already knew. Theo must have told her.

"However you put it, I won't be dancing long."

"Nothing pop, of course," Ellen goes on to cover her embarrassment. Her nose is turning red and beginning to run. She's going to cry after all. "She prefers the blues."

The chainsaw sounds high above them, which makes the chill hunker down. All across the city, people will remove their screens, and the ambitious ones will hoist storm windows. The birds will gather to discuss migration, and the animals that hibernate will move to their winter burrows. Duncan can tell from today's effort that he'll have to hire someone to help him with the winter chores. The thought dismays him.

"You and Theo will come?"

"Dancing?" Ellen says. She nods. "On one condition."

"What condition is that?"

"Don't tell her until after."

"After the dancing?"

"Until after we've moved." She drops the cigarette and keeps her eyes on her shoe as she snuffs it. "Otherwise, I can't see myself going."

Duncan is surprised and baffled by this response. Inside, the front door noisily opens and shuts. Greta has already made the short walk to their house and driven back.

"It might be easier on her, though," he says softly, "while you're still here."

"Easier at first," Ellen replies.

He can hear his wife crossing the living room and coming to the
stoop. There's no time to argue.

"All right then." He agrees to her terms.

Greta joins them. She holds a book in her hand, a hardback novel.
"How can you possibly give these up? Are you certain?"

"They're too heavy to move," Ellen says. "Besides, I don't plan
to read in Florida. No one there reads."

Greta plucks her husband's cigarette from his mouth. "Are you
crying?" she asks. "Has it finally hit you how much you'll miss us?"

"It's just the cold," Ellen says. "Thank god I'm leaving it behind."

Dancing with Andrew Holzman hasn't helped Greta's sore calves.
She steps into the backyard of the party house to smoke in peace.
She's carrying her shoes again, which makes lighting the cigarette
awkward. The trip to Ellen's gym is still troubling her. She hated
their reflections, how their muscled torsos spoke not of youth or
beauty or even health, but something she can't—or won't—name.
Men like the way Greta looks. She has known this all her life and
it's still true. She's gone out with several men since Duncan died.
Contrary to the dire predictions about dating after forty, she's had
no trouble finding suitors. But her body in the gym's mirror had
seemed like the body she used to have in caricature.

During a slow dance, she convinced Andrew to come to Ellen's
later and smoke a joint. Getting him there by seducing him is not a
strategy that will please Ellen, but Greta is confident she can pass
him off at the house. A few years ago, she and Ellen had made their
husbands take them to a blues bar on Chicago's South Side. The
men had quickly given out, but she and Ellen danced together until
closing, talking the whole time, yelling over the music. Greta cannot
fathom how they saw each other so often without using up all their
stories. The long-distance calls had been compelling at first, until
the gaps began. Greta repeated herself, caught herself exaggerat-
ing, occasionally outright lying. When they lived inside each other's
lives, they had no end of things to discuss and analyze, reconstruct
and dismiss. Now she feels the need to entertain her friend.

A giant palm dominates the yard, the squat kind with leaves like spikes. A figure steps from the tree's complex shadows. A woman, Greta can tell, although she can't see her face. As she draws near, Greta recognizes her—the bartender with the ponytail. Before she can greet her, the girl says, "I know who you are." She stops walking and crosses her arms. "I know what you're doing."

"I'm a friend of Ellen Riley," Greta says and corrects herself. "Elle Forsythe."

"That may be true," the girl says, "but it's beside the point."

Greta feels a quiver of fear and smokes to hide it. "I don't know what you're talking about."

"I knew it the second I saw you." The girl's eyes are bloodshot, her face puffy.

"You spilled that drink on purpose."

The girl's eyes shift to one side and back, the most laconic dismissal Greta has ever witnessed.

"I don't know you," Greta insists, "and I don't know who you think I am."

"If you don't want to consider *her,* fine." She spits out the words. Real spittle strikes Greta's cheek, as well. "But what about *me?* What about my brother?" She takes another step and the porch light turns her face green.

Greta drops her cigarette and grinds it into the dirt. The girl starts to rush past, but Greta puts out the hand with the shoes to make her stop. The girl backs away from the heels as if they're spiked with toxins. Greta searches her purse and then offers her driver's license.

"I don't live here," she says. "You poured a drink on the wrong person."

The girl seizes the card and studies it.

"Okay," she says reluctantly, "you're not her." Her tone is not apologetic. "But you're exactly like her. You're one of *them.*" She tosses the license back.

Greta snatches it out of the air, as the girl rushes past and slams through the door, bumping Andrew Holzman as he pokes his cast through.

"What's her problem?"

"Mistaken identity," Greta says casually, as if it happens to her all the time. She swings the shoes against her thigh, feeling drunk and sweaty, barefoot, scorned, and sexy, as if she's Bette Davis or Marlene Dietrich, a woman with intrigues and desires and a taste for trouble. She feels bold. "Are you married?"

"At the moment?"

She laughs and puts her arms around his neck, kisses him on the lips. She tastes bourbon on his tongue. She slips her fingers inside the waistband of his gray slacks and whispers in his ear. "You don't move for a second. Let me do this." She unbuckles his belt and pulls it partway free. She slides her arms around his waist, puts her mouth to his ear. "You missed a loop."

On the front lawn, they join Ellen and a few others, including the hostess, "the consummate bitch," whom Greta has only briefly met. Her name is Penny, and the straps of her black dress have slid down her shoulders, revealing the white of her breasts. The V in the back shows her panties. It's a dress aching to come off.

They begin the trek to Ellen's house to the tune of "Hotel California," sung by a stray man from the party. His voice has range but he lacks control, emoting through the song as if the lyrics have no meaning. Greta has seen actors perform this way, milking each scene even though it makes the character incoherent. There have been times in her life when she felt the conflicting urges: to behave sensibly, to make the most of the moment.

When they pass an elementary school with a colorful plastic slide and jungle gym, Greta recalls the playground at Euclid Square where she first met Ellen, where they watched kids and talked about their lives.

Oh, how they had loved each other.

Ellen strolls a few feet away, her arms wrapped around her thin torso, lost in calculation. Does she really want Andrew? Something subterranean is guiding the evening; Greta guesses it must be love. What does she want herself? For Ellen to seduce him? That will leave her with the bad singer or one of the other men. Sex with strangers often interests but rarely compels her. With Duncan, sex served an additional purpose. It reminded her who she was. It taught her who she loved. It fed the flimsy and hard-to-hold thing she came to think of as her soul. Sex with strangers inevitably disappoints. It feels good some of the time, but it is momentary and meaningless, like any other workout.

Penny continues to play hostess, even as they distance themselves from her house. "There used to be an estuary here. It's underground now. Been that way for ages. But they left the bridge, a metal bridge that had gone over the water. It was here a long time."

"I remember that," Andrew says. "I didn't grow up on this side of town, but I remember a bridge over nothing."

"It was only a foot or two off the ground once they filled in under it," Penny continues. "The joke in high school was to jump off the bridge. How we dealt with heartbreak."

"Where was it?" Greta asks.

"You're standing on it, toots."

Greta nods but doesn't smile. She gives herself permission to dislike this woman. Why on earth has she left her own party? The road shows no traces of the bridge. A street lamp blanches their faces. Up the way, fog drifts across a yard, a simple oval, like a white hole in the fabric.

During what turned out to be the final month of Duncan's life, Greta threatened to divorce him. He blamed it on Ellen. "You hear her talking about lovers and lawyers, and it sounds dramatic." He wanted her to quit calling Ellen.

Greta refused. She had brought up divorce after he signed a legal form to be put on a ventilator when the time came. It would operate his lungs, permitting him to live indefinitely. He would not be able to speak by that time. He would not be able to move more than an eyebrow. Greta took the children and went to her mother's house. She doesn't know whether she would have gone through with the divorce. Duncan wheeled his electric chair onto the back stoop and veered off the ramp. He suffocated in the snow.

"I jumped out a window," Andrew announces, indicating his cast. "I landed badly." He has spoken softly, but everyone hears.

"Were you trying to kill yourself?" Greta asks.

"My, my," says Penny, "aren't we direct."

"I was trying to kill something," Andrew says. "Not me literally, it was only the second story. But I had to make a point."

A surprisingly complicated man, Greta thinks, handsome, damaged, confused—a worthy companion.

"Greta's no stranger to stunts," Ellen says. "Ask about her divorce sometime."

The others make noises to convey the sensation of being startled and enticed, a consensual apparition of emotion rather than the real thing. Greta, though, feels genuinely stunned. She doesn't know what Ellen's talking about.

"Let's do hear some divorce stunts," Penny says. "Give us the down and dirty."

"I don't know how to respond," Greta says. Her husband died before she could divorce him. "I wasn't a saint. No one would accuse me of being a saint."

"We don't want whining," Penny says. "*Stunts*. Exploits. Humiliating whatnot."

"We were happy," Greta says. "Ellen can testify to that." She will not describe the way Duncan's body quit little by little, how it became a substance, a stone. The immovable object. How it repulsed her. Every moment of her day was concerned with that weight, its comfort, its functions, its awful greed. "When Ellen moved away, well . . ."

Andrew and Penny speak at the same time. He raises the cast to stop her. "Sometimes we need an outside party to keep the inside steady, like . . ." His face tilts skyward. His head makes small jerking motions, as if he's searching the constellations for words.

"A *voyeur*," Penny suggests. "Every family needs someone staring through its windows. It's the only thing that keeps you from seducing the mailman."

They laugh to let Andrew off the hook, but Greta doesn't laugh and neither does Andrew.

"She had a fling with a boy," Ellen says, making her eyes wide. "They were upstairs while hubby was down!" They have almost reached her house. She points to it, and her voice takes on the approximations of excitement. "Our destination: Florida's official Bacchanalia site—Elle's Den of Iniquity!"

Greta is too bewildered to move. She never had sex with any boy or man—not while Duncan was alive.

Andrew hangs back with her. "Like a spoon," he says at last, "in a cup of coffee, that keeps it from spilling over the rim. An outside person can do that. A spoon. That really works, you know."

"I know," she says. The sudden affection she feels for him is troubling. She takes his arm. "We're falling behind. We should catch up with the others."

AJ can't stop trembling. The men help him from the harness. He wants to describe the look the snake gave him and how it stared at him a second time after it was cut in two. It had a cruel face and then an awful, impossible face. There is no way to tell anyone this.

They wrap him in a coarse blanket. They're treating him as if he's injured. Could this blood be his? He touches his ribs as he walks, a man on either side of him. He pats the bloody places, feeling for wounds. They put him in the cab of the truck. He can't remember the boss's name, but he's driving, talking about bathing and fresh clothes, taking a day off. They're not going to the hospital, which tells AJ he isn't hurt.

It's a long drive and no one is at his house when they arrive. His boss asks when his parents get home. AJ doesn't know. He thinks they should be home now and wonders whether they're in the right house. On the end table is a picture of himself as a boy standing between his mother and father. No one else would have that.

"You ought to get a shower," his boss says. "You've got blood on you." After a moment, he adds, "I never should have put you in that harness. I have experienced men. They wanted to see how much they could slough off on you."

"It was okay," AJ says.

"Get some clean clothes," his boss says. "Soak in hot water. I'll wait out here. Go on. Wash off."

AJ understands something is required of him. He heads down the hall to turn on the bathwater. In his bedroom, he finds clothes. When he returns, his boss is by the front door, talking on a cell phone. AJ piles the fresh clothes on the toilet lid. The water is hotter than he normally likes, but he feels it's his job to soak as his boss suggested, and isn't he a good guy to be so concerned? All that happened was a snake . . . a snake in a tree . . . a snake he sawed in two . . . a snake looked at him and ruined his clothes.

The bathwater turns pink with the snake's blood. A surgeon could sew the snake back together. Doctors can do all these things now. They could get blood from other snakes to fill its body. But there's no way to make it alive again. Which makes AJ wonder what that means, to be alive.

He dries off and dresses, discovering that he took two pairs of pants from his room and no shirt. When he steps from the bathroom he finds his boss on a kitchen chair in the hallway, his cap in his hand. The cap is green. His name, AJ recalls, is Tom Stewart.

"You look like a new man," Tom Stewart says almost too softly for AJ to hear. "Did you a world of good, I bet."

It occurs to AJ that maybe he missed something in all the action. What else could have happened?

He says, "You didn't have to wait, Mr. Stewart."

"I owe your parents a word or two about what happened."

AJ doesn't know how to phrase the question he wants to ask. "I cut up a snake," he says. "Did something else happen?"

Tom Stewart raises the hand with the hat, pauses, and then fits it onto his head.

"No, son," he says. "You did fine."

"That snake was alive," AJ says. "It makes me think how you can't put life back into something once it's gone."

"That's right," his boss says. "That's how it is."

AJ wants to describe the commotion inside him. He wants to say the encounter with the snake is the most important moment of his life. But how can that be true? He was born, wasn't he? He's had sex with two completely different girls. He won a drawing for a color television and sold it for two hundred dollars. He went to Disney World and tried to kill himself. How could sawing up a snake compare to any of that? He realizes he himself was the one screaming. That makes the most sense. A snake, even if it isn't sawed in half, can't scream. That's why his boss is here. To make sure the screaming and trembling are done. He can't decide whether his hands are shaking. It might just be his eyes.

He says, "Why am I so . . ."

"There's no telling," Tom Stewart tells him. "What scares us, we don't have control over that."

"After I cut it in two," AJ says, "it was ugly." He wants to say more, explain that the snake had a second and horrible face, but the door opens. The sun is all but set and his father's shadow across the carpet is gigantic.

As soon as the joint is lit, Penny decides she must get back to her party. "I don't require an escort," she announces, a statement that demands a volunteer.

"Grab Andrew," Ellen whispers to Greta. "Let's hold on to him."

As the joint is passed to Andrew on the couch, Greta intercepts it and sits on his lap. She inhales to make the lit end glow. The one who sang "Hotel California" offers to walk Penny.

The Talking Heads sing over the speakers. A slight chronological advancement over Motown, Greta thinks, as she rises from Andrew's lap. By the end of the album, the joint is gone and all but four have returned to Penny's party. Besides herself, Ellen, and Andrew, there's a dark little man she has hardly noticed. The pot is not so potent that she fails to see her duty. She kicks off her shoes and traipses over to his chair. She sits on one of the wide arms and puts her bare feet on his knees.

"Hey, sport," she says. "I've forgotten your name."

He has a serious face with intense black eyes.

"We were never introduced," he says softly.

"I'm Greta, like the immortal Garbo."

"Not too often I meet an immortal," he says. "You're only the second."

She laughs at that. "Tell me something about yourself."

He bends his finger. She obediently leans in. "I'm in love with your friend." He points.

On the couch, Ellen and Andrew use a mechanical device to roll another joint.

"Which one?" Greta asks.

"Hah," he says without any humor. "Your sister. This whole evening is for my benefit. I'm supposed to be crazy jealous."

Andrew holds the rolling apparatus while Ellen tucks cigarette paper in its vinyl saddle. They look intimate already.

Greta says, "Sorry, but I don't think so."

"Oh?" His eyebrows rise, and the pouches beneath his eyes vanish. He looks a decade younger. "Watch this."

He runs his hand along her leg and under her dress.

"Hey, now," she says.

At the same moment Ellen says, "I know," and hops up from the couch, spilling pot over Andrew's lap. "Let's move the furniture and dance."

AJ pedals his bicycle to the house where the tree is coming down. He has stayed home from work two days, and it has taken most of the morning to ride from his neighborhood, which has few trees and no snakes. He watches from a distance. He doesn't want the crew to see him. All of the branches have been removed from the tree. The top of the trunk has been lopped, but the tree is still incredibly tall—and bare now, like a single monstrous thought.

He pedals farther, to the house with the red tile roof. A station wagon fills the driveway. The house is brick—nothing any bad wolf could blow down. It would take something huge, as big as the tree, to knock it over. The sprinklers are on and a man is on his knees in the wet grass, getting soaked.

"Can you help me?" the man says. He is trying to turn off the sprinklers.

AJ gives the spiked knob a twist. It's not really that tight.

The man is effusive. He drips on AJ's shoes. "Are you handy?" he asks. His name is Duncan, and he offers work. "A few hours a week."

AJ starts immediately, hauling trash to the curb, mowing the back lawn, raking leaves in the wet grass. He is not quite finished with the leaves when Duncan tells him that's enough.

"My wife and kids will be back soon. I don't want them to see you."

AJ doesn't know how to take this.

"They don't know how weak I am," Duncan explains. "I don't want them to know. Not until they have to. The children . . ." He loses his voice. His face changes shape. He searches the grass, as if his voice has fallen there. AJ imagines what the voice might look like. In the raked pile, a jagged red leaf turns away from his gaze. Finally Duncan says, "Once they know their father is dying, their childhood's over, you see?"

These words don't just strike AJ's ears but take to the sky, which pales and wobbles. He swallows an uncomfortable gulp of air.

Duncan pats him on the back. "How are you at carpentry?" He describes ramps for a wheelchair. "I want to have them ready when I need them."

In the weeks that follow, Duncan gives him a set of keys to the station wagon. They shop together for plywood and two-by-fours, which they take to a neighbor's garage. Duncan is a patient teacher. He brings AJ iced tea and makes him wear protective goggles. He doesn't mind when AJ confuses measurements or makes a cut so ugly it has to be redone. AJ learns to maneuver a circular saw. He hammers nails, drives screws. He builds two ramps. They go together in sections. He paints them a brick color to match the house. When he shakes Duncan's hand, it does not feel like a hand but a soft bag holding something lighter than bones—pretzels or Pixy Stix.

He thinks he will finally see Greta when he installs the ramps, but Duncan is taking his family out of town.

"Are you good with this?" he asks. "Should I hire someone to help you?"

AJ declines the offer. The sections fit together like the plastic connecting blocks he played with as a boy. He has retrieved these blocks from his closet and built a house much like Duncan's, adding plastic ramps to the steps.

"Keep track of your time," Duncan tells him.

AJ spends the morning loading the sections into the back of the station wagon and unloading them down the street. The sections are heavy and difficult to maneuver. One set is for the front, another for

24

the back. He has visited this house to clean the gutters, shovel snow, put up storm windows. He has never seen any of the family but Duncan, yet he feels connected to the place—the shape of the lawn, the rumpled roots of the sycamore in the backyard, the handprints in the sidewalk out front. These shapes and sites put him at ease, but the sections of the ramp fail to align. AJ drives to a pay phone to call his father. When he gets no answer, he calls Tom Stewart.

"I'm not much of a carpenter," he warns.

It takes them an hour to figure out the problem. AJ confused a section meant for the back with one meant for the front. A simple problem, but he has nailed the sections together. It becomes a complicated setback. They do not finish until after dark and admire their work by flashlight.

"These are well built," Tom Stewart says, kneeling to knock on the lumber.

"The guy they're for designed them," AJ explains. "I just followed directions, and I messed up a lot even then."

"That's all right," Tom Stewart says. "These are good ramps and you built them."

"I guess I did build them," AJ says, surprised somehow by this information.

Headlights appear on the street and pull up to the driveway.

"They're not supposed to see me," AJ says.

They climb into Tom Stewart's truck and drive away.

Greta and Andrew Holzman are stationed at the front door. He offers her a tired smile. "Why don't you give me your number?"

"I'm staying here," she says. "But I only have the weekend, and I want to spend it with Ellen. Then I'll be in cold, cold Illinois, while you'll be in warm, warm Florida."

The door is open, which lets in the smell of the outside world: grass and trees and the soft, soporific southern air. The night is fully dark now, and she is tired.

He says, "Hot and cold don't mix?"

"They become something terribly bland," she says, "or a tornado."

He places his hands on her hips. She leans in and lets him kiss her. It carries a tiny charge. She glances at Ellen, who is slow dancing with the dark little man.

"Did you know about those two?" she asks.

Andrew nods. "Elle tells me everything."

Greta's understanding of the night is shifting. She can almost feel the movement. She doesn't know what to think, except she doesn't want to be alone with Ellen and her strange partner. She initiates a second kiss and lets Andrew press his body against hers.

"I could be persuaded to stay." He wags the hand with the cast. "This doesn't prevent me from doing anything."

"What do you know that I don't?" she asks. "You can start with that guy's name."

"It's Stan. He's in the process of leaving his wife. She was at the party. Maybe tonight was *it,* you know, the parting."

"That girl who was the bartender—"

"Stan's daughter."

"*Jesus,*" Greta says. "I thought Ellen was after you."

"Me?" Andrew makes a face. "Didn't you wonder why Penny left her own party to come here? The wife is her best friend."

This talk makes her dizzy. She clings to him while she works to fit the pieces together. Penny hired Stan's daughter to tend the bar, which was meant to stop him from attending to his mistress. Greta understands that she misjudged Penny. She left the party to stop Stan from seeing Ellen, to shame him. The night makes sense, just not the kind of sense she expected. It's Penny and the little man's wife who are friends, not she and Ellen.

"I'm trying like hell to get your attention," Andrew says. "What do I need to do?"

"Love me," she answers. "Give up Florida and move to Chicago. Buy snow boots and earmuffs. Live for me and me alone."

"Hmm," he says.

"You asked."

"What the hell. Let's do it."

She expects him to laugh but he doesn't. "You're almost serious."

"I turn fifty next month." He looks at his watch as if it keeps track of his age. "I was married once, but that was done with years ago. And you look like . . ."

"I'm the wild friend from out of town."

"When I jumped out the window, it was at my daughter's house," he says. "She has a drug problem. I had to let her know what she was doing to all of us."

"A stunt," Greta says, and it sounds like self-accusation. She realizes why Ellen said she was no stranger to stunts. All those things she invented to prolong their friendship. She mentioned a boy—one of the tree men—who began appearing on her street, staring from his bicycle at their house. She had the vanity to think he was there to catch a glimpse of her, but she discovered a canceled check to *A. Jack* written in Duncan's nearly illegible hand. Duncan was using him to do the chores he could no longer do himself. The kid had built the ramps she had yet to remove.

Then Greta used the boy, too. She'd only told Ellen that she kissed him, but that was bad enough. There was the real stunt, telling such a lie.

"I left my husband when he was dying," she tells Andrew. "I left him because he had chosen *not* to die, and I couldn't face it. When there seemed no end to it, I couldn't continue."

Andrew nods without comment. He has no interest in judging her. He behaves as if the person she's describing no longer exists, as if by admitting her bad behavior she erases it. She knows this is not true. All of the people she has been do not merely trail her like a wedding train but envelop her like the layers of an elaborate gown she can never entirely shed.

The player changes discs. Motown is back. Marvin Gaye and Tammi Terrell have tracked her down. "Ain't no mountain high enough," they claim, "ain't no valley low . . ."

"I'm so weary of this music. Why can't we take the pledge and move on?"

"Hey girl, I'm with you." It's Ellen. She and Stan join them at the door. They're holding hands. He wipes at his nose with his sleeve. "I'll take the pledge," Ellen says as she marches to the stereo. The music dies. "Open the door," she calls, but it's already open.

They step aside and she flings the CD, Frisbee style, into the yard. The silver disc catches the moonlight as it flies across the short stretch of grass, gleaming as it strikes a parked car. The door to the car opens. The dome light illuminates the girl with the ponytail who tended bar. Beside her sits another woman.

"I have to go," Stan says.

"Close it," Greta says as soon as Stan passes through. "Don't watch."

Duncan takes Greta dancing as Ellen advised. Ellen and Theo come along as Ellen promised.

Except for the stage, where a band is immersed in golden light, the bar is dimly lit. Duncan keeps time with his wife on the crowded dance floor. He is worried that he will fall and give away his condition, and yet he's enjoying himself. Greta used to make fun of his dancing when they were dating. "How can a musician have no rhythm?" she'd say. The memory adds to his pleasure. He loves the way his wife dances, the large and fine movements of her body, even her mouth, puckering and grimacing with the beat. He stomps a little to make his awkward shuffle seem intentional, but it leaves him unstable. Greta bumps him as she does a spin, and his body tips like a great timber.

Yet he doesn't fall. Theo and Ellen have been dancing beside them all night. Theo's hands grip him, balance him, and let him go. Greta doesn't see a thing.

He understands he will not dance again. This is his last night for dancing. When the song ends, Theo pretends to be tired and takes his arm.

"You gals dance together," Theo says. "We want to drink."

Theo was the first to know. He noticed something in Duncan's golf swing, convinced him to see a doctor. Probably he told Ellen right away. What else would explain her reaction at the house? It can be hard not to tell your wife everything. Immediately he amends the thought. Some things are easier not to say.

They sit beside each other at the table, drinking and watching their wives. When the band announces its last number, Duncan is drunk enough to ask. He takes Theo by the arm.

"When did you tell Ellen about me?"

Theo sighs and shakes his head wearily. "I can't keep a damn thing from her."

Duncan smiles, nods. He has another question. It coils in his mouth, ready to spring out. The transfer to Florida was so abrupt, their decision to move such a surprise. He thinks it's his illness that made up their minds. It wouldn't have taken much effort to research the disease, how it dominates the lives around it, all the work it takes to care for a human who can no longer move. Families fall apart. Friendships dissolve.

He holds to Theo's arm, but he does not speak. To ask is to accuse. He prefers to believe in their friendship. He takes a long drink of beer and searches the dance floor again for his wife. He's determined not to let his illness destroy his family. Already he's hired a kid to do chores, build ramps. The beer is still cold and just bitter enough. His wife dances into view. She's talking with Ellen even as they flit and shake to the music. His life swirls deliciously inside him, like the smoke in the stage lights. He merely has to keep one step ahead of the disease. That's all.

How hard can that be?

On the day of Greta's return flight, the Florida sky opens and rain pummels Ellen's car. They leave the house hours early. Neither wants her to be late. Ellen drives incautiously, skating over street ponds, passing on the freeway ramp. But traffic grows thick and they come to a standstill.

"There must be an accident," Ellen says.

"It was smart to leave early," Greta agrees.

Since the party, Ellen has had nothing to do with her. She stayed in bed on Saturday morning, claiming a hangover. Yet when Greta got out of the shower, she was gone. A note explained that she was at the gym. She didn't return until lunchtime and arrived with friends. She announced in front of the others that Andrew had invited Greta to dinner. "I accepted for you," she said casually. Greta took the hint. She had dinner with Andrew and spent the night at his apartment. A siren sounds. A patrol car passes them on the shoulder.

"Andrew is really taken with you," Ellen says.

"He's nice," Greta replies.

Andrew had grilled tuna on his balcony and lit candles in the bedroom. The sex wasn't entirely satisfactory, but she enjoyed seeing his apartment. She asked him why Ellen wanted to hurt her, but he did not attempt an answer. She told him about Duncan, how he'd had rages near the end, accusing her of intentionally hurting him when she got him dressed or took him to the toilet. They went to a counselor, but they could not make the therapist understand how they felt. He used words like *codependency* and *enabling,* feeble words that did no justice to the tragedy of their lives. Greta had wished Ellen and Theo could be with them. Why shouldn't friends go to therapy to save their happiness? But she cannot imagine sitting with Ellen and talking to a therapist. Instead, she sees them in Chicago with their husbands and children, bundled for winter, chatting about their lives.

When the reverberation of the siren dies out, there's only the sound of the rain.

Ellen says, "I don't care what you think of me." Her voice is soft, almost apologetic. She grips the steering wheel with both hands, her knuckles turning white. "How many more chances will I have?"

"I'm not judging you," Greta says.

"You met him. You could see it. He's a cut above."

As far as Greta could tell, Stan was as ordinary as they came.

"People *die* for love," Ellen says. "They fight wars for love. So what if I'm willing to break up a marriage for it?"

"Why didn't you just tell me? Why the big story about Andrew?"

"You made out all right there," Ellen says. "You wound up pretty entertained by that little ruse."

"Oh, please stop."

They sit in silence. Ellen turns on the radio. An oldies station, the Turtles: *I can't see me lovin' nobody but*—Greta switches it off. The traffic begins to move.

Finally Ellen says, "I couldn't risk it. I couldn't have you throwing yourself at him."

"God*damn* you," Greta says. "I hate you, you know. I really do."

One evening, near the end of Duncan's truncated life, he lets it slip that he told Ellen first. Maybe he means to hurt Greta with it. Maybe he wants to turn her against her friend.

"She wouldn't let me tell you until she'd gone south." He's hard to understand, his mouth no longer fully under his control, the muscles in his body burning out one at a time. The disease encourages them to be petty, to attend to minutiae, anything to avoid the havoc of misfiring nerves, the husk of his body. It doesn't help that their sleep is ruined. Greta has to get up if he needs to pee or merely turn on his side. She has to feed him and watch him chew. Twice a day she pours a protein drink into a tube surgically connected to his stomach. He says, "She told me to take you out while I could still dance."

Greta feels a wide sea of responses. She understands her friend has perhaps betrayed her. She understands her husband is looking for a fight. But this day she does not get angry. This day something else prevails.

She says, "You could *never* dance."

He lets out a laugh. He no longer has the fine muscles to produce a smile, but he offers the skeleton's gape.

"Don't I know it," he says. "But *this* is ridiculous."

It's a rare sweet moment, yet Greta can't seem to convey that in the telling. Describing it to Ellen, she claims they danced, woman and wheelchair, about the cluttered house, knocking over a TV tray, Greta performing an unlikely striptease, her body undulating like a serpent's. She claims they had sex in the living room. (Duncan still could have erections all the way to the end. What feeds desire is not muscle, evidently, but some more resilient force.) She describes to Ellen the cold arms of the wheelchair against her thighs, how she pressed his gaping face to her breasts.

In reality, they just touch hands. He wants to hear one of the tapes from his class. She finds the cassette. The lecture is on the beautiful and mortal Medusa and her immortal sisters, who were so spectacularly ugly they could turn a man to stone. During the actual class, when Greta recorded the lecture, Duncan had asked a question. She remembers holding his hand aloft for him. He had wanted to know what became of the immortal sisters after the mortal one was slain. What did they do for the remainder of eternity? The teacher had not come up with a good answer, although Greta can't recall exactly what he said. On the tape, he talks about the notion of some scholars that the hideous faces of the Gorgons were representations of female genitalia. That had made Duncan laugh in class, and she can hear his laughter on the tape. Nothing about the female anatomy—about her body, anyway—was ugly to him. She puts her hand on his chest, ready to direct the afternoon toward sex after all, but he has fallen asleep in his chair.

She clicks off the tape, noticing the creases in the carpet left by the wheelchair, a long path from where he sits to the opposite end of the living room, branching off to the bedroom in one direction, the bathroom in the other, a heavy crisscrossing foliate crown. She gets out the vacuum to erase it all.

Greta is in a Florida airport during a rainstorm when she is wakened in her Chicago bed by the thunder of a sledgehammer. She is in Florida and she is home from Florida. She is two places at once, and she needs a drink.

In Chicago, her pajama tee is damp with sweat. The new season has begun and the morning is warm. She changes into one of Duncan's white shirts. She has not thrown out his shirts. In Florida, she gestures to get the bartender's attention. The bar has a view of the airstrip and an assortment of junk on the walls—old oars and snowshoes, rusty signs for Esso Oil and RC Cola. She doesn't care for the decor, but the weather has shelved her flight. She has time to kill. She is home and her home is changing shape. She is stranded far from home, and the distance she wishes to travel is growing.

Her mother and daughter have ravaged the newspaper, and the coffeemaker holds a simmering carafe of her mother's watery brew. She can't bear her mother's coffee without a shot of Baileys. She searches for the bottle in the liquor cabinet. The men dismantling the wooden ramps have finished out front and appear now on the back stoop, two young guys in jeans. They sweat just beyond the kitchen window. Now and again they peek in at her. The bartender leans in her direction. "What'll do you?"

She orders a gin and tonic. "Strong," she says. "Mighty. A powerful drink, please."

"I'll make it as strong as you can take it," she replies, a young woman in an ugly green vest.

Greta cannot stop thinking about the disastrous visit—the gym, the party, the whole ugly mess. She backs up to their life in Chicago, their long friendship, the parting. They had been like family. Greta's mother fills the kitchen doorway, saying, "Sleeping Beauty rises." The tone is disapproving. She wears a floral dressing gown, a garish and threadbare garment the kids gave her one Christmas, a display of fidelity wasted on Greta's daughter, and if her son were home, it would be wasted on him, as well. Her children are sweet but inattentive and self-absorbed like almost everyone their age.

"So?" her mother says. "Did you have yourself a time?"

Greta shrugs as she grabs the Baileys. "It was pleasant."

Her date the night before had been with an attractive stockbroker who means nothing to her. They ate dinner in the Palmer House ballroom. The occasion included a jazz band and speeches by politicians and actors—a fund-raiser for an obscure malady. Afterward, they had drinks and sex and a drive in his convertible. With her mother at the house, Greta could have spent the night with him. She had no responsibilities calling her home, and she'd been only mildly bored—a gentle, yielding brand of boredom she was coming to appreciate.

She chooses a cup for her coffee and Irish cream, and tells her mother about the celebrities in the audience, their clothing, the courses of food, the alderman who shared their table. She enjoys the night more in retrospect than she had while she lived it.

"Hair of the dog?" her mother asks, eyeing the bottle.

Greta finishes pouring the Baileys. "You can call it that."

The back door opens. One of the workers nods a greeting, taking in her bare legs. He holds a sledgehammer. "We're about to get serious out back. Thought I ought to warn you." He offers an abbreviated wave, two fingers flicking. Lightning divides the sky over the runway. Greta observes it through the bar's wide window, a brilliant forking flash, followed by a tremendous percussive slap. The lights shut down. The room turns the gray of the sky. The girl in the vest rolls her eyes as she gives Greta the drink. "This always happens. The control tower has a generator. There are emergency lights in the halls."

"The bars are on their own?" Greta says.

"You got it."

The tonic is flat. She barely tastes the gin, but she's happy for the dim room, the quiet, the time to think. The bond she shared with Ellen was physical, a belief in the bodies of children and men, a faith that resided in their own flesh. She cannot keep her friend without her family. For that matter, Ellen could not keep her marriage without Greta and Duncan. They had all come together in a complex harmony, and now they can't help but attend to everything that is missing. Is there a word for this kind of loss? She's acquainted with the grief of losing her husband, the shame of deciding to leave him, the guilt from knowing how he died. What's the word for losing a dear friend? She tries to find one with the right sound and texture. She can almost feel it on her tongue.

A man on the next stool speaks to her, "Buy you a drink?" She hadn't noticed him, though he's in pilot's uniform. His cap is on the bar and he's touching the emblem—white wings—with his thumb, as if to wipe it clean. His eyes are appraising and curious. Smiling, he adds, "I get a discount."

She declines his offer. "I just want to be left alone."

"There's a wish," he says. He jostles her stool as he stands. She lifts her G&T to keep it from spilling. The transparent liquid rocks in its transparent container. One of the men dismantling the ramps— the same one as before—pushes open the door again. She has moved her chair into the sun, her feet up on the windowsill, and the door nudges her chair. "Sorry," he says, his eyes steering themselves along her legs to her thighs. The second man wedges his face into the space between the jamb and the door. The two heads in the opening look connected, like a mythological creature.

"Something wrong?" she asks.

She removes her feet from the window ledge and the men enter. They want water. Greta fetches cups and ice. It's only when she's handing over the drinks that she realizes one of them is a woman— hipless and flat-chested but undeniably female. She is silent while the man talks about the assembly and heft of the ramps, their sturdy design, the clever interlocking parts.

"They're impressive," he says, "like building blocks."

"My husband was an architect," Greta tells him, but she cannot explain why the pieces are nailed together so haphazardly they have to be sledged apart. "I'd have removed them earlier but my son used to skateboard on them. He's in college now."

"*You* have a son in college?" he says.

Even as she smiles, she recognizes the tedium she felt the night before. It seems this will be the dominant feeling in her life, this somewhat gratifying monotony, like a boring song played especially for her.

"I guess we ought to get back to it," he says.

The woman never says a word.

The pounding resumes. Her mother has abdicated the kitchen. Her daughter is upstairs in her room supposedly conjugating French verbs. Greta experiences a vague sense of desolation and gloom despite the brilliant sun on her skin. She doesn't let it affect her too much. The coffee is bad, even with liquor in it, but otherwise what does she have to fret about? Some feelings exist to be ignored. Just beyond her window, the man and woman examine a crowbar. They are siblings, she decides. She wonders whether they notice the gouges where Duncan's wheelchair skated off the ramp.

Meanwhile, out front, a car slows as it approaches. AJ drives by the house every weekend. He's in college now and barely passing his classes, but he likes the campus, the grass, the paths between buildings. He feels better about the course work from week to week. He can almost see himself as a college student. He can almost see himself as something he already is. On his way over, he drove past the house where the great tree had stood. He cannot count the times he has seen the snake in his dreams. It doesn't bother him now as it used to. It bothers him in a new way. Which must be a kind of progress, he reasons. The sections of the ramp he built have been separated and removed from the steps. They're stacked on the driveway.

AJ understands that Duncan is dead.

He would like to take those sections of the ramp home. There must be a use for the lumber. He doesn't want to see it wasted. This is the reason he gives himself for parking the car and walking to the front door of Greta's house.

In the dim airport bar, she pulls again at the thread of her reasoning. What she comes up with makes sense to her, even if she cannot find the right label for it. When she and Ellen are together now, they feel diminished and nostalgic, like the members of any group who regret their solo careers. And that is what's left for each of them now: a solo career. Greta's husband is dead, her son is in college, her daughter will soon follow. She'll have friends, but none like Ellen. She'll see men. Maybe she'll marry one. But none will have the presence in her life that Duncan had. None will have the gravity. Her life is thinning, tapering. She takes up no space in the world, so light that the slightest breeze will stir her. Even grief will give up its hold, and she will be like the children who mocked their sorrow by jumping from the bridge that spanned nothing at all.

Thinking this through does not make her happy, and yet she is pleased to figure it out. She would like to tell someone about it.

A long mirror backs the bar. People hunch over their drinks. Strangers stuck in a terminal, everyone waiting to be somewhere else. There is no one here for her to talk to.

It is Greta's mother who answers the door, but AJ doesn't know this. She is a woman who looks like Greta but far older than he remembers. Time, he understands, is tricky. You think it runs downhill like water, like a great wide river. But time is no river. It shoots up from a central source, but it isn't one thing, it's many things that fork and fork again, and you find yourself almost grown one moment and a child at the same time. The minute he spent with the snake seems like less than yesterday, and the hours he worked as Duncan's hands seem now ages ago.

The woman is waiting for a response, but he didn't hear the question.

"Oh, I know who you're looking for," she says. She leaves him on the doorstep.

Time is not a river, he thinks. Time is a tree. Branches, roots, limbs, the leafing. Time defoliates. Time buds. Time cracks. He doesn't know what he means. Yet he believes it.

Greta finishes her drink and orders another. "Stronger, please," she says.

"You're the boss." The girl in the green vest looks a little like the bartender at the party who drenched Greta's dress. Maybe *she* would listen. There should be some way to advise this girl, to tell her what Greta has discovered.

Which is what? That friendships end? That love dissipates? That people die? That there is nothing to trust in this uncertain life? Happiness, love, friendship, even one's own body—all the enduring bonds finally cannot endure. Nothing is secure. Nothing keeps. What is the good of knowing that?

The bartender sets a glass of ice before Greta and pours from a bottle of gin. She says, "Tell me whoa."

Greta feels the blood rush to her face.

"Yes," she says, "that's it."

The girl stops pouring. Greta nods. The bartender has it right.

"*Woe*," Greta agrees. "Woe."

The person who comes to the door is Greta's daughter, who is seventeen, who is Greta all over again, brand-new.

"Do I know you?" she asks.

AJ's world is tumbling—branches, roots, limbs, leaves, rings of time.

"Are you all right?" she asks.

From the way she asks, he knows she wants him to be all right.

"I built those ramps for your dad," he says.

"Oh." Not just her face but her whole person softens. "My mom's getting rid of them."

"He's dead then, I guess?"

She doesn't react for a moment. "My dad?" She nods.

This confirmation does not sadden him as much as he expected. He's not just in the doorway with this girl, he's at the base of the great tree and across the street from a beautiful woman who is walking his way. He is the boy he used to be and the man he is about to become.

He says, "I don't know why I'm here." A spot on his arm grows warm. Unexpectedly, he adds, "You must think I'm a jackass."

Her face opens now and AJ senses a world there in the trembling gap between her lips.

She says, "How well did you know him?" and "Do you want to come in?"

She is not merely holding the door for a stranger, she's holding it for her father, she's opening it to a future she can sense and almost see. A thousand moments from her life crowd into this one. She feels their rush. Until this point, she never imagined that life could be so rich.

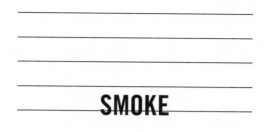

SMOKE

Three boys smoke and talk about sex.

Even her back, says Lee. *She had this incredible back with these shadows by her shoulder blades . . . I don't know how to tell you.* He flicks his cigarette to the plank floor of the porch. The spark from the butt could consume the graying wood of the shack, but it merely smolders. *I touched every part of her.*

They are taking their spring break in the mountains, alone in the wilderness. They spend the whole time talking of girls when they could have gone to a beach to pursue them.

She made me wear a rubber, Lee continues. He taps another cigarette from his soft pack. *I felt like I'd put on a spacesuit, while she was completely naked.*

The word *naked,* like an explosive, creates a silence after it. It is a word he loves to say.

That's one big condom, says the next boy, Greg, snickering and staring at the silver clouds above the pencil tips of pine that hide the moon. He puffs on his big cigar.

The trip has consisted of one error after another—getting lost on the drive up the mountain, the car stuck on a muddy shoulder near a lake, the boys without a fish after hours in an overstocked reservoir because they packed the wrong bait. Through it all they've relished their incompetence, talking the whole time—on the drive, at the lake, in mud up to their ankles as they pushed against the Plymouth's trunk—about sex.

They stand now on the porch without their coats, the night turning cold, their beer and food inside the cabin, because they've locked themselves out. They will have to make a decision soon—to break in or hike a few miles up the road and ask for another key—but for the moment they smoke and Lee describes the girl who permitted him to have her body against his.

It felt so—he strikes a match, as if to complete the sentence. He lights his Camel and shakes his head as he inhales, as if his lungs fill with wonder. Lee's father, a half decade earlier, was caught performing an abortion and stripped for three years of his license to operate. His father's crime colors every aspect of Lee's sexual life.

He blows a long spine of smoke, continues his tale of the naked girl, her naked opening, his tunnel vision. Much of it has basis in lived events, involving a girl with braces on her teeth and a feeling inside him, a tenderness he knows instinctively to disown.

Then she made this noise. Her moan had startled him, frightened him, made him worried, made him come. *I wish I had a tape of that noise. You don't know,* he says, his head shaking again in astonishment. *I can't tell you.*

Greg touches thumb and finger, making a circle, the signal for "okay," now a symbol for something else, the burning end of his cigar thrusting into it and out. Its aromatic smoke he associates with the men his father would bring home after the children were supposed to be asleep. These men would gather in the kitchen, which would smell, come morning, of smoke, despite the pancakes his mother would have bubbling on the griddle, standing in her underwear with her flipper, red marks marching up her legs to her slanting panties, the cleft in her buttocks beneath the silky fabric visible to this boy even now every time he inhales smoke—a slight and shimmering ravine loosed in his memory from his actual mother, ready to furrow into any girl passing before his imagination.

When it's his turn to talk, Greg describes an uncurtained window *(I had to roll a wheelbarrow over and stand on it to get a good look),* the forked body of a naked woman prone on her woman's tummy *(tan all over, and I mean a perfect tan on every inch of her)*, the panorama of her body before him *(her toes hung over the edge, and her feet were spread way apart and had really deep arches)*, his eyes upon the widening gate of her sex *(her legs made a vee, like the point of an arrow, like a path that gets narrow and then more narrow as you get closer to where you need to be)*.

This is not an image Greg has actually witnessed but a picture from a magazine. Yet it speaks to him more powerfully than experience. He doesn't know that he isn't talking about sex. Neither is he trying to recall his mother's satin panties at the kitchen stove. Through a keyhole one night as a child, he witnessed his mother being passed among a throng of men in the kitchen, gently fondled by each. She took a hatted man's cigar and dimpled her cheeks sucking smoke from it. His father's bright voice called out, *First!* as he kneeled among them. On hands and knees he crawled behind his wife to make a ladder of kisses up her thighs, his tongue a serpent bent on pleasure, her panties at half-mast in its honor. His mother tugged the other men close to her, whose mouths touched her neck and breasts and parted the pink of her lips. And later that night, after the boy had returned to bed, the sound of applause came slapping down the hall.

Greg does not remember this night, but it lives inside him. The weight of it straightens him like a plumb, holding him erect, a tension in the long ligaments of his back. Its heft is what first settled his eyes upon the photo and now limns his description of the splayed woman with excited affection. He pulls on the cigar again, tries to blow rings, but cannot tame the smoke into recognizable shapes.

Even lying like that, her bottom was, her ass—the cheeks were not flat, but kind of round, not like bubbles, more like those packets of sugar. You know that sugar?

The third boy of the group hesitates on the edge of the splintered porch, leaning against a knotty post. This boy would be me, thirty years ago, seventeen and posing with a cigarette, hoping to look untouched by anything in the wide world, including my own history, the distance between what I know of myself and who I actually am—roughly the same as the distance between who I want to be and what I'll become.

I say nothing for the moment. My Lucky Strike I treat like a date, fondling it, making a display of our familiarity, watching smoke curl from its burning end. I stall long enough for silence to slip onto the porch. The mountain air chills us, the stars flaunt their ancient light, creatures move in the piney distance just beyond our apprehension.

I would like this moment to prevail. I want for these boys to finally recognize the cold and feel their need for shelter. In the bracing air comes the sweet and predatory fragrance of decay, and it is not impossible to believe that boys might smell it, might hear the gliding complaint of an owl, which directs their attention to the night sky, the million burning things hovering above their heads. They might, at last, stare at the world around them and see, unfiltered by their shared obsession, the actual world around them—the sky, moon, stars, trees, a brown patch of earth, three kids with uncombed hair and mud-spattered jeans. They might witness these things for what they are, emblems of nothing, yet freighted with a terrible beauty.

Instead, when they lift their eyes to the dark heavens, they see a universe nippled with light, the crescent moon, that luminous curve of ass, riding seductively above the phallic pines. Their litany of extremity and orifice must continue, the push-me pull-you stories of suck and satisfaction, the wagging bravado of boys alone in the woods. Their every word returns to the feminine body—the ones they have witnessed, the flesh they have beheld with their own flesh, how the friction of skin on skin lights in them the spiraling fuse that they mistake for their souls. It's too simple to say they describe the roundness of women's breasts because they cannot say they love their mothers. Neither can they say that they love the world, nor that they feel the rending weight of it. But they can say *buck naked* and *big tits,* and if they need to say something that has nothing to do with sex, they speak of sex anyway: annoyed, *screw it;* pleased, *bitchin'.* When forced to speak of their love for one another, they say, *fuck you, man, you suck the big one.*

Lee's father, by this time, once again practices medicine. When the trouble came down, Lee had been led to the guest bathroom in their large house, where he settled on the rim of the tub, while his father sat on the lid of the toilet. It was the final week Lee's parents would live together, although Lee did not yet know that. His father's hands and voice shook as he explained why he had done what he had done. *No money changed hands,* he told his son. The woman, almost forty, married, mother of four, had wept in his office. *A good friend,* he said. *She needed help.* Yet it had been her husband who turned him in. *How he knew . . . ,* Lee's father began, but he let the sentence fade away.

Can Lee ever forgive himself for what he did next? He asked not about his father's arrest or why his father and mother yelled at each other; he did not ask about the law or about justice; he did not even ask how his father felt, or if there was anything Lee could do. Instead, he asked, *Was she naked?*

Lee cannot forgive himself because he can no longer name the transgression. But the awareness of this betrayal rides with him: in his shoulders, there in the dark space between the blades; in the narrow gap between bucket seats, the gulf that separates him from the girl with the braces; in the delicate silences among the words of his every sentence, words that shimmy about a girl's torso more roughly than his hands. The actual touch of his hands on the girl's body had been compassionate and laden with his father's shame, his fingers gently strumming her ribs, tracing the flared bones of her hips, his heart brimming with a rapacious delicacy.

When he seeks words to describe the encounter, he can only say, *She was . . . she was so . . . such great pussy.*

When it comes my turn to howl into the chasm, I describe my night of wonder. *At the party, after the Chandler game,* I begin, the cigarette a lever in my mouth, *she found ways to let me see her panties, just me.* I tap the end of my Lucky; flakes of ash float on the frigid air.

The story I tell my friends is true, but what I tell is only a fraction of the story. The white flash of the girl's panties from across the crowded room stirred in me a sleeping longing, a desire that hibernates in the marrow. I didn't remember my favorite aunt but *relived* her jaunty walk across the porch of my childhood home, a walk I witnessed through gaping blinds, her man of the month grasping her shoulder, spinning her into his arms, his hands sliding beneath her skirt, revealing the white planes of her secret skin. What can a boy do with such information but store it in his body?

At the end of the party, that girl and I found an empty room. *And I put my finger there, right there, right right there. I felt like my whole body was in that finger, warm, wet, and just where it wanted to be.*

I think my turn is over, but they won't let me quit. *Did you fuck her?* They want to know. They need to hear it. When I say that I did, it's only partly a lie. The power of that encounter speaks louder than the simple facts.

Yeah, I say. *Yeah, I fucked her, all right.*

Don't hold back, Greg says. *Describe the deed.*

Because I'm a virgin, I cannot describe the love I made with that girl. I describe, instead, my favorite landscape, the contours of a wheat field bordered by a canal, how wild the flowers grow along the bank, how bushy the patches of grass, how ready the field grows for the thrasher, and how, after the harvest, the stubble has to be burned, ash enriching the soil, preparing it for next year's crop. Lacking the words and experience to tell it right, I substitute the body of woman for the body of earth, the geography of an upturned hip and slanting slope of skin for the blue-green landscape of wind-blown wheat whose stalks genuflect and rise, a billowing movement that engages more than the eyes.

At least that's what I think I did. We didn't know what we were saying, and yet we knew we were saying more than what was said. Talking about the slender ribbon of dark hair on the taut surface of a girl's abdomen, I knew I was describing a thing whose real meaning was beyond my grasp, like a child who dreams of sex before he knows what it is, describing the mounds and valleys of his dream and the impossible wish to walk among them.

We were boys of no particular distinction, inventing our own history, perpetuating a species of desire as common as the cold weather that made our bodies tremble. Into the morning hours we continued our allegory of the body female, until we thought to try a window, and one by one we tumbled in, where we built a fire and breathed the smoke, then crawled beneath our coarse blankets to talk again, elevating, as best we could, the fragile faith that our lives had meaning.

MISS FAMOUS

He was black, too tall to be a dwarf, too short to be normal. Monica had to show her driver's license before he would let her into his condominium. Her DMV photo she considered alluring, her mouth showing a little pout, head tilted at a tough-girl angle, bangs falling just right across her forehead. She generally liked to be carded, but not at work.

"I have my own vacuum," he said, wanting her to leave the Merry Maids Hoover in the carpeted hall. "Follow me, please." His voice had the melodic lilt of strangeness, and there was something in his walk, a wobble, as if the floor beneath him were shifting. Monica's daughter Sally, not quite three years old, ran with that same rocking motion, her arms lifted and flailing at the air.

Monica regarded all black men as personally threatening, but she knew this about herself and tried to compensate. There weren't that many blacks in Albuquerque, but she had dated one for a while. His lips had touched the soft skin below her ribs; his tongue had explored her belly button. But while they were together, she found herself suggesting barbecue ribs, Kentucky Fried Chicken, even water-melon. "I love the blues," she had said, and then found herself un-able to name a single performer. "The one Diana Ross played in that old movie," she had added. She would have been humiliated, but he'd had no interest in the blues, which she found annoying. He

47

had been disappointing, hardly black at all. However, she hadn't trusted him with her daughter. There was that.

The black man she now followed down the hall went by the name of Mr. Chub. He intimidated her: his blackness, his short-ness, the swaggering teeter of his walk, the cut of his expensive clothes—pants ballooning at the waist, tapered at the ankle, as if to emphasize the brevity of his torso, and his white shirt, buttoned to the collar, cuff links (cuff links!) in the shape of gold coins.

"This is your first house of the day?" he asked, his voice smooth, like someone from radio, like Brian, her lover. Not actually her lover at the moment. Brian was her former and, she was confident, future lover. A smooth voice like Brian's, but Mr. Chub's voice was strange, too, haunting.

Monica assured him this was her first stop of the day. He paused before a closet, his hand on the brass knob, thin brows arching. Above his large head, a tight nest of dark, curly hair. *Natty* was the word that came to mind, natty hair and *nattily* dressed, but she thought they might be racist words. Her mind seemed to insist that she was a bigot, but she didn't feel it in her heart.

His big head nodded slightly. "And you . . . pardon me, but you did bathe this morning?"

"You don't have the right to ask me that," she said, suddenly defiant, fearless, then immediately afraid. She had showered and shampooed her hair. She bought shampoo from her hair stylist. She didn't scrimp on her hair.

"I apologize," he said and removed the vacuum from the closet, a Kirby Deluxe with a chrome case, brand-new and gleaming like a car just waxed.

"It's beautiful," Monica said.

"Sis-sis-sis," he stammered. "Sis-sis." He looked away, com-posed himself, his shoulders rolling mechanically. "I . . . have . . . a . . . stutter," he said, as if announcing royalty. "Rarely."

"My husband stutters," she said, dismissive, half shutting her eyes, imagining it were true. She could almost picture him, his hair rumpled, his sweet and naked mouth unable to fix on a word. "I'm used to it."

Mr. Chub seemed charmed by this. His smile grew large and rect-angular, teeth white and perfect. From the neck up he was movie-star handsome, a peaked mustache feathering his full upper lip. "If you have any questions, you may call me," he said and showed her the intercom mounted low on the wall—his level, the Chub plane. "This button is tricky," he warned, pushing it with his black thumb, pink in the creases. Not really black, of course, a shade of brown, with some red in it, like a dark oak stain, a tobacco color. The black man she had dated had been a waiter in a seafood restaurant. He had been getting a degree in economics. Uncircumcised. He pre-ferred V-neck sweaters. She made a mental note to look through Mr. Chub's clothing.

She stripped the bed, bundling the expensive pinstriped sheets, imagining this man's life, then imagining her own—a woman with a husband who stuttered, a woman who cleaned condominiums as a way to get close to the mysterious Mr. Chub. She could write an ar-ticle on him or even a book, either exposé or biography, depending. When Brian finally reappeared in her life, she would reveal that she had begun a biography, but she would refuse to divulge her subject's name. *He insists on anonymity,* she would say.

She vacuumed the big closets first, noting the shirts, identical ex-cept for color, all facing the same way and evenly spaced, like men marching in a parade. They would fit her, she thought, and wished she could try one on. There were only two sweaters, crew necks, folded and stacked on a shelf, but many belts—twenty-six—wide ones with enormous buckles, thin ones with elegant latches, belts made of metal, belts ringed with turquoise, a crude leather belt with little silver figures on it—*milagros.* She had a cross at home covered with milagros, silver shapes that healed whatever was broken—damaged arm, chronic headaches, bad marriage, loneliness. In the center of Monica's cross was a silver heart milagro. She would rub her finger over it daily and ask that her heart be healed. On Mr. Chub's belt were silver legs in a pair, one leg longer than the other. Monica touched the silver image to her lips. She would put a photo of this belt on the cover of her book. Maybe an actual milagro could be pounded into the cover of the hardback.

She knelt to inspect his footwear: six pairs of identical black shoes, polished, mounted on sloping wooden blocks. The soles of the left shoes were an inch thicker than the soles of the right. Custom-made, she thought, imagining a man kneeling and measuring her bare feet, then stretching the cloth tape to calibrate her legs, her thighs, to make shoes that would balance her perfectly, even her keel, flatten the world.

She would not sleep with Mr. Chub. No matter his grave pleading, his crooked legs bent beneath him. She inhaled sharply as she pictured it. On his knees, he would only reach her thighs. He'd have to stand, his natty hair blending with her pubis, his enchanted voice humming through her torso.

Monica cleaned houses most thoroughly when they were not dirty to begin with. Mr. Chub's spare condominium looked as if it had been cleaned the day before. She concentrated on grout in the tile lining the shower stall, grime on the chrome legs of the sink, dust at the base of the porcelain toilet.

He entered the bathroom while she knelt before the toilet, which made her gasp.

"I didn't mean to startle you," he said.

She clutched her heart, panting convincingly. "I'll be all right." She offered him a smile, which he returned.

"You work very intently," he said, that rhythmic singsong—but smooth. How would she ever find words to describe it?

The Man with the Magical Voice, a working title.

"I just thought I'd look in on you," he said.

"I'm fine," she assured him.

On her knees, she was only an inch or two shorter than he. She was on the Chub plane, the world around her instantly altered.

"You know how to reach me," he said.

He might have looked down her blouse. He turned too quickly for her to be certain.

Dear Chub, the letter began. *Have you forgotten the way to El Paso?* Monica found the letter in the trash, slipped it into her basket of cleansers, touched it several times to be sure it was still there. Even while he commended her work and promised he would ask for her again, she had slid a finger past the plastic bottle of Lysol to feel the crinkled texture of the paper. An unauthorized biography, and here was the first clue. Each week she would add to her store of knowledge about him.

She drove directly to her next customer—her next john, she used to say, as if she were a hooker, but no one had found the term provocative or funny. She parked in front of the Stalker's house, a red-brick bungalow inhabited by a middle-aged man who followed her, watching her clean, a computer genius she guessed from the mess he kept, who lived alone. "My wife died of a strap infection," he had said slyly, expecting her to be curious, a stupid joke hiding in the mispronunciation, in his watery eyes, but she had refused to ask. She thought of him as a stalker, a creep, a Heffalump; although, he had given her a set of china, unchipped and almost complete. "I've no need for it," he had said, hiding his secret motives so well she still could not name them.

She sat in the front seat of her blue Corolla under the shade of the Stalker's giant sycamore and flattened Mr. Chub's crumpled letter against her knee.

Dear Chub,
Have you forgotten the way to El Paso? We all would
like to see your ugly self some of these days soon. Does
anyone there call you WaterBoy? Have to come home to
hear the words that go straight to the heart. I am doing
alright. Really, I am. I know you heard they cut out that
lump I had that you did not know about. Which is why
I am writing, because I know somedumbody told you.
Which I didn't want. My own way of telling you would
have been more fun for the both of us. Anyhow, it is
out, and there is a little cut like a smiley face under my
nipple. You will like it.
Come see the girl who loves you no matter what.

Hear me? I love WaterBoy. I love Chub. As for Mr. Chub, he is a stranger I don't or even want to know. Don't step on my heart.

Your Only One,
Missy

Monica pressed the letter to her chest. The book would write itself. It would win all the prizes. She and Brian would cruise to Hawaii, Greece, Fiji. Sally would need a private tutor.

The curtains in the Stalker's house parted. She would keep him waiting another few minutes. The suspense would be good for his heart.

There was no question whether Brian would show up, only when. Fate being what it was, she guessed it would happen soon. His wife was already so explosively large, Monica could hardly bear to watch her wade into Casa Azul and drop onto her chair. Their baby was not due for two more months. One day Brian would come to Monica, appear at her trailer door, just before the baby was born or shortly thereafter. He would resurface in her life like a man in a boating accident who has held his breath too long: gasping and clutching, weeping over the good fortune of merely being alive.

Monica didn't volunteer at Casa Azul in order to see Brian's wife. It was important work. She had gone there the first time to gawk at her, but then she saw what they were doing. Food for the hungry. Shelter for the abused. A woman and her baby had spent one night in Monica's trailer. She had forgotten their names, but they had been dark-skinned, and the woman spoke with an accent. Monica had let them have the bed, while she slept on the sofa, next to Sally's crib—which was too small for her now. Brian would buy Sally a new bed when he came back.

Monica lunched in Waffle Park, sharing a picnic table with a guy in a black suit, red tie. His chin was too strong, pulling his face out of proportion, but Brian might be jealous, anyway—he was younger than Brian, closer to her age, and his suit was pressed and creased.

If she showed any interest at all, Brian would be jealous—if he had some way to know about it.

"Are you through with that section?" she asked the man with the chin casually, lightly touching the folded newspaper at his elbow.

"Help yourself," he said, pushing it her way.

Business section, but she glanced over it.

"Investments?" the Chin asked her. "Checking on your money?"

"I like to be informed," she said.

Her tone was brush-off, but not too brush-off. She didn't want to ever see him again, but she didn't want him to know that yet.

He returned to his lunch—a sandwich, no vegetables at all. She gave up on the business section, pulled her book from her bag. Poetry. Monica had studied poetry for a while, taken classes at the community college and through the library. She had published two poems in the college magazine. She had given up poetry to write fiction, and then given that up to paint. She sold two paintings, one to a boyfriend for twenty-five dollars, the other to a man in Santa Fe who wanted her to pose in the nude, for fifty. She had been surprised when he didn't make a pass at her. Just painted. She had spent hours at his house naked, even after he paid her. She watched *The Sopranos* naked on his couch, the artist beside her but not touching her. His painting had included the slight stretch marks on her stomach, the memory her body held of being pregnant, the way her hair remembered the hot iron with its curl.

She read her book:

> A nervous glance as eyes meet
> stare beyond
> the wide canyon

She glanced up at the Chin, who was studying the sports section now, his newspaper folded down to a little square.

"Are you nervous about something?" she asked him.

"Me?" he said, lowering the paper and beginning, then, to appear nervous.

"You look nervous," she said.

"How can you tell?" He flicked one eye oddly, a tic in the early stages.

"I bet I know your nickname," she said. "Do you have a nickname?"

"When I was a kid, I had one," he said. "What's your name?"

"That's not important," she said.

"I've seen you, though. Before. You bring your lunch here often?"

"I used to," she said, which was true.

Before Brian, she had come to Waffle Park twice a week, directly from the Stalker's house on Tuesdays and from the Colonel's on Fridays. Then she met Brian, and he had wanted to take her out so much—ethnic food, expensive places, once to a hotel in the middle of the day. He had been crazy for her, and she had quit coming to Waffle Park.

It wasn't really called Waffle Park, of course. She gave things names.

"So what do you think my nickname was?" The man with the chin shoved the paper aside. She had his complete attention.

"Water Boy," she said, smiling, cocking her head.

"Water Boy?" He sounded shocked, or tried to, then attempted a smile, but he was disappointed, that much was clear. What she said to him mattered.

"You were hoping I'd say *Romeo* or *Mr. Beautiful?*" She rolled her eyes dramatically.

"Well, no, but Water Boy?" Flicked, and flicked again, that nervous tic.

"Did I get it right?"

"Skeeter," he said. "My father—"

"I had a nickname, too," she said, though she had not yet thought what it might be.

He hesitated. His eyes wandered over her chest.

"I bet I know," he said. "I bet it was *Foxy.*" His eyes were bright now and zeroed in on her.

"Oh, please." She made a face to convey disgust. "My mother started it—the nickname—then my sisters used it, my girlfriends. It was a female kind of nickname."

"So?" he said. "What was it?"

"*Sting*," she said. "Mostly. I mean, my mother would say, 'My little Sting,' and my sister would call me 'Stinger,' and the girls called me 'The Sting.'"

She made a bridge of her fingers and let her chin rest there, happy with her invention.

"How . . . why'd they call you Sting?"

"They called me Sting because I have a big nose. It is big, isn't it?"

"I think you have a great nose."

"My ex-husband used to say that. He loved me for my nose."

"What did the boys call you?"

"Some called me Sting, the rest used my name."

"You're not going to tell me your name?"

"I come here twice a week," she said. "I'll tell you another time."

The Chin smiled again, a knowing smile, which she didn't like, and no tic. She could read him already. She would not come here again for at least a month. This idea pleased her, and she raised her book, as if she had forgotten about him.

"You must like the Police," he began. When she lowered her book and frowned, he added, "The band, you know. Sting is the lead singer, or was. I don't guess they're a band anymore."

"I hate them," she said. "They're so insipid. I quit going by that name when that band came out. That, and the last boy who called me Sting stepped on my heart."

"I have to go," the Chin said, gathering together his paper and lunch bag. "But you'll have to tell me how he did that, how he broke your heart."

"I didn't say he broke it. He stepped on it."

"Durable heart. I like that." His smile was full of self-appreciation. "See ya," he said. "I'll be looking for ya."

She gave him only a twist of her head to indicate good-bye. Already, she could hear herself tell Brian that he, Brian, had stepped on her heart, which he had, after all. He would know that already if his wife hadn't intentionally gotten pregnant. Blinding him. The idea of a baby, of becoming a father again, blinded him. Monica had meant to tell the Chin that her ex-husband stuttered, that she liked men who stuttered but she didn't like facial tics.

One time Sally's father had said to her, "What you don't know would sink a ship," which had made her think love was dependent on what you didn't know—a kind of blindness. Myopia, glaucoma, amblyopia, heterotropia, esotropia—she'd written a poem about it, eons ago, back when she had loved Sally's father and been seeing a guy named Eddie, not sleeping with him, just seeing him. Eddie had been to Nicaragua right when it was interesting to go. He had been desperate to screw her, which was why she had not let him. She had seen him twice a week for almost a year. Just petting, a little hand play.

Petting, what a funny word. She took her notebook out and wrote down the word *petting* and then made a list of the things that one might pet, starting with dogs and then describing the places on her own body that men liked to touch.

Her last house of the day was Mrs. Nighetti, whose apartment was as cluttered as Mr. Chub's was empty. Photographs of her nine sons lined the mantel of her fireplace, black-and-white photographs of beautiful young men.

"And only Vincent makes his mother happy with a grandchild," she told Monica, as she did every week. "Nine of them. Boys the girls go silly over. My phone never stopped ringing. Now their papa's dead, the phone is quiet, and what do I have to show? Only Vincent makes his mother happy with a grandchild, a girl, no less, Carlotta, which you may not know, but Carlotta is my name. Names her after his mother, my Vincent."

She did not look like a woman who had borne and raised nine sons, did not really look old, except for the bags beneath her eyes. She was confined to a wheelchair or Monica doubted she would permit someone to clean her apartment.

"Do you have any new pictures?" Monica asked her.

Mrs. Nighetti, from her wheelchair, showed Monica her palms. "You'd think that wife of his would know I want new pictures of my Carlotta every week, but she's too busy getting famous. 'I'm going to be a famous model,' she tells Vincent. To hear her talk, the baby set her back years." Mrs. Nighetti waved her hands as if to push away the very idea. "But I may have some old ones you haven't seen."

Of the three hours Monica put in weekly at Mrs. Nighetti's, half would be spent in conversation, often over cups of hot tea. She handed Monica a photograph.

"Here's my girl sitting in the lap of Miss Famous."

Miss Famous. Monica liked that. She felt sort of famous herself, a private sort of fame. A secret celebrity. It was the one real thing she knew, while the rest of the world was ignorant. She recalled, for an instant, the trip her senior class had made to Disneyland, how she had liked to pause behind people while their relatives snapped photos. All over the country, she appeared in pictures, the mystery woman in dark glasses at the border of the photos.

"Now tell me," Mrs. Nighetti said. "This Brian, has he come to his senses yet? Has he come rushing to you with an armful of roses?"

"Not a word," Monica said and sipped her tea.

"I've written my Pauly, my youngest boy. Handsome like Clark Gable, but with better skin. An electrical contractor with his own truck like they've got to have, and dating a woman whose name he won't remember in a year. Trash, forgive me for saying it."

She quickly made the sign of the cross, touching her fingertips to her lips at the beginning and again at the end. Monica had made Mrs. Nighetti teach the gesture to her during one of the visits. It took some flair to make it compelling.

"I forgive you," Monica said, which made Mrs. Nighetti flap her big hands and laugh.

Monica let her eyes roam the photographs for the one that might be Pauly. She had never met him, but his mother had written to him about her. No doubt he pictured Monica in his mind, thought about her, imagined her body, her life. What was that if not fame? The Chin was picturing her right now, she guessed. Not to mention the Stalker and Mr. Chub. Brian. She touched her fingers to her lips and crossed herself in the quick solemn manner that Mrs. Nighetti had taught her.

Sally ran her slow gallop, arms flailing, across her father's grassy yard to Monica's open arms.

"She took a nap," the new girlfriend called out, sitting on the steps, keeping her distance. "'Bout an hour and a half."

A frightened bird, Monica thought, eyeing the girlfriend. "Chirp," she said aloud but beneath her breath. "Thanks," she yelled, her voice as vibrant and happy as she could make it. She lifted her daughter into the car, buckled her into the car seat Brian had given them. "What did you do today, sugar?"

"Play," she said, taking on her car personality, the sweetly quiet child who stared out the window and clapped for dogs and trucks.

Brian would be upset about the car seat in the front—the instruction booklet recommended the rear—but Monica thought it only fair to Sally to let her ride beside her mom. What did Brian know about raising children, anyway? His own daughter was a mess. A fat, moody adolescent with pimples and an attitude. It occurred to Monica, as she pulled into traffic, that his daughter, when she'd been tiny, had probably seemed as sweet and perfect as Sally. It was not possible that Sally could turn out so badly. Monica had gotten high with Brian's daughter a few times. All after Brian had left her. A way to keep in contact with him, even though he didn't know about it, and his daughter didn't know who Monica was. "I'm the love of your father's life," she imagined herself saying.

From her car seat, Sally clapped at a passing truck, saying, "Big."

Her life is in my hands, Monica thought, steering them down the freeway, her hands resting at the bottom of the steering wheel. *My hands*, she thought, picturing a close-up of them: her fingers fill the screen, the delicate bones almost visible beneath the skin. Some actresses had stand-ins for their bodies, she'd read. It was never Nicole Kidman's breasts you saw, but some perfect girl without a face. Did her lover know that her breasts were famous?

Monica planned her evening as she drove. She would stop at Casa Azul briefly to see how huge Brian's wife was, to see if his daughter wanted a ride somewhere. She would stop at Alpha Beta to get milk and Pampers. She would drive by Brian's house without even glancing at it. She would get to the trailer in time for the last half hour of *Sesame Street*. She would read Mr. Chub's letter again. She might begin the biography. Notes about his condominium, the way he walked, the way his beautiful breathless voice rode the air. He had wanted to know whether she'd bathed, which meant he had pictured her naked. She would mention the shiny vacuum, and the belts in his closet, the custom-made shoes that gave him balance. And his shirts, all those shirts, the way they faced the same direction, one after another, identical but for color, one spaced perfectly after the next, like promises kept, like a series of snapshots all the same, like the days of a life.

A WALK
IN WINTER

Snow weighted the limbs of trees. Mounds of snow lined the shoulders of the county road and cloaked the adjacent fields. Snow lathered the air. Snow brought Conrad home.

"You have to like the cold to live up here," Sheriff Mallon said. He slipped a hand from the steering wheel to remove his hat and dust snow from his jacket, the finger of his glove erasing a dozen years from his eyebrows. The official vehicle, a huge Suburban, was forest green, inside and out.

Conrad positioned his hands before the heater vents. He had left his gloves on the plane. The township of Chapman, North Dakota, had no airport. In this weather, the drive from Grand Forks could take four hours.

"I never liked the cold," Conrad said. "Not when I was a child, not now."

A pier of electronic apparatus separated him from the sheriff. A queue of red lights flashed on the slender face of a police radio. Saddled to the radio was a louvered microphone and cochleate cord. A second screen displayed digital numbers shifting from 00 to 05.

"That's the radar," Sheriff Mallon said. "The trees are growing at five miles an hour." He indicated with a nod the plastic trumpet on the dash. Without his hat, he looked like a boy. "It sounds slow, but if they really did grow that fast, a seedling in the a.m. would be taller than Everest by nightfall."

"You must spend a lot of time alone," Conrad said. He tucked his hands inside his jacket, under his armpits. He was a chemist and spent a lot of time alone himself.

The Suburban gyrated slightly on the ice.

"I should have chained the tires," Sheriff Mallon said. "You have to drive so slow with chains, I didn't want to bother."

The road wound through a broad valley. The river that dictated the road's curves had vanished, turned to ice and laminated with snow, as solid now as any other piece of the frozen world. Beyond this rolling esplanade, on either side, lay forest. Conrad had learned of his mother's disappearance in such a landscape. He had been ten years old. The farmhouse in which he had lived had a handmade ladder that led to the unfinished second story, the walls framed but only the exterior covered. Conrad had leapt over straw insulation from one joist to the next. Frost made the lumber slick. Twice he fell. The noise, he feared, would alert his father.

Beginning with the south window, he searched for his mother's path through the snow. No one could walk on snow without leaving a trail, he reasoned, not his mother, not even Christ. Beyond their farm stood the forest, as dense and dispiriting as a roar. The only clear footpath led to the chicken coop and had been made by his father's boots. The tractor, their one functional vehicle, had a heap of snow on its black seat, the great tires buried. Conrad could not even see evidence of the road that led to their house. The only possible paths were two runnels in the snow that curled out to the forest. The wind might have softened their appearance, and new fall disguised them. Or they could have been made by animals, a funnel of wind, a trick of the underlying geography.

If she did the smart thing, she cut through the woods to their nearest neighbor. Conrad ran to the next window, stumbling again, the straw slapping his cheek. He couldn't seem to catch his breath, yet it fogged the window. There was no sign of a trail, but he resolved to hike to the neighboring farm to search for her.

His father waited at the bottom of the ladder. He took hold of Conrad's head to examine it. "Straw," he said, pulling loose a twig. Gripping the waist of Conrad's pants and the collar of Conrad's shirt, he carried him down the hall and locked him in his room. The drift beyond the bedroom window reached almost to the top of the glass. Conrad threw himself on his bed and wept.

"Snow has always been a civilizing factor in history," Sheriff Mallon said. "Compare the north to the south, Scandinavia to the tropics." He pointed a gloved finger at the landscape, but Conrad saw only the rumpled white blanket of winter. His window held a cornea of ice. "Deer," the sheriff said.

As he spoke, the deer materialized by the side of the road, a startled doe racing alongside the Suburban.

The sheriff lifted his foot from the accelerator. "They do the damnedest things."

The deer cocked her head and the sheriff braked. The vehicle began to skate, turning to one side, sliding forward at an angle, the running deer suddenly framed by the windshield. As the front of the Suburban crossed the centrifugal line, the engine's weight whipped the vehicle around. At the same moment, the doe made her crossing, darting in front of them, the swinging rear of the truck gliding magnetically alongside her body. But the trailer hitch caught the deer's back leg and upended her, sent her skidding into the high white bank left by a state snowplow. She flew into the mound headfirst and snow collapsed over her. She vanished.

The Suburban rolled backward to a stop, all four tires on the road.

"Be careful with her," the sheriff said.

The outside air, brittle glass, splintered in Conrad's lungs. He nudged his door shut, afraid to touch the metal with his bare hands. On the other side of the truck, the sheriff paused at his door to flip a switch. The flashing lights on the roof shone blue and white. Appropriate colors for the cold world, Conrad thought.

He reached the snowbank first and shoved aside loose fall, cursing himself again for losing his gloves. A furred flank appeared.

Conrad touched the leg hesitantly, then gripped it and pulled, his feet sliding. The animal was larger and heavier than she had looked. The sheriff uncovered another leg. Together they freed her.

"She's not breathing," Sheriff Mallon said. "Watch her."

Conrad thought they might gut this deer and lash it to the metal rack on the truck's long roof. His father had been a hunter. Conrad had eaten a lot of game as a boy.

The sheriff retrieved a metal box from the vehicle. The open lid revealed columns of switches and dials. Sheriff Mallon lifted two disks from the box, each with a black cord and Velcro straps. Mallon slid the straps over his hands.

"When I tell you, hit that green button." He knelt over the deer and placed the disks on the doe's chest. "Now!" he yelled, as if Conrad were far away.

Conrad punched the button. The disks sent a shock through the doe's body. Her four legs kicked. She raised her head and peered about, back from the dead. She stared at Conrad, her face inches from his. For an absurd moment, Conrad thought she might speak. Then she got to her feet and began running.

Conrad's laughter caused him to teeter and drop onto the ice. He rose quickly to one knee to follow the doe's prance through the high snow. He was speechless with delight until he saw blood on the sheriff's face.

"She kicked me," Mallon said.

The right side of his face was split open.

Conrad drove the Suburban in the direction from which they had come. Sheriff Mallon lay moaning in the back. The snowfall grew heavy. Conrad kept his eyes on the yellow line dividing the road or on the slope of snow that marked the shoulder. He'd had an accident behind the wheel, five years earlier. No one had been hurt, but it had changed his life. He had been driving his girlfriend's son to day care. The boy was buckled into his safety seat in the back of the Taurus. They were talking, as they did daily. The boy said, "Remember that dream we had about those guys and those animals?"

It should have made Conrad smile. He recalled looking for the boy in the rearview mirror. He meant to ask the boy to describe the dream, but he could not complete the gesture. His stomach cramped and his hands trembled. This is fear, Conrad thought. He had to name it to understand what was happening.

Fear made Conrad double over. He threw his arms around the steering wheel and leaned against it. Tilting his body, he directed the car off the road, onto the shoulder. He failed to find the brake in time and ran into a chain-link fence. The poles of the fence remained upright, but the wires holding the links snapped, and the fence recoiled as if it were a living creature.

Conrad cut the engine and pushed open his door. He tumbled from the car while the boy called for him.

"I'm all right," Conrad shouted, but he did not sound all right, even to himself. The child cried and flailed in his safety seat. Conrad climbed to his feet. "I just have a tummy ache," he told the boy, a small part of the truth. He leaned against the car and walked hand over hand to the open door. The cramping eased. Lifting his knees to dust them, he expected to find snow, but he lived in Arizona and it was September.

It was not that he had recalled something he had forgotten. He would never forget the walk he took with his father. He did not like to think about it, but he had not forgotten it. He had suffered a moment of terror from that walk. Something had brought it back. He lifted the boy from his restraints and carried him to a parts store across the street. Conrad called his girlfriend. A *breakdown,* she labeled it. She spoke as if the problem were merely vehicular.

Conrad checked the gauges on the Suburban. He did not believe he would have another breakdown. He had managed his life more carefully since the accident. Ahead, he saw white and blue flashes. He couldn't see the car until he was almost even with it. Sheriff Mallon had radioed ahead. The window on the cruiser lowered.

"Follow me," said a young man in a ski mask. His siren sounded.

Conrad felt a funny thrill, driving the Suburban, following the police car, the few vehicles on the plowed city streets pulling off to let them by—all the moving things in the world scurrying to get out of their way.

The first decade of his life Conrad spent on a small farm outside Chapman. By the time he was old enough to have memories of the place, his father had quit raising cash crops. They had a vegetable garden each summer, and his father hunted game in the neighboring woods. They had no money, except the monthly envelope his aunt sent. She lived in St. Paul, Minnesota, where she cleaned houses. Eventually, Conrad would go to live with her. One of her clients, a professor at Macalester College, took an interest in Conrad. When Conrad graduated from high school, the professor came to their house with a present—a tuition waiver to the college. The life that Conrad lived he owed to that professor and to his aunt, but not to them alone. He owed his mother, who had protected him from his father. And he owed his father, who had saved his life.

His aunt liked to say his parents had not been well suited for each other. To others, she said horrible things about his father. Conrad's mother had a few slight deformities—her nose was asymmetrical and one of her eyelids drooped. In profile, her right side showed a disfigured woman, while her left side revealed a beauty. Her teeth were a mess, the bottom row listing like a stand of trees maligned by prevailing winds.

Conrad's father was no taller than his mother and almost as slight, but he was dark while she was light, and handsome while she was ugly. He had gone to St. Paul looking for a wife. His parents had died the winter before. He needed help on the farm. He was marginally educated and nervous among people, but he was healthy and good-looking, and Conrad's mother, who had been a cashier at a grocery, had been happy to give him directions about town and flattered to find him waiting in the parking lot when she finished her shift. He owned land and the farmhouse. At that time, he'd had a few cows and pigs. He likely told her about the animals and especially the house, how it looked complete from the outside, but the rooms upstairs were skeletal.

Conrad had no memory of animals on the farm, except for the

ragged hens in their stinking coop and the creatures his father would kill and drag home—rabbits, quail, deer, a neighbor's dog or goat, prairie dogs, ducks, fox, house cats. He presented the gutted creatures to his wife with a kind of magisterial silence. He spoke little and expected to be obeyed. He hadn't always been a harsh man. A bad crop of corn the summer Conrad was three had changed him. The pigs and cattle didn't survive the winter. They needed grain he couldn't provide. Conrad's mother spoke often of the winter their lives turned grim, as well as the time before, when she had held out some hope. Conrad was returning to Chapman to identify his mother's frozen remains.

"We got a room for you at the Motel 6," the policewoman said. She had a boxy head, a square smile. OFFICER PATTY, her tag read. Her police cap had flattened a recent perm, making it stick out on the sides. She looked deranged. She had bought him gloves and handed them over, along with the receipt and his change.

Conrad thanked her. They stood in the hospital cafeteria, drinking coffee. The room smelled powerfully of gravy. Everyone had taken a table near a window to watch the blizzard grow near. The snow had let up, as if in anticipation of the storm, while the sky turned solid, a thick metallic lid the color of pewter. Conrad asked about the sheriff.

"He'll live," Officer Patty said and finger-waved to someone seated nearby.

One of the nurses had flirted with Conrad, a young blond with straight white teeth and a full chest. She somehow thought of him as heroic, although she had heard the details of the afternoon. Nonetheless, he had driven up under the flicker of constabulary lights and delivered an injured officer to people who could care for him. She had hinted about dinner. Conrad had politely ignored her.

"I know your aunt," Officer Patty said. "Most of the people in law enforcement hereabouts know her. Quite a determined lady."

"She's a force of nature," Conrad said.

"You'd think, after twenty years, she'd give up. Finally we have something on our plate. I hope this'll put an end to her grief." She touched her hair. "Oh, flatty Patty."

"Can you give me a lift to the motel?" Conrad asked her.

"In the job description," she said, fluffing her hair. "Protect and serve. Around here, it's mostly serve."

She, too, drove a Suburban, a hula dancer wiggling on the dash. Wind lifted fresh fall from the drifts, but the impending storm still lingered outside the city. A peculiar light resulted, a solemn gray illumination that lent the drab buildings a dignity they did not deserve.

Officer Patty said, "Your aunt thinks maybe you spoke with your father back five or so years ago."

"She never said that to me," Conrad replied. His aunt wanted to find her little sister. She wanted justice when there could be none.

"Something in your behavior tipped her off."

"My aunt is a peculiar kind of conspiracy nut," he said. "She believes every detail of my behavior has its roots in a single bed. But the world is full of unpleasant catalysts."

"She's always putting two and two together," Officer Patty acknowledged, "and sometimes gets five. Or seven. Still, she says you went into a shell."

"I had an accident in a car. I haven't seen my father since I left the farm."

"*Seen* is a tricky word," Officer Patty said. "*Contact* might be the better word. Any contact whatsoever?"

"None," Conrad said.

"It may seem like ancient history, but if this turns out how we expect," she continued, "talking with him and not telling us, that could be interpreted as accessory after the fact."

Conrad said nothing in response to this, but shook his head contemptuously.

"I'd just hate to see that happen to you," she said.

At Motel 6 he said, "I appreciate the gloves."

Sheriff Mallon appeared at Conrad's motel room the following morning. A white square of gauze covered one side of his face. White tape held it in place.

"You're gonna have to drive," he said. "I'm taking Percodan."

"You look like a deer kicked you in the face," Conrad replied.

They had to take alleys to the edge of town. The chains on the tires would gouge the asphalt, Mallon explained.

"Policy is twenty miles an hour max with chains. I may lose vision in the eye."

"I can get someone else to take me," Conrad said.

The sheriff began to shake his head again then stopped himself. "I'm supposed to keep my head still. Had to pay a kid to put the chains on. My doctor will be in Chapman on Thursday, anyway. No point staying here."

At the highway, Conrad kept the vehicle on the shoulder until they came upon a stalled snowplow, a man in a fat coat examining its smoking engine. Sheriff Mallon studied the scene as they passed.

"This is an idiotic place to live," he said.

Once they had the chains on the appropriate terrain, the men rode in clanking silence. After a while, the sheriff said, "You know what I kept thinking the whole time they messed with my face? They didn't put me under. I wish to god they had. I kept thinking about that deer. She's out there wondering what the hell is going on. Pain's got to be a different experience if you don't know what it is, you know what I mean?"

"No," Conrad said. "I don't know what you mean."

"Maybe it's the Percodan talking, but it seems to me humans must feel pain differently because we can point to the source of it. A deer gets hit by a truck and it hurts. Fine. She knows the source of the pain—that great green metal monster that tried to eat her. That's what she'd think." He gestured with his hand, the open palm hesitating in the air. "But then, she gets up and runs away, sleeps through the night. Now it's morning, and she wakes up feeling real bad. What's the deal now? she wonders. There's no green metal monster—well, she wouldn't know what *metal* meant—there's no roaring green monster here to bash my leg. Why do I feel this pain? Me, I know why and I know what can happen. I can wind up needing cosmetic surgery, which my insurance won't cover. I can wind up blind in one eye, which'd mean I'd have to quit sheriffing. Hell,

I'm not even sure this will be taken as an 'in the line of duty' injury. In which case, I'll owe the hospital a fortune. But that's not the point. What was I talking about?"

"The deer."

"She's got to be thinking there's something inside her, like a rat—not that she'd know what a rat is. A forest animal, a squirrel or something. Maybe she'd think her thigh is frozen. That's my point. She can't know. It's like lightning striking when you don't even have a word for the sky."

"How many Percodan did you take?"

"Several. This thing hurts like hell. I just was trying to tell you what I thought was this profound thing. How a deer can't know what we know."

"Do you think deer have a concept of death?"

"Sure, they do," Sheriff Mallon said. It began to snow. "They know there's something that happens to the others—the deer they run with. The ones that die. They know that a body asleep and a dead body are two whole different things. I don't imagine they guess it could ever happen to them personally." He grew quiet again. The snow fell lazily like the snow in dreams. "I have a friend used to work in a slaughterhouse down in Iowa. Cows marched along this ramp to the killing floor where it was my friend's job to shoot them in the head with a rifle. Says those cows knew. They were scared as hell. Lowing like all get-out. Christ, I hate to think about it." He started to shake his head again, but put his hand to his chin to hold his head in place. "Iowa's an awful place. My buddy is my age, but you'd think he was fifty. How old are you?"

"Thirty-two," Conrad said.

"I shouldn't have revived that deer." The patch on his face made him appear unfinished, missing a piece. "It's out there somewhere in pain. There's a kind of code about this. You don't leave an animal to suffer."

The Suburban descended into the valley they had visited the day before, the white fields and hazy defoliated forest.

"I shouldn't be laying all this on you. You've got your own burden. Your mother found after all these years." He unbuckled his shoulder belt and shifted in the seat to lay the good side of his head against the headrest. "Had to clean out the freezer to store her parts. Everybody at the station took home venison. We don't get much actual crime. Graffiti. If it's summer, Mrs. Morrison's likely to run up the street in her nightie. But murder . . ."

"It was a long time ago."

"People remember your dad," he said. "Not till we found this body did people think he literally killed her, just that he made her run out into the cold, where she froze. A man matching his description in Saskatchewan operates a diner. Had a run-in with local authorities. They faxed a photo, but after twenty years who could say? I *will* ask you to take a look." He settled his head back and shut his good eye. "Nobody much recalls your mother. I hope there's enough that you can ID her." He remained silent for several minutes. "That poor creature," he said. "Out there in the cold. In pain. And not a clue."

In another moment, the sheriff began to snore. Conrad noted the place where the deer had been hit. The emergency gear still rested on the shoulder, covered now in snow. He did not consider stopping to retrieve it. As for the deer, Conrad believed she likely knew as much about death as he did. He would be able to identify his mother if they had the lower jaw. Her slanting teeth would make the identification.

The idea that his father might run a diner amused Conrad. His father had cooked for him exactly once. Conrad had stepped into the kitchen one morning and found his father frying an egg.

"Your mother run off," his father said. He put the egg on a plate and handed it to Conrad. "From now on, cook for yourself."

"Is she coming back?" Conrad asked.

His father had said all he was going to say. Conrad ate the egg, fearing what his father would do if he didn't. He had never actually hit Conrad, nothing more than a cuff or slap, but his mother had always been there to intervene, to put her body between the man and the boy. Conrad ate the egg and climbed the ladder to the second floor to look for her, but he never saw his mother again.

He recognized almost nothing of Chapman, yet the general contours of the town were still familiar. The school had been remodeled, but he could make out the old shape hiding beneath the stucco. The county sheriff's office took up a corner of a strip mall.

"Oh, my heavens," the secretary said.

She put her hands to her face, as if she wanted Conrad to count the painted nails. She was a vaguely pretty woman. It might have been just her concern that made her attractive. She reached out to Sheriff Mallon but pulled her hands back. Blood had soaked through the bandage, and the sheriff's cheek was swollen.

"I've got to get him home," she said and then introduced herself. Abigail. Her fingernails were the pink of salmon. "Could you hold down the ship for me?" she asked. "There's only the two of us, and a deputy who's been on duty since Sheriff Mallon left to get you. Everybody and his dog has slid off the road. He's got his hands full with vehicular. I won't be more than an hour."

Minutes after arriving, Conrad found himself alone in the sheriff's office. He seated himself at the sheriff's desk and went through the sheriff's drawers. None of the reports he found related to the body. One drawer held a Polaroid of the sheriff with two people who might be his parents. They had chalky skin and prim smiles.

Conrad tried the deputy's smaller desk. The drawers held almost nothing—loose paper clips and cellophane-wrapped post-its, a can of soup, a motorcycle magazine. The cover of the magazine showed a woman wearing a bikini on a chopper. The photo centered on her buttocks, her bathing suit the same chrome as on the motorcycle.

Conrad found the file on the unidentified remains in Abigail's desk. She also had the most comfortable chair. Blanched photographs showed a stand of trees, the yellow ribbon of official business, and a vague shape on the ground, which must have been a piece of the body. It had been found by a farmer's son, the report said. Conrad already knew this. The boy's dog had brought in a bone with a scrap of clothing chewed into the marrow. The boy followed the dog's tracks through the snow to a wooded ravine where other bones lay scattered. The sheriff had found shot in the splintered pelvis.

> The unidentified victim appears to have been blown in
> half by the discharge of a shotgun at very close range. Or
> animals may have separated the body after the shooting.

The report was full of pen scribbles—someone, likely Abigail, making grammatical suggestions, revising for clarity. The county coroner had attempted to reach Chapman but had been stopped by the weather. By the coroner's name, Abigail had written *prima donna!* State investigators would arrive at week's end, weather permitting. A fax explained to what extent *presumed relatives* could examine the remains to identify the body.

Conrad closed the file. He found the freezer in the hall, long and white, large enough to hold an intact body. The lid of the freezer had a lock with the key in it. Conrad raised the freezer's hood. Frost covered Tupperware containers. The first he lifted held a bone shard, as did the second. The third had discolored skin and gray gristle attached to the bone. As he snapped the lid back on, he spotted a label and wiped frost from it. BONE, it read. Conrad laughed, and the laughter continued long enough to make him nervous. He squatted with his back against the freezer and slowed his breathing. What amateurs these people were. Yet he liked them. The cold air from the open lid slipped over the side of the appliance and chilled the back of his neck.

He took the containers from the freezer and stacked them on the floor. They were as tall as a person. He wiped frost from the labels, working his way down the stack until he found one that said JAWBONE. He pried off the plastic lid. The bone was in three pieces, but the angle of the teeth was clear enough. This was not his mother's body.

Conrad returned the containers to the freezer. He closed the freezer door and settled himself at Abigail's desk. He felt neither elated nor discouraged, merely fatigued. He lowered his head onto the desk and fell asleep.

"It's not good coffee," Abigail said, "but it warms you up."

He looked at his watch. He had slept almost two hours. True to her word, the coffee was terrible, but it felt good in his throat and warmed his stomach. Abigail had changed clothes. Conrad was certain of this, although he couldn't recall what she had worn before. She now wore a dress and black leggings. Earrings. Makeup. She looked ready for a date.

"I'd let you sleep longer," she said, "but it's time for me to lock up."

"The sheriff's office shuts down?"

"We have call forwarding," she said. The part of her lips revealed teeth as white as the snow. "The sheriff was gonna put you up, but he's passed out from Percodan and in no condition to entertain."

"Is there a motel?" Conrad asked.

"In Chapman? Are you serious? Have you made eating arrangements?"

"Can I sleep here?"

"There's only the cot in the cell, and that's just too ghastly." She sighed. "I suppose you're my guest."

"You have plans. You're all dressed."

"Oh," she said. "This is nothing."

In her car, navigating the frozen parking lot, she revealed that the deputy had turned up another bit of evidence.

"You should have seen the sheriff when I told him. He hates anything happening while he's gone."

"I looked in the freezer," Conrad said. "It's not my mother."

"Well," Abigail said, deflated.

Snow pelted the windshield. She slowed for a pedestrian standing at an intersection. He was bundled in black—shoes, pants, parka, woolen hat. Only his scarf had any color, a red like the lipstick from old advertisements. She brought her car to a full stop and waited while the pedestrian crossed the road.

"I guess I shouldn't be disappointed," Abigail said. "You can still have hope she's alive somewhere."

"No," said Conrad. "I don't have any hope of that."

The car slowly accelerated. "Who could this be?" She put her fingers to her mouth and tapped a tune on her teeth, pausing to add, "We just don't have people unaccounted for."

"What's the new evidence?"

The tapping ended. Her hand returned to the wheel. "The murder weapon. We think. A rifle. Right there with the bones. The handle was chewed up some, like an animal had dragged it about."

Conrad took a deep breath. He felt a specific, small elation, like being the first at a party to get the joke.

"It was a sawed-off shotgun," he said.

Abigail slowed the car and looked at him.

"It's my father you've found." He crossed his arms against a shiver in his chest. "You can show me tomorrow, but I'm certain."

"Who would have killed your father?"

"He himself," Conrad said.

Her gaze made her face naked. She stared so long that he had to reach over and correct the wheel. Her house was small and painted red, nestled among larger houses, hardly more than a cottage, but warm inside. She boiled spaghetti and heated sauce from a jar. Conrad told her a few things.

After his mother disappeared, his father gave up language almost completely. In the past, he and his father had never been alone in the house—only in the vegetable garden or in the woods hunting for game.

"I know it sounds implausible," he said to Abigail, "to people raised in a house with a television and stereo, whose home was in a neighborhood, whose parents held jobs, but it's the truth. My mother never left me alone in the same room with my father for more than a matter of seconds. When she went to the bathroom, she took me with her."

"Unbelievable," Abigail said. Then, "I believe you."

Conrad and Abigail slept in the same bed. The shared bed was not about sex. The electricity in the house died shortly after dinner. They built a fire and lit candles. They kept each other warm.

"I'm tempted to entertain myself with your body," Abigail told him, her painted nails touching his neck. "But I shouldn't while you're here on official business."

Conrad recognized his disappointment in this dismissal. He hardly knew her, but he felt uncommonly alive in her bed. She fell asleep, the warm air from her nostrils ruffling the slight, bleached hair on her upper lip, her eyes moving beneath their thin sheathing.

He was too agitated to sleep. He ran a finger over the textured chambers of her insulated shirt. He traced a nipple, and it changed shape beneath the material. He thought of the emergency equipment left by the side of the road. He placed his hands just where the disks would go. She stirred but did not wake. The memory that had been summoning him for years blew against the dark windows.

His father had come into the kitchen where Conrad was building a fire in the stove. "Leave it," his father said. He made a gesture with his shotgun, the buttstock pointing to the door.

Midday, a dim sun lit the snow on the ground, the sky cloudy and cold, wind lifting the skirt of recent snow up and into the freezing air. Conrad carried the shotgun. According to his mother, a dog had made the teeth marks in the gun's buttstock. His father denied ever owning a dog. At the time of the walk, his mother had been gone four weeks.

The neighbor's livestock seemed their most likely prey, but they did not head in that direction. His father said nothing. The teeth of the cold air gnawed at the soft places on Conrad's face. He had to take two steps to his father's one, but he felt a pathetic surge of glee. He had been terribly lonely without his mother, and the only time he felt comfortable with his father was when they were hunting.

At the edge of the woods, they stopped. Conrad needed to pee but it was his custom to wait, out of modesty, until they were among the trees, even though there was no one within miles to see. It had begun to snow. His father gestured for the shotgun. Their farmhouse, in the distance, seemed to have a hole of light in it. It took Conrad a moment to understand the front door was open. He shifted his gaze to his father's face. His father appeared to be studying him.

He said, "You know what that word means?"

Conrad had spoken no word and, except to ask the question, neither had his father. His father seemed to think Conrad was privy to his thoughts. Conrad opened his mouth but only breathed. The cold air found his tongue, and he tasted winter. His father turned quickly. The barrel of the shotgun swung around. It would have hit Conrad had he not moved. He stumbled and fell, but got up quickly and dusted snow off his knees.

His father said, "It's what you do to a woman." He breathed heavily, the exhaust of his nostrils white and furious. "And there's no pleasure in it." He pointed to a tree stump covered in snow. "Over there." He wanted Conrad to sit on the stump. His father evidently had more to tell him.

Conrad shoved the snow off the tree stump. A thin layer of ice covered the wood, but he sat anyway and looked up to his father, who gestured for him to turn, to face the other way. Snow animated the sky and painted the world about him. He heard the shotgun crack open behind him, heard his father load one shell and then the other. It was then that he understood. The frozen world paused for him, the woods still and orderly under their white quilt. Even the snow coming from the heavens became stationary in midair, a white organism Conrad had never before seen whole, but only in its million parts.

The shotgun reunited with a snap. Conrad sensed creatures in the forest going about their lives, refusing to be his witness. The fabric of his father's coat made a little cry as he raised his arms. Conrad lost control of himself. Urine soaked though his pants and ran out onto the stump. It made a spirit of steam.

"You wet yourself," his father said, his words startling and heavy. "Get up or you'll freeze to the stump." He lowered the shotgun. "You'd best hurry."

The urine began to ice Conrad's legs as they retraced their steps. He tried to run. His pants froze to the fine hairs on his legs. He stumbled and continued. He fell to his knees, got up, and fell again into the crusted snow, which embraced him, held him as his mother had, a comfort and protection. Conrad tried, but he could not get back to his feet. The snow was no longer cold but warm, and the warmth spread throughout his body.

His father lifted him by the waist of his pants and hefted him into his arms. He carried Conrad the final distance home. When they crossed the threshold, his father shut the door that had been left open. He put Conrad before the stove in the kitchen and re-kindled the fire.

Conrad sat before the blazing stove in a kitchen chair. His father stood nearby, his back against the wall, his hands behind him, the shotgun at his side. He thought to bring the boy a blanket and then resumed his position. He did not speak. As Conrad remembered it, his father did not move. But he stayed there, watching while his son thawed.

Conrad was sent to bed. He heard the front door open and shut. His father did not come back until after dark, stamping snow from his boots, walking heavily to the bedroom door. The boy's heart beat so hard that he imagined he could make it out beneath his flesh, hidden but present. His father spoke through the closed door.

"Pig you have to cook clean through."

In the morning Conrad discovered that his father had stolen a neighbor's pig, a small thing that he had gutted in his arms while he held it like a baby. Conrad found his father's clothes on the porch, blood frozen into the fabric, and he reconstructed the butchering. His father himself was gone. Conrad would not see him alive again.

It occurred to him, while he lay sleepless in Abigail's bed, to wonder about the boy who had been riding in his safety seat when Conrad crashed into the chain-link fence. How had that accident become one of the stones on which the boy's character was built? The boy by now would be ten himself. He would no longer think another person might share his nocturnal dreams. Conrad understood that he had loved the boy.

Electricity returned to Chapman before dawn. Abigail made coffee. Conrad had slept little, but his head was clear. The coffee was strong and gratifying. He told Abigail about the walk in winter with his father.

"I feel better about it now," he said.

"Why?" she asked him. "Why on earth would you? Because you know he's dead? Because he can't harm you now?"

This would be what his aunt would think, what his therapist would think.

"It's more specific than that," he said. His father had meant all along to include himself. Conrad understood that now. He tried to explain. "It makes it less personal."

Outside, the morning snow fell onto the snow that had fallen through the night.

A SKETCH OF HIGHWAY ON THE NAP OF A MOUNTAIN

Let's forbear the usual drift.

Billy, the main guy in all this, has trouble of female origins. His dally this time entails no tangible scram. Never up, never in. But the attempt, her name is Karen, carries the same wave, and his old lady gives him the stroll. Which is what sends him to me. Back when I was one hundred per, I was the female organs Billy troubled.

He comes calling here with nickels in his packet and a plaintiff, he tells me, that still won't stand, even with a video in the mouth and women taking off their robes right and left on the big scream Mitsubishi.

"My body," he says to me, "kept the faith."

Did I convention how Billy and I were a pair for ten years? And he, I'm told, pulled the same stunt without me, and couldn't get it up then, either. Even with my sister, who, I can tell you, has beauty.

"Why did you take him back?" she asks me.

I say, "Ten years is a big chump of your life."

He arrives on the porch, hands in his golfing pockets, staring out through the mosquito screens at the groves of lemon backdrop and oriental oranges. I live in the citrus desert of Arizona, where, with enough laughter, anything will flourish. Billy used to live here with me. When I push open my door, he turns and stares. No one can believe I live alone.

"You know," he says, and his voice is one of those familiar things, like the way some people recall music, "who I am?"

I go, "Billy," and wonder how dressed I am for a man who used to be the one I was wife to. His car is clocking out by the porch steps, time running down as it cools. I'm in a nightgown but have a skirt under it, as if ready for the ball.

"It's good to see you," he says, and says more literal things that orbit my ears like the popsicle sticks and candy wrappers that swirm the dense water next to the canal gate. Suitcases lashed to the roof of his car make the picture crystal. He loves me again and he's got no other bed to rest his buddy, which can, after a workout, have a sour effect, like that bathroom in some car station I can't remember where, that had a wooden Indian ten feet tall and not made of wood.

"All of my parts still work," I say, smiling at what it means and how it must sound to people who cannot, anymore, wonder about such things aloud. Whenever I get irrigated with my life, I remind myself of all they can't say either.

Billy shows the teeth he's been hiding just as the sun dips under the wooden eaves of my porch, making him like that god people talk about. But how often do they see him ablaze on a porch with suitcases tied to his car?

A zithering rush of movement. And the dizzying things that take us to bed do their work—in the him-on-top-of-me fashion—his cheeks juggling with each ricochet, and the candy going on in my middle like it always has, that memory a part of my gravitation, and it builds and sifts into something almost horticultural.

It feels so much I scream.

When I wake up, he's got the car things in my drawers.

"I never," he says to me in that same voice he has, "should have left you."

I had sort of forgotten that he fled like a hat from a hive when the wind goes crying through. The memory winces down my atrium until I hear the timer that reminds me to eat. Food is one of the things not to do alone if you don't have to. We park at either end of the tableau, Billy skinning the plastic wrap from the scheming platters.

"I'll cook for you," he says, which makes me happy and worried for my timer.

That is a fine day, the day he parks by my porch and disgorges his car into my—what is it when it's more than a house? And the fellow days are the same—the good bright hallows and lighthearted skew. Nothing gets in the way of how he puts his hands on my round bottles and rubs a small circus. "Sweet Cheeks," he calls me, which makes me look at the cobbler around my wrist with the letters of my name. "Valerie," I say aloud, while he does with his mouth's finger my one thing and then my other, a whole alphabet of pleasure.

Early one deepening, we watch from the porch as a coyote crosses the swath, a black kitten striving in its mouth.

"My god," says Billy. "This place is a wonder."

He begins happily dissembling our past, our years in this house— the hawk coughed in chicken wire, the cumulus of rain that throttled the road, the tracing chill of splintered mornings. I pretend to remember more than I hold on to. But the taste of flesh on my mouth when he kisses me is wish-making and longed for, like the satisfaction of eating when you don't know you're hungry.

Even if I can't frame what I'm missing, I can tell it's gone, and that makes it mine.

Billy was driving when the tree came through the window's shield. He has in his soft place beneath the pit of one arm, a skashing seam, crooked as a burble in a brook. I don't have mark one on me. Except the smile hidden by my trick of hair. Hair doesn't have to remember. It goes on like nothing ever tarnished the pot it grows in. Mine is wavy when it gets long, like a sketch of highway on the nap of a mountain.

It's a different day altogether when the fireplug—his recent ex— comes and returns his things to the roof of his Dodge. I don't get it for a while and even help with a few loafs. When it hits me, I'm at the car, divulging a black boom box.

"Oh," I say, "you're moving up."

"Out," he says, "not up."

Which makes me think for one monument that I have it all wrong. But, no, on this particular invasion, I've got it right.

Before they go, they show me how people look when they carry on in my bed. A more gentle stack than you might think. She offers me her bare hand. They disarray me kindly.

And they sleep, the three of us, in the following light. I dream a dream of waking, and flowers in the room, a set of shiny tools latched to the wall—silver pliers and bullet-peen hammer and a shiny crushing wrench.

When I really wake, it's to the scrubbing sound of Billy reaming the tub.

"Everything is clean," he says, streaks on his face as he erases me his arms. They have dressed. The girl skates my hand while he holds me.

Then wouldn't you if you weren't me know it? They and the car both papoose.

It's not "dravel," the little gray rockets that make up the road and hurt my feet, but all I have to offer is what's prattling around in my bag, and "dravel" keeps enlisting. So . . .

I stand in my dravel drive-away umbrella a sky as wide and dark as the afterward of a fire—a black with no bottom and yet scarred with light. It's a cool night and I'm naked, but a steeling warmth comes over me. The green scent of the groves and the canal's artificial water hole me still. In this fraction of the country, people staple ranches from the desert. They burn crops out of land most people wouldn't bother tasting. It's where I below. And where I'll stave.

I know I will not come fully to.

But what I think right now is, *This is beautiful.*

I'm unsure that I've got it right, what all this means—Billy's sudden aperture and the hostly gray of the road, the white shaft from the kitchen wind row, the green orange trees, and the way I posture naked and skinflint in the sky's widening yawn. For tonight, anyway, I'm willing to cast my trademark on faith.

There's no shortage of wander in my life.

It's a big house and getting around in it can be surprising, like when you discover it's the next day. Unless there's evidence, how can you know the difference from one to the next? We all need evidence. We need a life that is evidence-making.

Anyway, what house this is I know is mine. And that dingling noise is the timer, which means it's morning and I'm hungry. Even when you're alone, you're requested to eat. Or you'll forget and become so thin even the wind won't notice. And then nothing in the wide world can move you.

SUPREME BEINGS

Father McEwen knew the advantage of his height and used it for God's work. He leaned heavily on the jamb, filling the doorway. He was nearing fifty and more of his bulk shifted each year from muscle to fat, but he knew how to exhibit himself. In the presence of one who had faltered in faith or deed, he became the immovable object.

"You haven't done much with the place, Teddy," Father McEwen said. The front room displayed only a scarred coffee table and an old sofa losing its stuffing. Across the dusty floor, a television and VCR rested on a metal filing cabinet turned on its side. The calendar put out by the refinery hung crookedly on a nail and hadn't been changed for two months.

Teddy Allen squinted at Father McEwen's round red face as if looking into the sun. "This is a rental," he said. "Don't see the point in fixing up what isn't mine." He had lived in the apartment two years, since graduating from high school, and the priest's comment felt like an attack on the whole of his independent life. He wasn't even wearing his clerical collar, as if Teddy were not worth the trouble. "You want to come in, I guess." Teddy's head gave a sharp sideways nod as he spoke and his neck cracked. He was little more than bone, a slash of hair across his head, a faint mustache above his pale lips.

"Thanks for the invite," Father McEwen said, stepping in and shutting the door behind him. He liked to say that a priest, like a vampire, should never enter a home without an invitation. People liked their priests with a sense of humor.

He picked one end of the couch to give Teddy room to join him, as there was nowhere else to sit. The springs, though, were shot, and as he sank into the sofa's pocket, he slid to the center. His knees rose up to his chest. The cushions exhaled white, fluffy filament, a raveled floss like fiberglass insulation.

Teddy Allen liked seeing the priest hunched up like a cold man before a fire. His spirits had plummeted upon recognizing the giant in his doorway. Until he moved out of his mother's house, he had gone to mass every week of his life. He hadn't retained much, though, and didn't care to ever go back. Now it occurred to him that he might have some fun at the priest's expense. Teddy had an appointment in less than an hour, and he guessed the father had come to make him miss it. But Teddy knew that no one on earth could make him miss it. Such certainty can make the worst coward willing to gamble.

"Want a drink or something?" he asked.

Father McEwen looked at his watch, though he knew the time.

"I don't think a whiskey would hurt me," he said. "Have you got whiskey?"

"Everybody does, so why wouldn't I?" Teddy said and left to fetch the liquor.

McEwen worked to get himself free of the couch. He dusted the seat of his pants and strolled to the window, which was covered by a soiled vinyl shade. The stains looked to be sweat, but he knew that was impossible. The spring in the roller was busted. McEwen pushed aside the sheet of fabric.

The afternoon light had just made the turn toward dusk. Children in the playground below huddled around a dark-haired boy who held three oranges. The oranges made Father McEwen wish Teddy would hurry with the whiskey. Thirst exerted real power over him. Down below, the boy spread his arms, and the oranges one by one lifted into the air, cutting arcs above his black hair. The oranges hopped from the boy's palms as if electrified.

The window needed washing. What was this grease that settled on glass? Human oils? We leave traces of us everywhere, Father McEwen thought. Teddy's mother had asked him to make this visit. "He don't talk to me," she had said. The misalignment of verb and noun had surprised her, and she repeated the sentence to correct herself, becoming flustered by the betrayal of her own words. "That girl he goes to does some kind of spiritism," she said. "He sees her every day of the week."

One of the oranges struck the boy's fingertips but bounded free. He tried to nab it, which permitted the others to escape. The first orange lost its shape on impact with the ground. While he was watching the fruit bounce about the children's feet, Father McEwen realized that Teddy was not coming back. He dropped the shade.

"Teddy?" he called.

The refrigerator began vibrating as Father McEwen entered the kitchen, making a hum like a giant insect. The room's rear door hung open. Except for dirty dishes stacked by the sink, the kitchen was orderly. It did not suggest that Teddy was damaged, as the bare living room did. That room shrieked of omission, of screws loose, a deck a few cards shy.

On the Formica table, a shot glass with a finger of cheap bourbon awaited him. The glass wasn't clean. Inside the refrigerator, Father McEwen found a stick of butter cowled by its partially opened wrap, maple syrup in a plastic bottle, a head of iceberg lettuce turning a rusty brown, and two cartons of beer—good German beer—with only two bottles missing. Father McEwen decided to investigate the boy's bedroom.

The "spiritism" Teddy's mother had described concerned a store-front fortune-teller on Division Street, a business that had appeared the month after Browne's Shoe Repair closed. The big window facing Division was now painted black with stenciled lettering advertising the woman's craft. Father McEwen had never met her, but he couldn't believe this kind of bother was serious. The bedroom door swung noisily open, its hinges complaining of abuse and neglect. A mattress lay on the floor at an angle to the walls. The sheets piled upon it gave off a sour smell. A heap of blankets lay like a dog at the foot of the makeshift bed. Peeking from beneath the blankets were the round toes of women's shoes. These feminine togs relieved Father McEwen. Sex out of wedlock was a sin, but he felt better knowing Teddy was not entirely alone. The smell, more than anything else, discouraged him from investigating further.

Even cheap whiskey burned the throat in that familiar, pleasurable manner. He put the shot glass on top of the stack of dirty plates. Of the ten beers in the refrigerator, Father McEwen took only one, a tithing he slipped into the pocket of his coat.

Teddy Allen celebrated his deception of the priest with a piss in the open mouth of a neighbor's trash can. The alley behind his building would take him to the corner of 34th and Palmer, where he could cross the street and wait for the Division Street bus. Normally he walked to Lucinda's, but he didn't like the idea of Father McEwen motoring up beside him, lowering the window of that old boat he drove, and beginning in on whatever sin Teddy had committed by running off as he had. He hadn't lied, really, having poured the man a drink just as he said he would. He'd only committed the sin of leaving things out, of telling half the truth. A partial sin, at best.

Since he'd begun studying Lucinda's trances, Teddy Allen's life had turned upside down, which made the trips to her parlor irresistible. He no longer hung out with his pals, and they had quickly discarded him. His bank account had dwindled to nothing, and he'd had to sell his furniture. He'd even stolen a backpack from an unlocked car, the opportunity too sweet to ignore.

He first took note of Lucinda one day at the supermarket and followed her about as she filled the little basket she carried. Something in her appearance began gnawing at him, her free hand groping a grapefruit, handling limes, snapping two green bananas from a bunch. Teddy wound up buying a lot of useless fruit that rotted in his refrigerator. Then one of the guys at the refinery mentioned that he had paid her ten dollars to hear his future. He claimed she'd held his hands and slid into a hypnotic state that made her rock up and back until her blouse loosened and revealed her breasts.

The day Teddy got up the courage to go into her place, she had worn a blouse whose buttons reached her collarbone, each one snug in its buttonhole. Men lied about women all the time, Teddy knew. The guy had needed an excuse to explain blowing ten bucks on a fortune-teller. Teddy had needed a similar excuse to convince himself he was there out of manly lust and not human loneliness. Her window read:

Lucinda
Mistress of the Future
Readings, Advice, Help

What man alone in the world wouldn't want to enter a building bearing such a sign? Especially when the Lucinda in question had eyes the faint blue of ice and a mouth that never quite closed, the endearing gap between her painted lips a dark, slippery shape like the reflection of a crow on moving water.

They sat opposite each other in her rattan chairs that first time, their knees touching.

"You're nervous," she said after taking his hands in hers.

That impressed him, although any fool could have felt his hands tremble. He managed to nod.

"A little," he said, his voice cracking.

Her lids slid over her eyes, which still roved about, their movement shifting the contours of their delicate hoods. Her body began to sway and her head tilted back. Although her breasts were wholly concealed, Teddy found that her bare neck, revealed so completely by this posture, became a sexual organ. The vertical furrows formed by the backward slant seemed so private and erotic that he could not quite catch his breath.

What she had to say to him does not matter. Lucinda had no power to reveal the future, and about this she had no delusions. Neither was she an out-and-out charlatan, as she did believe herself to be sensitive to the needs of others and a help in their lives. She had taken two counseling courses at a community college in the suburbs. She had read books on how the body and mind might be healed. She also knew instinctively that vague suggestions had more power than direct predictions.

With Teddy, she spoke a lot about his past: "There is someone important, a woman or girl, I think, who has never really understood you." She touched on the present: "You're not entirely appreciated by your employer, and you're not really fulfilled there." About the future, she hedged. "Someone is waiting for you to call. Only you haven't met her yet—or maybe you have met her but didn't realize how important she would become to you. She doesn't even know she's waiting. Poor girl."

That sort of rubbish. The traditional enticing murk.

From the moment that her sinuous neck caused him an erection, Teddy Allen was hooked. He was the sort of man who could not grasp for long any idea that was not tied directly to a physical object, and so each time he returned to talk with her, her ideas seemed new and fresh, enlarged by his inability to hold on to them. The initial visit had cost a mere ten dollars. He now paid from thirty to fifty dollars, depending on the intricacy of the session. He owed rent. He had hocked his stereo system. He had begun eating just once a day. The backpack he had taken from an unlocked Lincoln had provided a wristwatch he had sold for ninety dollars. A pair of women's shoes had taken up most of the bag, but he hadn't yet sold them to the thrift shop. They would not bring much, despite their obvious elegance and relative newness. They did not quite smell new. Better than new somehow. He kept them near his bed.

Lucinda opened the door before his hand could reach the knob. He knew she could see out through the dark glass, despite his inability to see in. He knew this, but he also credited her for fathoming his approach, the swinging door further evidence of her powers.

"My," she said, tilting her face to study his. "You have some kind of story to tell me, don't you?"

He thought, perhaps, she could see that he loved her. Then he remembered the priest and nodded.

"Someone's been to my apartment bothering me."

He hadn't even gotten to eat because of the priest's interference. Should he talk to her of his hunger? It seemed to him unnecessary to explain.

Lucinda took his hands, sending an electric tingle through his limbs as she led him to their chaste and conjugal chairs.

Because Mrs. Corbus had no Mr. Corbus, his disappearance an event of much local notoriety, and because Mrs. Corbus had become so arthritic at the age of forty that she could not do it herself, it had fallen to Father McEwen to be responsible for the thrashing of her children. Her requests rarely came more than once a month, and in five cases of six, Father McEwen could negotiate a settlement between mother and child—additional chores to be taken on, a period of time without friends over, a ban on telephone calls. But twice or thrice a year, he had to beat one of her kids. He knew she was not entirely stable in the head, and yet she provided for them. They owed her their help and respect.

His own father had preferred fresh-cut birch limbs the thickness of a large man's finger at the grip, narrowing to pencil width on the impact end. They had to be fresh cut or the limbs would break after the first laceration. Father McEwen had two permanent scars from such switchings. Mrs. Corbus, who taught seventh-grade history, supplied him with a paddle that a shop teacher had fashioned for her. The paddle had a handle with an indentation for each finger, and on the business end, five drilled holes each large enough to hold a cigar.

Father McEwen worked very hard to avoid paddling any of the Corbus lot, but when it came time to administer the swats, he rediscovered, each time, the pleasure that comes from having power over another. He did not like to see their fear as they undid their belts and lowered their pants, but he nonetheless enjoyed it. He did not like to hear them yelp, but gratification crept into his body anyway. This, of course, was not the whole story. He felt morally obliged to apologize after each swing, and despite the directions of Mrs. Corbus, he required that they keep their underpants on. That he found furtive satisfaction in this ugly act made him work all the harder to achieve a compromise between mother and child, which was what redeemed him. No one could entirely resist the pleasure of such dominion over another, but the good recognized the debasement of others as something to be resisted, while the evil and weak sought it out.

This evening in the dim light of the Corbus kitchen, Father McEwen attempted to negotiate between Mrs. Corbus and her daughter, Aluela, who had commemorated her seventeenth birthday by celebrating the night through, getting home at dusk the following day just after a policeman standing on her stoop had explained to Mrs. Corbus for the third time why they were unwilling just yet to file a missing person report. Aluela's arrival humiliated as well as angered Mrs. Corbus, her arthritic clubs flailing at the girl with such vehemence that the policeman had restrained her and advised Aluela to lock herself in her room until her mother calmed down. Once released, Mrs. Corbus called Father McEwen's number and left a message on his machine. He had not wanted to come. The whiskey he'd had at Teddy Allen's and the purloined beer he'd sipped in the rectory had encouraged him to visit Mallory's Room, a bar he often frequented with parishioners, the pretense of listening permitting him to drink, the drinking permitting him to listen. A boxing match on the tube became his excuse for coming. A few of the boys from the refinery had insisted he join them, and no one would let him pay for a whiskey or beer. He wanted sleep and the forgiveness of Christ. He had no desire to hear of the Corbus children's latest transgressions.

Aluela Corbus had come full into puberty, a feminine weight settling into her thighs, her breasts taking shape, acne pocking her face, a coat of cheap makeup covering her discolored cheeks. She claimed she had fallen asleep at a girlfriend's house, a lie so transparent that Father McEwen did not even attempt to get at the truth. He simply stated that she was too old to be spanked, which sent Mrs. Corbus into a rage.

During her rant, Father McEwen spotted one of the Corbus boys lingering by the kitchen door to witness his sister's subjugation. The priest in him cared more about the boy's pleasure in his sister's pain than he did about their mother's litany of accusations. It did not occur to him that this feeling stemmed from his own guilt.

He stepped to the doorway to run the boy off. It was Patrick, the younger Corbus boy, who had been arrested for shoplifting just last month.

"Get on with you," Father McEwen said to him. Patrick had been caught with a bra and panties stuffed into the tops of his boots. *Gifts,* he'd claimed. "You have homework, I'll wager," McEwen said.

Patrick pushed his yellow hair from his forehead and gestured for Father McEwen to come with him into the living room.

"I'm occupied."

Patrick said, "I know where she was."

"Sure, you do," Father McEwen replied, stepping to the hall. "Look, turn on the television if you have to. Just give us some room to breathe here."

The boy presented an exaggerated expression of exasperation. His brother, the father recalled, had moved out of the house. Only Patrick and Aluela remained.

"Go on," Father McEwen insisted.

"Fine," Patrick replied, turning his back. "Eat your peas with a knife."

The turn of phrase almost made Father McEwen laugh. He had a fondness for Patrick Corbus. The boy had once come to the parish to ask God to help him with his math. His sincerity had touched McEwen, and the complexity of the math had shocked him. That had been before the boy's father vanished, and in the three years since the disappearance Patrick had gotten into one scrape after another. In confession, he had failed to even mention the shoplifting arrest. Father McEwen had made the salvation of the boy a special project, but his duties had kept him busy, and he'd all but forgotten about it.

A slap and squeal came from the kitchen. Father McEwen hustled back. Aluela was bent over the table and her mother had spanked her bare buttocks with the flat side of a butcher knife.

"Stop that now," Father McEwen called.

Mrs. Corbus tried to swing the knife again, but it slipped from her hand and ricocheted off the wall behind her, landing on its point and sticking upright in the gray linoleum. She glared at him.

"I don't have the strength," she said. "You whip her. You whip her or I'll do to you. I'll do to you and her both. You whip her."

Father McEwen jerked the hem of Aluela's dress over her behind, but he jerked too hard and the dress snapped back. He pulled at it again and successfully covered the girl's pimpled butt. He couldn't see what had happened to the girl's underwear. Mrs. Corbus threw open the closet door. A broom handle fell forward against her shoulder, and she shoved it fiercely to the floor. The paddle hung from a metal hook.

"It's no use getting that," Father McEwen said, yanking the butcher knife from the floor and placing it in the sink. The girl did not move from the table. "Leave it," he said.

Mrs. Corbus could not wrestle the paddle from its hook. Arthritic pain brought tears to her eyes, and as she dropped her arms and leaned forward, a tear ran down her nose and fell onto her shoe. Father McEwen saw its descent and heard it strike the leather.

"You whip her," Mrs. Corbus demanded hoarsely, "or I'll take this mop handle to her."

"All right, then," Father McEwen said. "Leave us alone."

"Do I have your word?" Mrs. Corbus demanded.

"You do."

"Her father named her," Mrs. Corbus accused. She sighed then, regaining her strength, and straightened. Softly she added, "Little bitch."

She left the room by the back door, the same thing Teddy Allen had done earlier in the evening, leaving McEwen with trouble to ponder.

He might have struck the girl just to keep his word, although he was also considering slapping the paddle against his own hand to make enough noise to please the woman, but when he turned to Aluela, who still lay prone on the table, he saw that her skirt held a red streak of blood.

"God forgive," he said. When his hand went for her skirt, she tugged it up, expecting him to swat her. "You're bleeding," he said, the impression of the blade a red welt stretching across the girl's behind. The sharp end of the knife had cut into her, a thin incision on either side of the buttocks' cleft.

He did not consider calling the girl's mother back to tend to her, though he took a step to stare out the window. Mrs. Corbus had wrapped her withered arms around herself and walked huddled against the cold across the street. He returned his attention to the girl.

"Are you all right?" he asked her softly. "You must be bandaged."

Her eyes were already wet, and now she began to sob.

Father McEwen unrolled a strip of paper towels, dampened them, and laid them across the wound, covering the remainder of her nakedness with the bloody skirt. He stepped to the door and called for Patrick.

Patrick Corbus ran to the kitchen door, moved not by the call of his name but by the desperate tone in the voice. The red face and man's shoulder protruding from the door, the big hand holding the same door tightly against the body, spoke of secrets, of the illicit. Patrick's first thought was that his sister had done something to the priest, but he was standing there on his big feet, flustered yet unharmed. Which meant that the priest had done something, and that desperate tone had been one shaped by guilt and fear of exposure. These impressions flashed through his head almost too fast to leave a residue. Patrick was not merely a smart boy; in many ways he was brilliant. His gifts had gone unrecognized by the nuns who taught him; they could not penetrate his guises to see what lay underneath. By the time he pulled up just short of the door, he had deduced that his mother had lost herself again and left the priest to clean up her mess.

"What has she done?" he said.

Father McEwen mistook the pronoun. "Forget your prying for a moment and fetch me some bandages."

The human body, at times, must do nothing, must stand as still as the plastic torso on a crucifix. As Father McEwen saw it, the boy froze for a second and then regained his senses and ran to the bathroom to get the necessary medical supplies. But Patrick's mind ran faster than Father McEwen's in any case, and in a moment such as this, when the father was close to panicking, Patrick's thoughts rained while the father's dribbled. From the second that he stopped his forward movement to the instant that he reversed himself and began his gallop to the medicine cabinet, Patrick saw in the red orbit of the priest's face a dozen human failings—dishonesty, desire, drunkenness, delight in the suffering of those who opposed him. These failings did not distance the priest from Patrick but made him human. He could see the father had lost some faith in God. He guessed that Aluela was not fully clothed, and understood that their mother had stripped her for a beating. What a pounding reason took in the deluge of reasonable thoughts. The boy could see it all with a rapidity that made the most complex things appear simple. The priest was embarrassed by his own desire and fearful of it. Patrick's mother was tormented by her husband's desertion of her arthritic body. That her husband had abandoned their children did not bother her. She would not have hated him had he taken her along and left the children in the moldy house to fend for themselves. What other course could her revenge take but to seek the bones of those same children and break them?

His sister, in that frozen moment, stood naked in his imagination, her hand shyly covering the brown patch of hair between her legs. An image speaks volumes to an agile mind. He had stolen the bra and panties for his sister, but he could not confess this without revealing the intense derangement in the Corbus house. Their mother had shredded Aluela's undergarments, accusing her of a deadly sin she could not name. Patrick had known many names for it, though, and as he spun to sprint to the bathroom, those words appeared before him in red letters tumbling through the air like the rolling credits of the cinema: the sin of clear breath and heartiness, the sin of the unbuggered body, the sin of fine fettle, the sin of upright bones and pliant flesh, the sin of energy, the sin of the muscles' easy contraction, the unapologetic and hateful sin of health.

The priest's voice shook, as did the telephone in his hand.

"I cannot leave them here with her," he said. "She's gone off the deep end, and I can't permit her to harm these children."

He spoke to Liam Hitchens, a middle-aged man with a large family and modest income, a devout Catholic, bald but for the slap of hair he parted just above the ear to saddle his bare pate. His wife, Mary, was a woman so physically attractive that Father McEwen had more than once fallen into doubt about his calling in her presence, wondering whether he could still find comfort in a woman's arms. Liam had never been handsome, and time had been cruel, having stolen his hair and eyesight, silver glasses perching on a nose grown too large. Mary, on the other hand, was incapable of aging, no matter the number of children she bore. In Liam's secret heart, that place secret to even himself, he wanted her to succumb to age as he had; their six children were the products of this desire. He could never consciously conceive such a motive; he could only act upon it. Therefore, he had decided that it must be his Catholic upbringing that had made their family large, which encouraged him to consider himself religious. He became devout by failing to understand himself and substituting the handiest excuse. Which is not to say that he did not love his wife. Not even God held his heart so securely; without her, he wouldn't have needed a god.

"It has the sound of trouble," Liam said. "I wouldn't want Mrs. C. to know where they were staying. I'll have to check with Mary. She's at the Rexall getting hose. If she doesn't wear hose, the veins in her legs will pop and make blue streaks you can see with your own eyes. So she claims. Do you need me to come there? I'd rather not. My littlest is got some project about the earth's core due tomorrow and it involves magic markers and tracing dinner plates."

"I'll bring them," Father McEwen said. "It's just Patrick and Aluela. The other one's moved out. Living at the Y or some such place." He didn't want to give Liam a chance to ramble again and so added, "We'd better make haste. I don't want a scene." The dark window to the dark world that fronted the Corbus house held white flecks of snow. "It's snowing. Wouldn't you know it?" Before putting down the receiver, Father McEwen said, "Snow" instead of "Good-bye."

Aluela had eavesdropped on the conversation and looked up from the couch at the window. The snow stuck only to the corners of the glass. She had asked her brother to pack for her so that she could lie down. She kept to her stomach to avoid bloodying the cushions. Her backside did not particularly hurt. She simultaneously wished she had on underwear and wanted to pull the hem up and see Father McEwen's face again as he examined her behind. His hands, while taping on the bandages, had quaked.

As a birthday gift, a friend had given her a reading by the Division Street fortune-teller. Aluela had wound up spending the night in the shop.

"You're in trouble," Lucinda had said to her while studying Aluela's face. "Is it at home? I think it has to do with your home."

Aluela had burst into tears and begun describing the extent of her mother's madness, the rages, the inconsolable sadness and weeping, the sleepwalking, the self-mutilation.

"She sticks herself with pins," Aluela told the fortune-teller. "She won't let us talk or move while she does it."

Lucinda dropped the girl's hands and threw her arms around her. "I live here," she said. "In the back rooms. You can stay with me tonight."

Aluela had called home and told Patrick where she was. "Don't let on. I don't want Mother to know," she said. "I called so you wouldn't worry."

"Are you coming back?" Patrick asked.

Aluela had offered no answer. Now she believed she should have moved to her older brother's apartment. James had fled the house as soon as he turned eighteen. His roommates, though, Aluela didn't trust. They made grabs at her, pinching her butt and nipples, talking dirty every chance they got. She wasn't a prude, but she didn't like idiots. She'd had sex a few times, all with her father, whom she and Patrick both missed terribly. She suspected her mother had found out about them. It was true that she had been only thirteen when it started, which was too young, she knew. But her father had been lonely, and she did not hold it against him. The gentle way he had parted her legs had pleased her. He had put his hand over the scant, dark hair that curled about her vagina, and slowly, ever so slowly, maneuvered a finger into her opening, talking all the while about men and women, about what he called the "hang-ups" most people had about sex. After each visit, he had said, "We won't do this again until you ask me to." It was only that final time that he had stripped himself. She had told him she wanted to, that she was ready.

She had not liked the physical sensation of his prick inside her, but she had liked the experience. She'd felt very close to him. A day or two later he was gone. He had packed only his clothing. The laptop computer that he always kept with him was left on his desk in the bedroom. He had not written them a note, but Aluela found three hundred thirty-four dollars under her pillow. No explanation accompanied the bills.

She had expected him to contact her, or maybe Patrick. Their elder brother, James, was not bright. He liked to fool with cars and that, luckily, redeemed him. He had work as a mechanic across town. She and Patrick were smart, like their father. She believed he would call or show up somewhere and wave her over, tell her to get Patrick and they would all run away. She did not imagine living with her father as man and wife. She had no interest in that. She simply missed him. That she had fucked him played only a small part in her present emotional turmoil.

At the fortune-teller's Aluela had sat in the kitchen eating soup while Lucinda kept appointments with her clients. "These are my regulars," she'd said. "My bread and butter." One, she claimed, came to her every day. "He must spend half his paycheck on me," she boasted. Aluela had been surprised to hear that it was Teddy Allen, who was a friend of her brother James's. He didn't seem the type to embrace the future.

The next day, just as Lucinda predicted, Teddy came again. When Lucinda left to read Teddy's future, Aluela put a glass to the wall and listened through it—a trick she had seen in a movie—but it did no good.

"What did he talk about?" she asked after the appointment was over and Lucinda had returned to the kitchen.

"Privileged information," Lucinda said and then laughed. "His mother is harassing him to quit coming here. She sent a priest to talk to him."

"Father McEwen," Aluela said. "Mother calls him in to paddle us when we've been bad." It was no coincidence that she thought of this. She knew she'd have a beating coming. "Mother doesn't have the strength to hit us as hard as she thinks we deserve."

"He does that?" Lucinda seemed astonished.

The priest's paddling had not seemed the least bit strange to Aluela until she witnessed this reaction.

"He barely taps us," Aluela said shyly. "He's the only one who has a chance of talking her down. Patrick used to could, but since the shoplifting thing, she won't listen to him."

Lucinda fetched them beer from her refrigerator and seemed to really listen as Aluela described her life, which, as she spoke of it, became astonishingly exotic. She'd had no idea her life was so color-ful. She hadn't talked to people about it before, and even now she had not told Lucinda about screwing her father. She saved that, say-ing only that he had disappeared without a trace.

Then she said, "Can you really see the future?"

They had switched from beer to hot tea by that time, and Lucinda set her cup on the table to concentrate. She cocked her head and stared off at the wall for a while, and then eyed Aluela, leaned for-ward, and kissed her hair.

"I can see that you have better times ahead of you," she said, as if it were a bold prediction and, at the same time, making fun of the whole enterprise. It had served as a cue for Aluela to gather herself and head home.

Patrick entered the living room with a single suitcase he had packed for them both. Father McEwen extended his hand to help Aluela up. His palms were sweaty. He had written a message to their mother, which he pinned to the couch with one of the needles their mother used to pierce herself. He ushered them out to his big black car. The walk was icy, and Aluela hoped Patrick had thought to pack mittens. Snow lighted against her face and in her hair. She was surprised to find the car warm inside. The father had gone out and warmed it up for them. For *her,* she thought and looked to her brother, who was having the same thought. Her sideways glance at the priest and Patrick's purse of his lips conveyed it all, each to the other. Father McEwen's interest in Aluela was more than priestly. Although, as she saw it, not more than fatherly.

Masturbation humiliated Father McEwen, but it was a compromise he'd worked out with himself decades ago. The girl was barely pubescent, he told himself. This was the kind of exaggeration that suited people who needed to argue with themselves but did not wish to win; its exaggeration permitted the libidinous side of him to dismiss it, while the priestly side held tight to the indignation. Meanwhile, the actual Father McEwen pulled out his penis and began to rub it between his thumb and forefingers. The cleft in the girl's behind appeared first to him, and then he had a recollection in his fingers of the soft resiliency of those feminine cheeks. He had bandaged her quickly, but he'd had to press the tape down, and he could not miss the pucker of her anus and the tuft of hair below.

Father McEwen, some years past, had entered into an amorous affair with a married woman. She was not of his parish, not even a Catholic—not that such facts excused anything. He had known that it was a significant sin, and he had also known that this fact contributed to his pleasure. The woman had not loved him. From the very beginning of the affair, he had seen that she relished the thought of seducing a priest. Later, he realized that she had been promiscuous throughout her marriage.

He had confessed this affair to no one but God, and he did not believe God had forgiven him.

Liam and Mary Hitchens had taken in the Corbus children as if there were nothing unusual in it, as if the kids were merely there for a sleepover. Liam had almost no talents of consequence except this ability to embrace others, but it had served him well. His wife was, to Father McEwen, the most remarkable person in his acquaintance. If he had met her in his youth and she had been amenable, he would have given up the cloth for her. He liked to believe as much, anyway. He liked to think of himself swept away by his passions. The image of Mary Hitchens mixed in his mind with the image of Aluela's young bottom.

His affair could have proved that he was a passionate man. He had, after all, risked a great deal to pursue it. But he knew that his desire had been all but generic. She had been available, attractive, and out of the Catholic loop. Lucky for him, she no longer lived in his city. He did not like to recall her in detail, would not picture her when his body demanded its sexual urge be placated. He tried not to permit her name to be uttered by the voices that tirelessly went on and on in his head, the many-layered soliloquies of a typical adult mind. Diana. Like the pagan goddess. The mole on her inner thigh would press against his tongue like a button.

He didn't take long to come, catching his unholy seed in his meaty fist. What pathetic creatures were men alone, he thought, rinsing his hands in the dark bathroom. A siren sounded outside, startling him, so loud and near that he stepped to the narrow window and pushed aside the terry-cloth curtain. It scared him, that judgmental noise, as if it were an omen, a sign that his mortal sins were worse than he imagined, as if the world—as well as God—had caught on to him.

He let the curtain go and ran himself a bath. Father McEwen felt dirty.

Teddy Allen often peeped into Lucinda's window. She made it easy for him. The green flag she used as a curtain in the kitchen had a gap at the top. All he had to do was push a garbage can in the alley close to the city dumpster, climb up onto the dumpster, set his feet on the metal rail the garbage truck used to lift the giant metal box, then lean forward until he could catch himself against the brick wall of her building. This position provided him a good view of the entire kitchen. The bedroom window would have been better, but she had actual curtains there and no available dumpster. The green flag had an image of a man on it, and the words "Redemption Songs." It had to do with recycling, he figured. She looked the environmentalist type.

Was Teddy, human lean-to in an unlit alley just to glimpse this woman he saw every day, merely a fool, or was he something more dangerous? He had violence in him, but it was deeply buried, cushioned by strata of fear, self-loathing, sloth, and a thin slice of humanity. He had never hit anyone in his adult life, nor had he taken advantage of a girl. Which was not the same as saying he was a good man or even one of average ethical standards. Prying in this acrobatic fashion caused him not a second's pause. He worried only that a police cruiser might decide to check the alley, and he could get arrested. Questioning the morality of his actions didn't occur to him.

He had not expected to see Jimmy's little sister there, and he wished that she would leave. There had been one time when Lucinda had come into her kitchen in panties and a blouse—just to flick off the light, but still. It didn't seem likely he'd get to witness that again with Jimmy's sister present. An angry, urgent sensation clutched him at the thought of this interference. The feeling had more to do with his empty stomach than annoyance with Jimmy's sister, but he didn't know that.

He couldn't think of the girl's name at first. She and Lucinda talked and drank beer. He'd love a beer. And a sandwich. Good beer pleased him. It was the one thing in his life about which he was a snob. He would not drink American beer even if it were offered to him free of charge. He would eat most anything, though. He cursed the priest for making him miss his meal. Teddy did not have the kind of body that could go long without food.

The girl's mother had run off, Teddy recalled—incorrectly, as it had been the father of Aluela who had disappeared. Teddy remembered that there was something wrong with their mother, as well. MS, he thought. No wonder she ran away. Probably offed herself. This made him think of the suicide of Lot's wife and prostitutes shinnying up the cross to sponge blood off the holy feet of Christ.

While the ingestion of certain drugs had caused many a temporary disarray in Teddy's mind, the current and ongoing confusion was not the product of chemical experiments but of infrequent mental exercise. He thought of himself as an outlaw but acted like any other person whose passions were shaped largely by television. Lethargy was his byword, or would have been had he the vocabulary and the self-knowledge to name his creed. His desire for the fortune-teller had become the first exceptional event in a life so tawdry and yet so ordinary as to have no texture whatsoever.

All that was about to change.

His arms grew weary, and he felt faint. He had to push himself back with enough force to right himself, but not so powerfully that he fell into the dumpster or onto the alley floor. He executed this push successfully, then settled down against the metal roof that covered half the dumpster, and let his arms take a rest.

Visions have come to less likely characters than Teddy Allen. Drunkards commonly see God, and drug addicts are known for their quixotic whatnot. Prostitutes have witnessed wallpaper moving in a rhythm countercurrent to a john's meaningless thrusts and understood that their lives had to change. Judges have observed their reflections in the gold cuff links of prosecutors and suddenly apprehended what it actually meant to be judged. Pilots have seen clouds take the shape of Christ's holy countenance; they have seen the blue become transparent as glass, revealing brilliant bricks of gold and gorgeous bare feet separated by clusters of wing tips. Even priests have had moments in the dark, holding their aching cocks, thinking of girls whose blistered buttocks they earlier tended, when they discover themselves concentrating on the girl's pleasure, as if this imagined scene, to be made real enough to satisfy the body's desire, demanded of them not only arousal but compassion and something like love.

Teddy Allen leaned against the dumpster's metal roof, hunger no longer a sensation in his stomach but a constellation of deficiencies in his head, pinpoints of loss, the brain's craving for nutrition making these modest stars of desire to prickle the gray matter. Teddy stared intently at the mouth of light above the green flag, when suddenly the image of the man on the flag began to move. Teddy could not know that the heater in Lucinda's kitchen had kicked on, causing the flag to flutter. Visions often need a little help to get started. The dark man on the flag turned his head to stare at Teddy, his lips pursed, and he began to whistle. Did it sound like a teapot's trilling? What whistle does not? Teddy couldn't see Lucinda putting tea bags into porcelain cups. He could see nothing but the dark whistling man on the flag. His narrow chest tightened and he held his breath.

The man's initial speech was unintelligible, a rumble of words that had begun before Teddy realized it, the sentences running together like the rattle and buzz of traffic. But as he listened, meaningful language began to reach his ears—words, random at first. "Interior," he heard quite clearly. "Afterburner . . . hopeless . . . indigestion."

Synapses fire so rapidly in even the dullest of brains that one suggestion can free a mountain of hallucination; what else, after all, could account for seeing that which cannot be seen and hearing that which cannot be heard? The voices of angels are in all our heads, down there next to that Alka-Seltzer jingle we can't seem to forget, the one that played on television decades ago and showed all those bellies.

Teddy Allen heard at last a straightforward sentence come from the black man's lips: "Christ lives in your city."

The price of natural gas being what it was, Lucinda had the thermostat on low. The heat cut off. The vision ended. Teddy Allen slid down to the edge of the dumpster and hopped off. He stared again at the green flag. He made a mental note to look up *redemption* when he got to somewhere that might have a dictionary.

His legs wobbled as he walked on the unsteady ground of his new life.

Patrick Corbus rose from the sofa where the Hitchenses had made him a bed and slipped into the narrow hallway where he had earlier spotted a telephone. The house was quiet except for the snoring of Mr. Hitchens. Patrick imagined that flap of hair that Mr. H. swept over his head during his waking hours: Did it lie on the pillow beside the man's bare dome? Did his wife touch this thin book of tresses, page through it in the connubial dark? Patrick thought she might. Unlike Father McEwen, Patrick could see why the lovely Mary loved this unlovely man. She required the weight to keep her from ascending directly to the clouds.

Patrick took the lamp and phone book from the little table and put the lamp on the floor to restrict the spread of the light. He looked up the number, killed the lamp, and dialed.

By the sound of the priest's voice in the receiver, Patrick guessed that the call had wakened Father McEwen.

"Who is this?" the priest asked, adding too late the compensatory "please."

"Patrick Corbus," Patrick whispered. "I need to know something. It can't wait."

"She hasn't called," Father McEwen said. "I made the note to her very clear. I thought she would have called by now."

"She doesn't want us back," Patrick said. "Anyone with half a brain . . ." He caught himself. "I need to know where my father is."

"Why are you asking me that?" Father McEwen wanted to know. "At one—almost two—in the morning? And him gone three years. How should I know?"

"He left Aluela money," Patrick said. "He left me a riddle."

"A riddle?"

"Where does a man," Patrick took a breath, "a good man, who loves his children, where does he disappear to, even though he knows his wife will mistreat the kids he loves?"

The telephone line offered a steady *shh* like an ocean with a single long wave or like some all-hearing thing asking eternally for silence. Father McEwen felt himself come fully awake as he tried to think how to talk to this boy.

"He did love you and your brother and sister," McEwen said at last. "You're right about that. He was a loving man."

"Why do you talk about him as if he's dead? He's not dead."

"I didn't mean to suggest that he's dead. He's not here, is all. Not around. I'm sure he's alive, and he still loves you. But I don't know where he is." McEwen glanced around his own dark bedroom, as if the man might be concealed there. "I don't have clue one."

"I just gave you one," Patrick said.

Father McEwen thought he heard exasperation in the boy's voice. "Sorry, son, but you'll have to repeat it."

"He loves us and knows that without him we'll be mistreated."

"And yet, Patrick . . ." Father McEwen felt a sadness descend into his gut. "He did leave."

"He's waiting for us to figure it out," Patrick said. "He left my mother something, too. And you. He left you something, as well. I need you to think about it."

"He didn't leave me a thing," McEwen said and stifled a yawn. "I'm not much good at this. I'm not a Sherlock. What did he leave your mother?"

"A crucifix. I took it away. She doesn't know."

"How can you be certain he left it for her?"

"It was under her pillow, just like the money under my sister's pillow, and the thing on the crucifix—the towel that covers Christ's, you know, his dick? It's red. Painted with fingernail polish."

"It was under her pillow?" Father McEwen's head hurt. Why did he love drink so much? "Come again. What did you say he left you? A riddle? How can you leave a riddle under a pillow?"

"Think about what he might have left you. We could make a deal."

"Patrick, you're not making sense. We should talk in the daylight."

"You find the clue, and I'll get you Aluela."

Father McEwen took a long breath and did not let it out, which made his speech shallow. "What are you talking about?"

"You know exactly what I'm talking about." Patrick hung up the phone.

Father McEwen heard the click but still spoke. "That's a sinful lie," he said as he could not have said with the boy listening, his voice turning thick in his throat, dirty water becoming sludge.

He thought he again heard a siren, but it was just the sound of a car alarm somewhere far off. He staggered to his bed and lay in the dark. Had he ever found anything in all his life beneath his pillow? A nickel for a lost tooth. He lifted his head and then the pillow. Not a thing underneath. How could Patrick Corbus know he had imagined his sister's naked legs and pimpled ass this very evening? Was he so obvious?

At the same time he understood something else. The girl had no real power over him. Arousal for a man did not necessarily connect to the deeper instincts. He was a man, after all. All priests were men. Father McEwen was a priest. Therefore, Father McEwen was a man.

The boy wanted to find his father. That was the real issue. Father

McEwen took that palliative to bed with him and it permitted him slumber.

Teddy Allen roamed the rooftops of the city in search of the savior. He reasoned that the most efficient way to find Christ would be to climb to the top of a building and look for a person with a kind of glow. Christ would have some kind of glow, wouldn't he? Teddy tramped across the connected roofs of Division Street, coming upon a couple fornicating in the cold, the boy saying, "Get the fuck going with you," and Teddy obeyed, stumbling later to his knees against the asphalt tile from his failure to eat or sleep. At daybreak he took to the streets, staring in windows, knocking on doors.

"I'm looking for someone," he said to the middle-aged black woman whose visage appeared behind the little square portal on the big wooden door.

"Who you looking for?" she asked him.

A metal grate separated their faces.

"Jesus Christ," he said.

"He ain't here," she said. "Used to be he live down that way." She pointed but Teddy couldn't tell in which direction. "But Baptists don't know to pay their bills, and that church is as cold as the bottom of the ocean. You wait."

She shut the little door and left Teddy shivering on the stoop, his eyes watering from the morning chill. It occurred to him that what he was doing did not fit into his life, that it was a crazy thing to do. He had this realization on a redbrick stoop while a sullen boy delivering papers bicycled past on the asphalt's black ice, the boy's face bundled in cloths of many colors. This moment of insight might have been enough to send Teddy home and to bed, but wind moved through the bare branches of the single tree of any size on that city block. The oak limbs creaked their wooden misery, which became in Teddy's mind the baleful mourn of a man on a cross.

The big door opened and the woman appeared with a steaming bundle and a tattered down vest.

"You put this on," she said to him. "No, *under* your coat. Use your head now." She helped him dress in his vestment of rags. "Eat this here. Get to a church got heat in it." The package she gave him was wrapped in aluminum foil and warm to the touch. "You shouldn't see no preacher's breath when he's ministering," she went on. "Christ don't want his flock frozen."

Teddy nodded to all of it, aware now of his hunger. He tore open the bundle as he started off again down the street. He needed to get hold of Father McEwen, he understood, whose church, no doubt, would have heat. Biscuits and brownies, crumbling curls of bacon, quarters of apple, he ate from the silver parcel. The food formed a knot in his stomach. Teddy did not know where he was, having wandered into a part of town he had never visited before. He walked and ate, the knot in his stomach slowly coming alive, growing limbs, a head and tail.

A man stopped him on the street, speaking gibberish as far as Teddy could make out, a tall man with a dark mustache whose ends drooped past his chin. He touched Teddy's ear with his hand, and the ear began to sting as if the man had bit it. Then the man crowed something else and walked on. What miraculous interaction had taken place, Teddy could not say. The thing inside him grunted and squealed.

Snow filled the air before him, dusted his shoulders and hair. When he had emptied the package of its precious food, Teddy began to chew on the aluminum foil. The beast in his stomach snorted its approval. What did it mean to have a pig in your innards? It kicked at him and wallowed in his belly, causing a dark and dull pain. And yet he felt he must accept this swine. After all, it breathed the air that he inhaled. He felt he must embrace its pink stinking buttocks, the scant black hair that curled like wire and scoured the lining of his stomach. He decided he would love even the corkscrew tail that Teddy could feel as he trudged through the cold, poking through his anus.

Father McEwen found Teddy Allen passed out on the church steps, his clothes smelling of feces, his forehead stippled with blood, a fine layer of snow coating it all.

"God forgive," Father McEwen said tersely and put his fingers to the boy's neck to check for a pulse.

Teddy's heart still sent steady messages to the distant arteries. Father McEwen slipped his hands in the boy's armpits and lifted him up. He chucked him a little higher, until he rested over one shoulder like a sack of flour. He did not weigh enough to contain life within him, McEwen thought.

Where Teddy had lain, a patch of ice in the shape of his body glistened in the faint sun. It made no sense that ice would form beneath a warm body. McEwen tapped it with his foot and the transparent mantle cracked.

He carried Teddy inside the church and laid him on a wooden pew. Ice lined the seams of his pants. McEwen ran to fetch a blanket. The modest cathedral had been built at the turn of the century and the cold leaked in at every join of brick. He slid the tiny lever on the thermostat forward, pushed the door through which they'd entered shut, and took a heavy blanket from the stack by the portal. The radiators began their ancient rattle and hiss as he hurried back to the frozen boy. He must call an ambulance, he thought. He might need to administer last rites.

"Is there anybody here?" McEwen called out as he ran, but the only answer was his own diminished voice, the half echo of a gaping room.

He found Teddy pushing himself upright.

"Praise God," McEwen said automatically, crossing himself and dropping the blanket in the process.

"How did I get in here?" Teddy asked. His voice was hoarse, and he touched his throat as he spoke.

"I carried you," the father replied, retrieving the blanket. He spread it over Teddy and spanked snow from the boy's hair.

"From where?"

"The yard just there. You picked a patch of ice to sleep in."

"My memory is fuzzy," he said. "My throat is dry."

"Just wait," McEwen ordered.

He hurried through the nave and past the crossing, where a red dolly held the cardboard cartons wine was shipped in and a stack of cellophane-wrapped boxes on top. He took a box of communion wafers and the corked bottle of consecrated wine left over from mass.

He did not think to bring the chalice or to look for the ready sack of plastic cups.

"Your head is bleeding," Father McEwen said as he passed Teddy the bottle of wine. He took a white handkerchief from his pocket and wiped away the red smears. As he tore open the cellophane package, he saw caked blood on the boy's left earlobe. "Did you have an earring?"

Teddy nodded and tipped the wine bottle up.

"You don't have one now," Father McEwen said. "Let's get you some dry clothes." He passed him a stack of wafers.

Teddy chewed on one of the dry crackers and shook his head. "I'm fine, but I don't know why I'm here." Bits of the wafer flew from his mouth as he spoke. He took another drink from the bottle.

"You stink of excrement, son." Father McEwen waited, but the boy didn't seem to catch his drift. "Let's clean you up a bit. Really. I insist."

Teddy shrugged. He corked the bottle again and returned the wafers. "I can't eat this."

Teddy followed the father outside and to the rectory, nothing more than a cottage on the church grounds. On their way Teddy witnessed trees limned with snow. He did not know what kind of trees they were, or what kind of snow. Were there kinds of snow? A tree with gray limbs and white snow, he thought. All he knew was that snow on tree limbs held a kind of attraction for him, something like the face of a pretty girl he knew he would never get to meet. The sensation was captivating, but what could he do with it? He did not yet know. He had only recently become interested.

Father McEwen's place struck Teddy as being a lot like his, only smaller, the one room and a bath, as far as he could see. He did not know the father had taken a vow of poverty and refused better accommodations. Teddy was not ready to conceive of such a thing. He sat on the commode and stripped off his clothes as the father directed. A tub filled with water. There was no shower. Cheap, Teddy thought. He recalled then that he had been on the tops of buildings. He had searched for the living Christ. He remembered that he'd had a vision. He realized he had made a mess in his drawers.

"Don't know how this happened," he said.

Father McEwen shut off the rushing water. "I can't be too hard on drinkers."

"I haven't drunk nothing," Teddy said.

He didn't reek of alcohol, but Father McEwen assumed the smell of shit had overwhelmed it. "Not drugs again, son?"

Teddy shook his head.

Father McEwen eyed him carefully. He seemed to be telling the truth. Moreover, he did not seem to be the same boy McEwen had recently visited.

"I'll step out while you wash yourself."

"Something happened to me," Teddy said.

"A fight then?"

Teddy shook his head and pulled down his soiled pants.

"Sorry," he said.

Father McEwen carefully picked up the boy's clothes, which left a puddle on the tile. The odor of feces almost made him gag. He carried the soiled clothing to the front door, and tossed it out into the snow. A volunteer did his laundry on Tuesdays. He would rinse the garments later in the toilet. He returned to find Teddy in the tub, turned round the wrong way, his back against the metal faucet. The backward pose spoke volumes about the lad, McEwen thought. He stepped to the sink and examined himself in the mirror, dampening a washcloth to wipe traces of the boy from his own clothing.

"What happened to you then if it wasn't a fight?"

"I seen something," he said. "And heard it, too."

"What was it?"

Teddy submerged in the water. He did not immediately come back up, and Father McEwen thought the boy might be in some kind of shock. He leaned over the tub. Teddy's eyes were open beneath the water. He slowly surfaced, then pointed.

"Where'd you get that?"

Father McEwen followed the aim of Teddy's finger. Above the tub, a small plaster Madonna and child hung on a nail. The child had been painted red with fingernail polish.

"It's not possible," Father McEwen said.

The late night conversation with Patrick Corbus came back to him. He reached for the Madonna but didn't yet dare to touch it. Could it have been left by Patrick and Aluela's father years ago?

Father McEwen reasoned that he might never have looked at that spot on the wall, given that he sat the other way around in the tub. But he didn't believe he was quite that blind. He lifted the Madonna from the wall. It weighed almost nothing. On the back three tiny squares cut from a photograph were glued to the plaster. He could not make out what they were at first, finally realizing they were breasts and a triangle of pubic hair. A woman's naked genitals glued to the back of this Madonna at the anatomically correct places, but on the flat side of the miniature.

"I been told something, and I'm working on fixing my life," Teddy said. He ground shampoo into his hair. "I'm quitting my job. You can have the rest of my beer. And whiskey."

"Did you put this up here?" Father McEwen asked.

"No, sir, but it's another one of those things I've been talking about."

Father McEwen could hardly do more than stare. His mind could not get around everything.

"I think I got a message from God," Teddy said. "Or someone like him. That thing there is another part of it."

Father McEwen nodded. He guessed that the boy had taken a fall of some sort.

"Christ is more alive than you think," Teddy said. "And he's got a place somewhere in town."

"A place of worship," Father McEwen said. "You were just in it."

"I mean a house or apartment, a condo. Who knows? If I was his real estate agent, I could tell you." Teddy smiled. He had made a joke.

"Teddy, you don't seem to be yourself."

He agreed. "It's a wonder, isn't it?"

"I'll find you some clothes. You bathe."

Q: *Who, besides the omniscient one, was privy to this conversation between Teddy Allen and Father McEwen?*
A: *The boy beneath the bed.*

Patrick Corbus had sneaked into Father McEwen's quarters as soon as he saw the priest vacate it. He had taken his time in selecting the spot to hang the Madonna. He had not expected the priest to come back so quickly. That he returned with a stinking bum was, he figured, the nature of priestly work.

Teddy got up from the tub and began drying himself with one of the church's towels, while Father McEwen brought him clean clothing.

"These are going to fit you big," McEwen said, hearing the awkwardness of it as he spoke. "Christ *is* present, Teddy. But he doesn't need an apartment."

Teddy stopped drying his hair with the towel and scooted it back to reveal his face beneath its cowl.

"He needed a manger, didn't he? He had to stay in that chicken coop thing you see at Christmas to get born, didn't he?"

"You've been away from the church a long time," Father McEwen said. "I hope this means you'll be returning."

"Christ himself is wandering around this city, checking it out," Teddy said, imagining the holy savior strolling the streets with a newspaper folded beneath his arm. "He's got a place of his own with running water and, I bet, cable. He'd want to be up on things, wouldn't he?" Teddy could see him in a room lit by both the television screen and his own glowing flesh. "He eats, he takes a piss, he likely has a drink now and then, although I've quit myself. You need a clear mind to track down a savior."

He could not fill the priest's shirt. The bulky roll of the pant cuffs made his slacks sway as he walked, as if he were swaggering, as if he were a sailor. Teddy liked the sensation. Hadn't Christ himself been a sailor?

"When I find him," Teddy said before departing, "I'll bring him by. You'll see."

"Get some rest," Father McEwen said. "Will you do that for me? Should I take you home?"

"Let me see that thing again," Teddy said.

Father McEwen held up the Madonna, but did not let Teddy take it. He didn't wish to reveal the obscene side.

"I can't yet hear him," Teddy said. He dipped his head, as if to get water out of an ear. Then he turned and trundled off.

Patrick Corbus had to remain beneath the bed while Father McEwen dialed the Hitchenses' number. "When Patrick gets home from school, let him know I called. Tell him I've got something to show him." The receiver clanked back into its holder, while Patrick's glee circled wildly in his chest, although he did not know what to make of the next thing the father said: "Poor little fool." The words stung like a slap across the face. Patrick thought that the priest must be thinking of the bum who had just departed. But some part of him didn't entirely accept it, and the wound from the words ached inside him.

Wide as the ocean, goes the folk song, are the mysteries of the human heart. What sea could span the mystery of disappearance when the disappeared is a boy's father? What gulf could be larger than the mystery of a daughter's love for a father who made her his whore? In all the billions of stars and planets in the universe, there is no other world that supports life; only the earth has sentient beings: the people who pronounce their scant wisdom in words, the animals whose acumen lives in the musculature of their bodies, and the plant life, most articulate of all, whose turning to the sun and from the cold is never subject to question or doubt. The great expanse of the universe is not for the creation of more life, but to permit the already living to grasp the enormity of the spiritual mysteries. Once astronomers reach with their artificial eyes the universe's ultimate end, people will begin to see the reason why they love who they love, why the innocent suffer, why desire endlessly escapes its own description, why some are tortured and others spared, why we abandon the light and pursue the cold, why we all must die.

Patrick Corbus was a foolish boy, an attribute quite separate from lack of intelligence, and it accounted for his tireless pursuit of the very thing that oppressed him. He wanted Father McEwen to become convinced that the vanishing of Patrick's father had to do with the church and specifically with Father McEwen and the god Father McEwen loved. Patrick's own belief, as worn now as the knees of his jeans, was that an adult could find his father if he was sufficiently motivated, if

117

his desire to seek out the missing were a holy mission. This child longed for his father. He believed there were things about the disappearance that were being kept from him. He had to believe that. How could a boy think otherwise without coming to hate himself and take the fall for his father's egress?

Before Father McEwen left his home, he hung the plaster Madonna once more over the tub, then groaned at the ring of filth left from Teddy Allen's bath. There were, in fact, many concentric rings of brown around the porcelain tub, the flecks of foul matter against the background of white like the negative of a photo beamed home from space revealing the ultimate union and secret order of the many million disparate worlds.

A sponge wiped it all away.

Can a creature as bound to words as man apprehend a thing beyond words and understand without words that this commodity of the exalted has meaning?

Teddy Allen examined the exposed neck of Lucinda the fortune-teller while her hands grasped his. How white the flesh; how resilient the cylindrical tides of movement down and up its cherished tower, arriving nowhere, not even where it had begun, a peristaltic habit of the throat's architecture, like a pattern of uneven flight produced by a drone that neither returns to the hive nor tastes of the nectar.

"I got a message from God," Teddy Allen told Lucinda's throat.

Lucinda lifted her head upright. "Beg pardon?"

"It was outside your window." He began the story with such enthusiasm that he did not recognize the expression of fear on the fortune-teller's face, did not realize the crazed gleam that inhabited his eyes, or the bizarre effect the priest's clothes had on his appearance. "That guy on the flag was the first messenger—or really the second. I count you as the first."

"You threw yourself against the wall to stare into my kitchen?"

"My whole life is topsy-turvy," Teddy agreed, nodding enthusiastically. "It's first talking to you, then the flag guy, then I'm up on rooftops eyeing the streets, then I'm in the bathtub at the priest's house and he's got a bloodred baby on his wall, and on the way here I caught this radio station that was no radio station saying that the snake's still in Eden, which makes me think *wow*, and—where you going?"

"I'll be right back," she said, stepping through a door and locking it.

Teddy walked over to the door and called through to her. "It's like I've got a lot of these pieces and if I can get them to snap together, I'll have, well, I don't know what, but it'll be important, like one of those tools you snap around into different shapes and you can fix most anything." He heard her speaking to someone. "Is that Jimmy's little sister?" He did not guess that Lucinda was calling the police. "I saw her here, too, which I kind of forgot about." More words erupted from his mouth, a flow like lava from a source that had been building for generations. He talked about god, language, earrings. After a spell, the flow took a turn. "So it must be clear," he said to the door, "how much I love you. Don't let this supreme being thing I'm going through scare you off. I'm just a regular guy otherwise, like you know about me already from the way I come in here after work. Although, I quit work."

His confession of love had about it the awkwardness of the pelican's land-bound stroll, and Lucinda, whose real name was Lucy Sullivan, understood that she had damaged this man. Perhaps it was good that he could speak so freely about his feelings for her, but she was certain he had not been a peeping tom before becoming her customer—her slave, she thought. What had she been thinking, letting him come every day, making him pay more than he could possibly be earning legally? *I've ruined him,* she thought, giving herself far too much credit, but believing it. She would have to quit this, she understood. She was tinkering with people's lives in an inhumane way. She thought of the comic book edict: *if only she had used her genius for good instead of evil.* But how can you know the effect you will have on others? She had a genius for consolation, and just beyond her door babbled a man damaged by it.

"Until I find out where Christ is holing up, we have to keep it plutonic," Teddy said, shortly before a police officer stepped through the door and called out his name.

Teddy turned to him, delighted. How could this man he had never before seen know his name? Another miracle was in the offing.

"Come with me, Teddy," the uniformed man said with such kindness that Teddy felt his eyes well with tears. He turned back to the door.

"I have to go, honey," he yelled, words that called to his mind a sense of television without providing an actual image. He felt his life had become a thing of clarity, the perfect reception of cable after ages with rabbit ears. It made him smile.

Father McEwen had requested only Patrick, but Aluela showed up as well. They had on new clothing, he noted. Mary Hitchens had provided it, no doubt. His heart inflated anew with appreciation of her. They were in the neighborhood grassy spot known as Berry Park by the locals because of the wild blackberries that used to appear in one remote corner each spring. There were no longer blackberries. Some park official had hacked them out, or the nature of spring had changed.

Aluela took a seat next to Father McEwen on the park bench without saying hello. She leaned her head against his shoulder. Patrick sat on the other side of her.

"What have you got for us?" the boy asked.

Father McEwen shifted to make Aluela sit upright.

"I can't stay long," he said. "I have to visit someone in trouble."

The voice on the answering machine had sounded ecstatic. "Come join me," Teddy Allen had said of jail. The police officer had sounded less enthusiastic. "He needs a rubber room, Father, and soundproof, too, if you've got one handy."

"I'm wearing underwear," Aluela announced. "Mrs. Hitchens bought us clothes."

Father McEwen produced the cough of the uncomfortable, although, this day, the girl and the image of her naked bottom carried not a glimmer of sexual power, something Patrick had already picked up on. McEwen didn't know about the shredded panties, and so found the remark disconcerting only for its strangeness.

McEwen had not brought the painted Madonna, having guessed

after the first moment of surprise that Patrick had invented his father's parting gifts. He could not guess why the boy had created this fabrication, but he had decided to investigate the father's flight anyway. He had spoken with the news reporter who had covered the story, a man with a self-important air about him and a beard like a sea animal on his chin.

To Aluela and Patrick, McEwen said, "I am not a fool. I'll not play the games expected of a fool."

Aluela slumped back against the bench. Patrick felt the grip of a man's fist at his throat, a sensation that meant he was on the verge of tears.

"But I *have* looked into your father's disappearance."

Patrick and Aluela became instantly more erect in carriage, their senses tuned in and alert. This moment of attentive anticipation pierced Father McEwen with sadness. How could a man leave these children? McEwen took a deep breath and began.

"A body was found in Canada that matches the description of your father. He'd taken an apartment, and found a job under an assumed name. I can't quite recall what it was."

He pretended to concentrate. The children stared at him with sickly deliberation. Was this cruel? he wondered. He did not feel the ugly, elated rush he felt when spanking them, which led him to believe his motives were pure. He threw his head back, as if engrossed in a mental process that demanded he exclude the outside world. He did not know that this was the same posture that the fortune-teller used for the same reason. He might have loved Lucinda had he known her. She might have loved him. But neither could divine the other.

"His alias was . . . Alluvial Sludge," he said at last, eyeing the kids again. "Or something like that."

He stared several seconds, long enough for them to know he was creating the story as he went. The reporter had known nothing, had hardly remembered the story, had stroked his beard with the urgency of sexual gratification, and McEwen had been forced to mentally toil against a growing hatred for the man. Without facts or leads, what was this priest to do? He had prayed, and in prayer a strategy had come to him.

"Auto accident," he told the Corbus children. "Last rites were administered. Body cremated." He paused once more, studied their faces. These children knew he was making it up. He needed to see that in their eyes and in their posture, and at the same time, he needed to see that they were nonetheless paying attention. "His apartment, you might want to know about. He lived alone, but he had three bedrooms. A bed in each. Like he was maybe expecting guests, or people to come live with him."

Patrick began to weep. Aluela turned her head and took a deep breath, disappointed and unmoved.

Father McEwen stood. "I've got to be going. Have you heard from your mother?"

Aluela nodded. "She wants us to come home." The girl began shaking her head. "Neither of us wants to go back there."

Patrick covered his face. His tears would not subside. How was it that this story he knew to be a lie could affect him so? Why was it that this man had figured out Patrick's tricks and then made up a lie that mattered to him? Worlds tumbled through the boy's head, whizzing by so fast a pressure gripped his skull. Why had this deception moved him? He needed to know.

Wiping his eyes, he looked up into the sun—the round flaming face of Father McEwen, who stood before him, eager to leave but waiting, Patrick could see, to be certain Patrick was all right. His face was not, of course, the sun, but the heavenly object that, this moment, blocked the sun, which lit his head as if his hair were on fire. These helio-optics unnerved Patrick and permitted him a new perspective: Father McEwen had offered Patrick that which supported McEwen himself, a story to have faith in even if he could not entirely believe it.

Patrick looked away and considered this revelation. He thought that every relationship of long standing had an element of this— husband and wife believing in marriage despite the ratio of bad days to good, a child loving his parents despite their malignant behavior, a priest keeping his faith despite questions about that old, unlikely story.

In these scant seconds, Patrick began his dedication to this question of truth and lies, of story and consequences, of faith and failure. He would figure it out, he pledged to himself, the only solid thought he could fix against the torrent of sorrow and relief flooding his mind. At long last, he had a new mystery to explore, one no less large and no less strange than the one it forced him to abandon.

Teddy Allen was lodged not in a holding pen but in an actual cell. He sat upright in the lower of two bunks, still in Father McEwen's ungainly clothes, talking softly to himself. On Teddy, the shirt looked more like a gown.

The boy's shrinking, McEwen thought.

Upon seeing the priest, Teddy leapt up and charged the bars, the heavily cuffed pants swinging wildly.

"I've done it," he said. "I found him."

Father McEwen guessed that more than a nod was in order, but he had nothing more to offer. Telling the tale he'd invented to the Corbus children had left him feeling flaccid and slightly scaly. He felt the fatigue of a man who has come to understand there will be no end to his duties. This weight made him slump.

"I'm talking Jesus Christ," Teddy said. "The real one. God *told* me he was in town, then he led me to him."

"I can take you home, Teddy," Father McEwen said softly. "Your mother would like you to stay with her awhile. She's lonesome, you know."

Teddy shook his head. "I got to stay here. It's my, you know, the thing I got to do. You understand. It's why you can't have a woman, isn't it? You got a call from God, and he said for you to lay off the pussy, right?"

The boy was utterly earnest, which made Father McEwen's fatigue deepen. He had to engage him, work him down from this high, get him to come along. No one wanted to press charges. He only had to agree to stay away from the fortune-teller and not look into the windows of others.

"Chastity is part of becoming a priest," Father McEwen began. "It's not what *I* chose, exactly, but what—"

"Right, and so I'm here with the same kind of wake-up call like you got from the Almighty. He already told me lots of things I don't understand." Teddy gripped the bars and rocked from side to side, the sway of the cuffs an instant behind the movement of the body, as if a second life shared the slacks. "He said it wasn't God who created man. God didn't do it. It's in the Bible that way by mistake, like a translation screwup."

"Have you eaten?" McEwen asked him. "We could stop at Mallory's on the way home. I'll buy you a cold beer and a hot sandwich."

"Hunger doesn't know me," he said, and for an instant it seemed to Father McEwen that the boy might be a prophet after all. McEwen's red face turned a brighter and more burnished shade.

Then Teddy added, "Except I did have a taco in the police car. That cop with the woman partner was a nice guy. Gave me part of his very own lunch."

"Your mother would like you—"

"Are you ready, Father?" The eyes of the boy flamed with a bright radiance. "Are you ready?" He had about him the frenetic charge of madness, but how else could a man look who had met Jesus Christ?

It occurred to Father McEwen that he *was* ready, ready for the next failure in his life, ready for the next foolish condition of being, ready for fresh blood to fill his boots, for spring to come and fill the recesses of his heart with wild berries. It was possible, too, that he was ready for something he could not anticipate, ready for the thing for which one could never ready oneself, for which only the circumstances of the world and the will of the all-knowing could make one ready.

To Teddy Allen, McEwen said, "Yes, sir. I'm that. I am ready."

Teddy turned, pointing. "That's him," he said.

A man slept in the top bunk of the cell. Father McEwen had not noticed him until now. The man faced the wall. His legs were bent. A coarse blanket covered him.

"That's Jesus Christ," Teddy said.

As Teddy spoke, a drop of saliva slipped from his mouth and fell to the jail room floor. The striking of the concrete made a noise, and that noise made an echo in the harsh, vacant room.

Father McEwen eyed the sleeping man. A tuft of dark hair was the only feature he could make out.

"What makes you think this man is Jesus Christ?"

"I put my hand in his wounds," he said, and he stuck the hand through the bars.

Father McEwen saw nothing on the hand, but he could smell, once again, the odor of feces.

"Oh, Teddy, please, son, let me take you home."

He felt himself losing his composure. His chest shook, but he contained himself. Whatever it was that wanted to escape him, he could not let it out just now.

"Eve did it," Teddy said.

Father McEwen shook his head. He did not understand and did not want to speak.

"What God created wasn't men and women. They was something else, like nobody we know or could ever run into. Jesus himself told me this. Eve created human beings. She did it when she bit that fruit. We owe it all to her. All this." His arms spread wide, up and down the bars. "Without her, we'd be nothing but horses and cows on two legs."

Father McEwen wept. The weeping took hold of him, multiplied his fatigue, and cast him down onto his knees. Fallen man was the only one this world had ever known. Love for mankind had to mean the love of Eve's children. Father McEwen knew these sentiments well enough, but it had not occurred to him that heaven would not be populated with people, but with cows and horses on two legs. It had not occurred to him that such was not life after death but the undead pretending to live. McEwen understood that there could be no afterlife for him as a human. In heaven he would become a sinless creature; which is to say, he would not exist.

"He's told me lots of things," Teddy went on. He reached through the bars to put his hand on the priest's head. "Some stuff, I'm sorry, you won't want to hear. Like a hundred years from now there won't be priests of any kind." Teddy made a confused gesture. He meant to ruffle McEwen's hair, not rattle his head. "I hate to be the one to break it to you."

One hundred years would pass as the blink of an eternal eye, Father McEwen thought. Everyone alive would be dead. Most of the buildings he knew would be decimated. New buildings he could not imagine would stand in their place. These things he could comprehend, but there came to him knowledge he had no means of apprehending; it settled in his mind with a sigh, as if weary from a long journey: one hundred years hence, the human world would still beat in its human ways; the far end of the universe would remain beyond the comprehension of woman or man; boys would still weep for fathers lost; girls would yet be seduced by men who knew better; women and men would love and fail, fail and love; what they could not grasp would remain the thing they most desired; what they could not see would remain the thing they daily strained to bring into focus; angels would still sing in every soul, yet none would hear the words and only a handful would move in time to the melody; but no priests would survive this future. Father McEwen understood this fact was beyond question. Beasts that cannot reproduce themselves are doomed to extinction. This insight, he saw now, came not from that heretic Darwin but from the fruit of shame, fruit of nakedness and genitalia, the fruit of humankind.

"He's coming to," Teddy Allen whispered excitedly. "Jesus, are you waking? He is, Father. Take a peek."

At what point is a man unable to continue a life based on the habits of a faith he no longer inhabits? At the point the knees give? At the point a fork in the path can be recognized? Father McEwen covered his eyes and made himself stand up on the jailhouse floor. He needed sleep. He could use a whiskey. He would like to be held.

On the top bunk, the man tossed off the coarse blanket and sat upright. He stared at Father McEwen, and Father McEwen stared back.

IN A
FOREIGN
LAND

A friend of my ex-wife's invited me to a party on the Upper East Side. The invita-tion surprised me because I knew she didn't like me and she knew I didn't like her.

I accepted, of course. What good is life without a bit of the devious?

The hostess wore a white satin bib sort of dress, open in the back to her sacral dimples. Not to my taste. I'm an advertising man and I'm not supposed to have any taste, but I can't seem to help it. "How," she said to me, opening the door. Howard Duel is my name, and she was being familiar, not imitating a Hollywood Indian.

Her husband, a stranger to me, had about him the ordinariness often ascribed to serial killers. Sort of a bland Regis Philbin, if you follow my drift.

As soon as the handshaking business was concluded, Judy Guevera came trotting up. She wore a strapless drop-waist dress and flat shoes that clapped too loudly against the hardwood floor: imagine a pretty out-of-towner in a piano bar. She smiled wryly at me, holding hands with herself at her abdomen, a single tan finger of one hand nestled coyly into the other's fist.

"I hear you gave Cyd the boot," she said exuberantly. "I never liked that bitch."

"The other way around," I said. "She disposed of me."

"Then she's an idiot *and* a bitch," Judy insisted, taking my arm. "They have Myers'."

With my usual lucidity, I gathered that Cyd was not present. Like most recently divorced men, I longed for my ex. If you have to ask why, you must be eighteen and of no interest to me. Judy Guevera was all of thirty-two and also of very little interest to me. I understand the attraction of young women, but I've never actually felt it. Another failing, no doubt, some misfiring in the pituitary, a failed synapse upstairs.

Judy surprised me. Not because she was brusque, but because she remembered what I drank. She was the younger sister of my ex-wife's closest friend, and if you put together every word we'd ever exchanged you wouldn't have enough for a decent quiche recipe. Also, I was shocked that she didn't like Cyd. I thought everyone loved her.

"You still selling opiates to the masses?" Judy nudged a bearded man out of the way and grabbed the rum.

"Something like that," I said.

"I heard the best ad man in history is the guy who convinced people to buy ordinary rocks as pets." She laughed through her nose, a half wheeze and half whistle. "I read that in a novel by this guy FTD. You ever heard of him?"

"No," I said. "And I don't trust people who go by initials."

She thrust the drink at me, the rum rising dangerously close to the rim, receding just before it spattered my white shirt.

"You must be getting old," she said. *"¡Salud!"* We clinked glasses. "You used to keep up."

"I do keep up. It's my business to keep up."

I should mention that I was, in fact, the oldest person at the dinner party by at least ten years. I was fifty and looked it, although that's not such a terrible thing. I still had a single chin and a strong mouth, which is all a heterosexual male needs. As a bonus, I had a full head of hair—utterly white, but plenty of it. Women old enough to interest me don't care much about the small details in a man's appearance. *Baldness, I can handle,* they say, *as long as he trims his ears.* Or, *Pocked skin is cute, really, provided he washes the algae out.*

Our hostess was roughly my ex's age, thirty-seven, and Judy, for those of you not paying attention, was five years younger. The others looked to be in their twenties. Our hostess—her name is Frieda Lasch, although I was trying to keep her name out it—was a talentless writer with one tedious novel about menstruation (essentially) and a nonfiction account of her ex-husband's vasectomy that she'd stretched like spandex to book length. I remember a line from it verbatim: "Bubbles of saliva grew on his lips, making me think of the third grade."

It was a literary evening.

I sat across from none other than FTD (not his real initials but from the same regions of the alphabet), a dark man with a ragged, intelligent face—something like Bruce Springsteen with an MFA—and beside another literary light, the bearded fellow earlier nudged, whose name escaped me even as it was spoken. He was a redhead-and-beard with a desperate stammer about his looks, like a clown with a migraine.

Judy sat on the other side of me, her chair close to mine, a pretty woman, with nothing of the bovine in her and only a tiny bit of the zebra. An ideal talking head in a deodorant commercial.

Frieda did the introductions as if awards were forthcoming, listing publications and print runs, enunciating with excruciating care, as if that were the latest fad.

Judy scooped her for my intro. "Howard Duel, call him How," she said, taking my arm with both hands. "He's got a big thick book on the outlaw Koos Vandermeyer, the Koos-Koos Kid. Did I get it right?"

I nodded. "He was the fastest gun in Creede, Colorado, for approximately a week," I offered, but they were too young to think a man my age might try to be funny.

The book had been a hobby, never even an obsession, about a Norwegian settler who'd misunderstood a sheriff asking him to "Dismount, there's a hanging about to start." He'd heard, "Dismount, we are going to hang you." He shot the sheriff in the kidneys and became an inept and doomed outlaw. My title was *In a Foreign Land,* and never mind what the publisher called it.

Frieda, after listing every piddling thing of hers that had seen type, introduced Judy as "my good friend," and began dishing out the food.

I leaned close to Judy's ear and whispered, "You was robbed."

"I saved you," she said, assuming a mildly sardonic tone. "*You* were supposed to save me."

Judy was a radio personality, not a disc jockey per se, but the steady sweet voice you hear between classical cuts on public radio. She told me that night that she did not select the music herself. As it turned out, her personal taste in music annoyed me. She liked the current music of people who were at their peak back when I listened to popular music—Neil Young and Stevie Winwood, Bob Dylan and the Rolling Stones.

Don't get me started on taste.

"Oh, yes, the Stones," I said. "Never have so few done so little for so long to so many and made so much."

"Right," the bearded one said. "I love the Stones, too."

Frieda had made the dinner herself—a pesto ziti, tomato and cucumber salad, and fresh sourdough bread with salt-free butter she had churned with her very own mitts. She was a great cook but undervalued her talent because she considered it too traditional, thereby discriminating against herself, and in the process creating a literary putz.

"I hear," Mr. Beard said cautiously to FTD, "that your new novel takes place entirely on the phantasmagorical plane. When's the pub date?"

"No, man, it's a historical novel. Set backstage of the *Cosby Show* in an alternative universe where they're all white—I didn't want to get into the race thing. September."

From this jumping-off point, conversation rollicked from the topic of first-person point of view to the current state of publishing, and on to the advantages of omniscience—"You'd know what liquor to stock for your guests," I offered, but no one even chortled. When FTD politely attempted to include me in the conversation by asking about the aesthetic distance of my narrator, I told him I was no writer and that the book was a fluke.

"I'm an ad man," I fessed up. "I work for S_____, V_____, and N__."

"Hey," beard said. "They couldn't use a young guy with fresh ideas who knows how to write, could they?"

"Yeah," a heretofore silent novelist I am otherwise omitting jumped in. "Ideawise, I'm tough."

And so the clamoring began. As author of *In a Foreign Land,* I was a pitiable hanger-on, but as an advertising man, I was Tut, Ruth, Marilyn Monroe.

To end my newfound status, Frieda brought up my divorce.

"Has Cyd's recent abandonment affected your work?"

"You knew she dumped him?" Judy asked her, a bit too quickly, with that overly surprised my-goodness-gosh tone that betrays a lie.

I guessed then that Judy had asked to have me invited. My spirits lifted. Not that I had any intention of going home with the girl, but I was suddenly certain that the whole dinner had been arranged to get me at the table, seated beside Judy Guevera. I moved from the cold and dismal periphery of belonging into the warm center of the action.

"How's Benj handling it?" Judy asked, lowering her voice slightly.

Benj is my sixteen-year-old son.

"He has complained about his eyes," I told her. "The optometrist and ophthalmologist say his vision is perfect, but he's started wearing big, black-rimmed, dime-store magnifying glasses. He claims he needs them." What he'd actually said to me was, "Everything's suddenly too little," but I wasn't going to repeat that and see it turn up in bearded-one's next family saga. "It's disconcerting," I said. "My son has suddenly become Woody Allen."

Judy laughed, bless her, through her nose, a melodic *phh-phh-phh.*

"Otherwise," I went on, "Benj is bearing up well enough."

"You know," Frieda said, and maybe I should start calling her "our hostess" again for anonymity's sake, "I've always wondered. Is that boy really yours? I mean, are you the father?"

Perhaps this is a good time to describe our hostess. Starting at the top, I'd say her hair was once brown, and now wavered between blond and yellow in a neverland impolitely known as green. Her nose, needlelike yet with cavernous nostrils, dominated a face otherwise lacking distinction, except perhaps for a rather handsome bleached mustache of ordinary dimensions. She was fashionably thin in a worn-out, oversexed sort of way, and her skin had the resilient tone and mock-tan coloration of cardboard.

Before I could respond to her, she added, "I've never thought he looked like you. I always believed Cyd trapped you. I've never thought Benj was yours."

What I thought was this: Judy had conspired with Frieda to have this dinner, agreeing that Frieda would be a hateful moronic toad to the both of us, which would endear us to each other and seal our sex-doing. What I said was the following: "Sperm and egg are the easiest, most entertaining, and least important parts of parenting. If it's true that I'm not his biological father, then I'm inordinately lucky because I certainly wouldn't trade my boy for any other child in the world."

She backed off.

Oh, well, I didn't say exactly the above, but a somewhat less articulate facsimile of same, and Frieda did back off. During the next lull in the conversation, I asked her why she hadn't invited any women writers to this liturgy. Just a light jab to keep her off balance. I had no intention of launching a haymaker.

I was, after all, a guest.

Cyd and I were married ten years. We'd first been lovers another seven years earlier, when she was all of twenty, and I, thirty-three. She had been a student at Johns Hopkins, and I an erudite reporter for the *Baltimore Daily News,* assigned to obituaries and crime—a niche in the journalistic hierarchy a half step above sweeping and mopping. I spent a good portion of my time at rest homes interviewing octogenarians about their late roommates ("Dead, is he?") and hating myself for not having gotten the scoop on Watergate.

Cyd did an internship with the paper, starting at the bottom—a euphemism for *me.* An hour into my training of her, I could see that she was already a better reporter than I was. She had a knack for getting to the heart of things. She'd see that so-and-so had been a grocer and now he was dead, and bingo, she'd be finished with the obituary. Meanwhile, I'd be looking for a human angle ("Did the deceased like large animals?") or some way to reveal his character ("His death mask divulged the wizened face of a philosopher, though his social security number belonged to a retired heavy machine operator"). I realized she could do my job, which took me every second of an eight-hour day, in about forty-five minutes.

I decided then we should marry.

I quit the paper and started dating her. She was given my job, and much sexual hilarity followed. Love came later, a fierce and jealous love, a big polar bear sort of love.

I had a flat downtown near the newspaper. There we practiced a lively brand of lovemaking and read aloud from *Lost in the Funhouse* and Carson McCullers (her favorites), and Cheever and Updike (mine). Otherwise, we didn't do a damn thing. Didn't travel, rarely went out to eat, never bought gifts for each other. We didn't even take the paper. I got a part-time job proofreading at a law firm. She did burglaries and obits. We were destitute. It was the best time of my life.

Then, of course, it fell apart. She became distracted, spent more time at the *Daily News*. Despite her conspicuous efforts, I wouldn't let her discard me. Finally, she disappeared. Quit her job and left town, leaving no forwarding address. After a month of torture and reading her mail, I chucked the proofreading job and tracked her to her parents' house in Columbia, Missouri. She was pregnant. She wanted nothing to do with me. She was thinking of studying cultural anthropology once breast-feeding was at an end.

I got hired by the local paper and hung around her as much as she'd permit. After the baby was born, she decided she needed me.

We moved to Philadelphia and lived there from the time Benj was three months until he was five years old, at which time I became employed by the ad agency. We decided to marry the same day I officially started work, grabbing strangers off the street to be witnesses (one Edith X. O'Connell, a retired telephone operator, and Jim Jennings, unemployed bricklayer).

I tell you all of this so you understand that our hostess's question had a history. I'm trying to be fair to the twit.

Following dinner, we adjourned to the living room. FTD and the beard began exchanging stories about graduate school, its peculiar intimacy and philosophical whatnot. There was "some something" profound about it, they agreed. They spoke learnedly about the manners, mores, and drugs of the times. Then began the inevitable agent comparisons and lamentations about the publishing world. Writers are a tedious lot. No wonder so many of them drink.

Judy sidled up to me, and I inquired about her sister.

"She is so happy about your divorce," Judy said. "She'd been pleading with Cyd to leave you for years. She and I used to argue about you guys all the time. 'Cyd deserves better,' she'd say. 'Cyd sucks,' I'd say."

"I had no idea our marriage generated such controversy." I was more than a little embarrassed. "I hope the divorce was sufficiently entertaining."

"Oh, don't get huffy. That's the only time I don't like you, when you become Mr. Huffy. Get me a drink. Liquor me up and I'll tell you wonderful things about yourself."

I accepted her offer. Her litany of compliments did, in fact, lift my spirits. I discovered that I had a kind voice, sexy eyebrows, and a graceful way of "bopping around"—something I'd always secretly suspected of myself. She also loved my book.

"Poor Koos-Koos," she said. "I identified with him completely. One misunderstanding and your whole life is turned around."

"Yes," I said, "but how does that apply to your life?"

"I completely misunderstood my parents. I thought they were normal," she explained. "I'm still playing catch-up."

"You'll have to be more specific."

"It's your basic younger sister story or Electra story, kind of a Gretel-and-Gretel-make-it-back-from-the-witch's-house-and-their-father-won't-believe-the-younger-one-until-the-older-one-puts-in-her-two-cents story."

She began to add something more about her sister but was interrupted by facial hair, who was quite drunk now, asking her to dance. Frieda and FTD were already fritzing about, as were a few others whose names I'm omitting to protect their publishers.

"Nah," Judy said to him. "I promised the first dance to How." To me, she added a seductive, "C'mon."

How should I describe Ms. Guevera's style of dance? An undulation with horns, perhaps, though that doesn't capture the distinctively postmodern charm of it. Meanwhile, the beard made it onto the floor with his second choice and immediately seemed to suffer electroshock convulsions. Frieda hula-hooped about, letting her bib-dress slide around her hidden parts. Husband of Frieda waffled between offbeat hand-clapping and a horsey sort of *clompity clomp*. Suddenly FTD yelled, "Limbo!" and—oh, you get the picture. A riotous time was had by all.

Benjamin and I were close, despite what his mother called "our opposite dispositions," which is an uninspired way to say Benj was polite to strangers. Since the divorce, our time together was restricted to Saturdays, and what I hated was that it robbed me of the everydayness of him: the nocturnal refrigerator plunderer, the six o'clock news-groping purist, the mealtime barbarian. When we meet now, he's on best behavior, and so am I. Our time is too short. I never get to see him with his hair uncombed, or when he's in his grubs doing the lawn. I miss my boy.

A week before the party, we'd met in a café near the subway stop, where we'd planned to eat before heading to MOMA for a highbrow day of chat-and-stare. However, he'd brought a disreputable-looking friend with him, and our plans were ruptured.

"I don't think my eyes could handle it," Benj said of the proposed excursion, blinking owl-like behind his cheap lenses. His magnified eyes made him seem especially the child, calling to mind a baby's exaggerated features—though the tiny post through one of his nostrils bearing a Guatemalan Worry Doll undercut the image somewhat. "Besides," he went on, "Ogle doesn't like art."

"How is it possible that you do not like any art?" I asked Ogle (not his real name; his father is a lawyer).

"Rack your brain, señor. I've racked mine and it's done zero, but there it is anyhow. It's all no-go artwise for me."

Unlike the skunk, who despite his bad odor and poor reputation is said to have impeccable table manners, Ogle ate beans by trapping a few in a bit of ravaged bread, then thrusting the dripping mass in the (approximate) direction of his mouth. Thank god he was garrulous; otherwise, we'd have been denied the sight of his amazing mastication.

"Your manner of eating is ghastly," I said.

"Funny you should bring that up," he began, and then launched into a defense of his eating like a buffalo (my simile, not his). His argument had something to do with the First Amendment.

Benj, meanwhile, wolfed down his chili cheeseburger quietly and with relative decorum. When Ogle finished his treatise, Benj said, "So you seeing anybody, Dad?"

"No," I said, startled. "Not really. Not at all."

Benj nodded, poking his glasses. "Mom's got a new boyfriend. Pretty cool guy, I guess. She says he's the first guy she's met since you who has backbone."

"Oh," I said casually. "Had a large sampling, has she?"

Ogle answered, "Backbone's way way overrated."

To which, I replied, "Such is the argument of most invertebrates."

"She goes out some," Benj said. "Pretty much, I'd say. I think she misses you."

I held my tongue and let Ogle launch into a directive about backbone and the poor and the superiority of unwaxed fruit.

We spent the day wandering about music shops, looking for a tape by the Revolting Cocks, a disc by Public Enemy, and Madonna's snake poster.

"No way it's Madonna who does the snake thing," Ogle pronounced late in the search. "We're barking up the wrong babe."

Benj just shrugged. To me, he said, "I don't much like him really. The guy Mom's seeing."

He stared at me plaintively, afraid he'd offended me earlier. I was touched.

Ogle agreed with him. "Major stooge," he said, nodding like a straining horse.

Cyd had sent me *The Good Enough Parent,* and at moments like this one, I almost wished I had read it.

"It's all right to like him," I said to Benj, "and it's all right not to like him."

"Yeah," Benj said. "Like I've got any choice, you know? How can you control who you do and don't like?"

Ogle, as if to prove the assertion, scratched athletically at his crotch.

A funny thing happened after the party, not directly after but during the following week: I quit my job. Call me impetuous, call me impulsive, call me unemployed. I don't know why I did it, but I told my immediate superior, V_____ himself, that I was ripe for a change.

"My marriage has ended you know," I said.

V_____ replied, "Metamorphosis is passé. Ninety percent of butterflies suffer from airsickness." His idea of humor, and evidence as to why he needed to change my mind: he had the creative repertoire of a tomato. "How, how 'bout a twenty percent raise?" he said. "The average butterfly would give his right wing for that kind of dough."

You see, I'm a very good ad man. I started the whole eco-ad trend, connecting the purchase of our brand of toothpaste, motor oil, and luggage with saving the whales, protecting the rain forest, and plugging up the ozone hole. I did the wandering-camera, narrow-focus ads, too, that elusive, suggestive darting that other agencies are still copying. I got Nike Michael Jordan. I'm *not* a let's-get-them-to-pay-for-a-rock kind of advertising man. I'm into big ideas. Laugh if you wish, but you're wearing my products. You've probably taken out a loan to purchase something that I convinced you you couldn't be done without.

V_____ insisted I take a two-week vacation rather than giving notice. He was certain I merely needed a rest. I walked a couple of buildings down the street and got a new job in twenty minutes. More money, roughly the same benefits. I don't know why I did it.

I preserved the two weeks of vacation, however, and tried to arrange to take Benj—sans Ogle—to Vermont to hike, but Cyd accused me of wanting to hog Benj's time, and though it wasn't the way I'd have put it, her analysis was accurate. I missed the boy so acutely I found myself weeping at anything even mildly sentimental: AT&T commercials or Robin Williams films. It was a pathetic business.

During those moments of helpless weeping I would hate Cyd for breaking us up, the way Beatles fans used to hate Yoko. Afterward, I would take it all back, in case some friendly god had been listening to my evil thoughts.

When Judy Guevera called and invited me to dinner at her apartment, I was free to accept. She lived in the Village, on the second floor of a three-flat, a nicer place than I had expected. She answered the door wearing only a robe, her hair wet and uncombed. Her mascara perfect.

"Would you believe I haven't even had time to get dressed?"

"No," I said. "I don't believe that for a minute."

Oh, well, you know what followed. Do I really need to describe the touching of fingertips to clothing and then to flesh? Or the staring, that nervous yet gooey brand of staring? We began the maneuvering of bodies and body parts, the strange little dance that precedes First-Kiss, our heads lifting and lowering, finding a parallel and then collapsing it—not suddenly but with little jerks forward, tiny retreats back—until finally our lips touched, our mouths opened. All of which served to create a dribble of sensation like a tickle or a lemon drop. Our tongues shyly collided, then less shyly commingled, and our mouths became sources of heat and sweetness—yes, *sweetness;* what a fine word for the pleasure of a woman's mouth against yours.

Okay, I hammed that part up a bit. She was the first woman I'd kissed on the lips since the divorce, and the only one, besides my wife, in seventeen years. We bopped right into bed. Which happened to be next to the dining table because Judy's absent roommate paid an extra thirty a month to sleep in the bedroom. I found that my sexual hunger had hidden an even more basic desire for food. By the time we finished the bed business, I was ravenous, too much so to cuddle, which seemed to suit Judy fine.

"Yeah," she said. "Let's chow."

I grabbed my shirt and began buttoning, but she brought plates to the bed and sat cross-legged and naked in front of me, eating fried chicken with her fingers, licking often.

It was not at all erotic, if that's what you're thinking. I've never questioned why restaurants require their patrons to wear shirts. A beautiful woman. Have I mentioned that? Judy is beautiful, and being naked certainly enhanced her attractiveness, but I couldn't look at her and swallow. I stared at her wall hangings and knick-knacks, making vaguely polite comments. I ate in a rush.

Without any prompting, she began telling me about Cyd and her sister when they were teenagers.

"Cyd always took Sis's boyfriend *after* convincing Sis to drop him." Judy shook her head over her chicken. "Sis was a sap."

Judy went on to explain that she had slept with many of the same boys herself, as well as her sister's first husband. It didn't seem to dawn on her that I was not the ideal audience for this confession. I came to understand that her hard work to win me stemmed not from great attraction to me for my mind or even for my body, but for my position in the constellation of her universe.

We got married a month later.

This is my first attempt at a comeback into the literary world since *In a Foreign Land*. (If you must know, the book was published under the title *Koos Koos, the Cuckoo Outlaw*.) Judy insisted I start with this, the history of our romance. I'm hoping FTD will give me a blurb, and I have left out several damning bits about his dress and grammar as a result.

I've been at my new job two years now and made my hours flexible to have time to write and to be home when Judy's there. At work, she comes over the speakers in my office, introducing Mozart and Sibelius.

Cyd has taken my sudden marriage to her best friend's little sister as well as can be expected, which is to say, she hates me with a deep and genuine passion. I would prefer Judy didn't have the old, long-standing connection with Cyd, though I know it's possible that some of my love for her has to do with her position in my constellation, too. And what of it? I find I care no more about the emotional origin of this love than I do the paternal origins of Benj. He is my son, and Judy is my wife. My love for Cyd has moved to some posterior chamber of the heart now, back there with cheap pizza, J. D. Salinger, Sophia Loren, Hermann Hesse, and, yes, the Rolling Stones.

Benj no longer wears magnifying glasses. He is out of high school and, against my wishes, enlisted in the army. Any day now he's going to be sent to the Middle East. He's waiting for his orders, waiting to discover his destination. Cyd claims he's doing this to impress us. (She's dating her therapist.) I don't think it's that simple.

When Judy gets in from the radio, she joins me on the floor in front of the Magnavox, and we watch the newscaster sanctimoniously describe the world. Between reports, my ads appear, and I've discovered that I'm proud of them—not for what they're doing, but for the care that went into their making. Then the newsman returns, looking solemn. "In Baghdad . . . ," he begins, or "In Afghanistan . . ."

We hold hands, Judy and I, and listen. We wonder to which distant country Benj will be sent, wonder what it was he misinterpreted that led him into uniform, wonder where the next unnecessary battle will be fought.

Marriage suits me. It's so red, white, and blue, but also *subversive*. We didn't understand that in the sixties. The subversive in matrimony will be the next wave in advertising.

You wait and see.

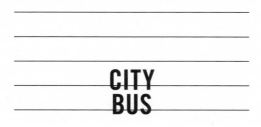

CITY
BUS

Helen Swann shivers in shirtsleeves at the bus stop, coatless and confident the day will warm. The city bus, as it lumbers toward her, cracks the ice that lines the gutter. Frost nubs its broad, bald forehead and clouds the immense windshield. Like glaucoma, Helen thinks. It's one of the old buses, which means the brakes will shriek and the heat won't work. She boards at City Self-Storage, a concrete bunker directly across from her apartment building. She rents units on either side of the street. From the front window of her living room, she can see the corrugated metal door of her storage shed. This fact pleases her. The vehicle's brakes bleat, and something under the great body rattles. The morning air is the gray of doves' wings.

The driver slumps behind the steering wheel, his head bulging beneath his city cap as if it were screwed on too tight. His name is probably Otis, but his name tag bears an extraneous u *(Outis),* and at each scheduled stop he bellows not the street corner but merely *Out,* as if to confirm his complicity in a divine pattern. He is her least favorite driver. His hand rests on the steel knob that operates the door, the first two fingers tobacco-stained to the second knuckle as if dipped daily in a secret vat. He keeps his eyes on the asphalt, does not nod or smile as she boards, the bus accelerating as the doors whip shut, his aftershave as pungent as poison.

The few passengers already aboard, veterans all, avert their eyes as Helen navigates the rocking aisle. She feels the urge to hike her skirt to her neck to see if any head will turn. They space themselves about the bus, each in a separate stall. Helen sits equidistant from the fleece cap three seats ahead and the fur coat three behind, inclining her head against the chilly window as the behemoth carrying them plods around a corner.

The view is too familiar to seem remarkable, and yet she looks for evidence of hidden splendor. High above her, the sun notches a gloomy body of clouds. Snow lingers in north-facing lawns and the scant sunlight makes it sparkle. Winter is finally coming to an end. The channel nine meteorologist has promised it. His kind voice and sly face (as if he knows more weather than he's letting on) visit her apartment five nights a week. She wears no coat as testament to her faith in him. He is a central figure in her secret life.

The bus slows and stops. Cars huddle at the traffic light, a woolly frost layering their backs. Helen's mother died earlier in the year, and Helen had not wanted to fly across the country to go through the possessions. A moving company delivered it all to City Self-Storage. The van was full, and she advised the men to stack the boxes to the ceiling. When she came home from work, she discovered that the crates and furniture filled only the back wall of the shed. She had room to park a car in there if she wanted.

She had planned to go through her mother's belongings quickly, discarding or selling most of the artifacts. But investigating the crates tired her. She pulled an overstuffed couch free of the pile in order to have a place to rest. She set boxes about as if they were tables. She bought a space heater, leaving the big door open, providing a view of her apartment window. One evening she fell asleep in the easy chair, as her mother had often done. She did not wake until after midnight, cozy in her friendly cavern. A light shone in her living room window across the street, the curtains slightly parted, as if the apartment itself were jealous.

The bus wheezes forward as far as the intersection. Helen's sigh hazes her window. She does not want to go to work. Her desk is in Public Records at City Hall, a room as mammoth as a toothache. Until last month, her job entailed filling the great room with papers—certificates of marriage and divorce, deeds to houses and cars, licenses for businesses and bureaus. Every civilization must leave a record of its existence, she had told herself. It was important work. But now she is required to empty the same wide hall, transferring documents to computer files. At her present rate, it will take another dozen years to erase the tangible evidence of the first twelve.

It seems to her that she has ridden this bus more than twelve years. Fifty, perhaps. Thirty, at the least. She can shut her eyes and describe the paltry buildings along the route: the white bank winged with a drive-through, the elegant brick courthouse warted by a concrete addition, the sleek silver supermarket on Laurel, the slate steak house on Sacker, the ugly new library spouting its shiny sculpture of the letter O, and the chalk white astonishment of her own City Hall. This daily edifice trail resides in her mind like something less than a city and something more than a routine, a coded sentence that is, at once, meaningless and beyond her ability to decipher.

"Out," Outis yells and a bundled-up man and child obey.

To be fair, it's her birthday. Thirty-five is a troubling age, especially if one is alone, a woman without husband or children. Helen doesn't particularly long for either, but she has always assumed she would have a few of each. Today, she has her doubts. When she was fifteen, she ran off with a boy. The police tracked them to a neighboring city and arrested him on *his* birthday. He had turned eighteen, which meant he could be charged with statutory rape, as well as kidnapping. Sometimes she believes they purposely waited until he was of age. The channel nine weatherman makes her think of him, although the weatherman looks nothing like the boy. Her lover had been short with a leonine mane, while the weatherman is tall, his premature white hair thinning and wispy, like cirrocumulus skies. *You remind me of the ocean,* the boy had said to Helen in the motel room, minutes before her rescue and his arrest, sirens already singing for them on the avenue. *Something big,* he continued. *Like . . . I don't know . . . the air.*

Her mother pressed charges. For years, until near the end, Helen and her mother were estranged. Malignant polyps brought about the reconciliation.

Today Helen feels that the remainder of her life may be like this very morning, a repetitious trip over familiar ground in an anonymous and nearly empty hovel of transport. She stares at her fingers' web on her lap as if it is literally her womb and feels suddenly weepy. Normally, she treats a maudlin thought like a stranger's sudden interest—something to flee. Today, she is defenseless. She pictures the weatherman bumping up against her in a tight-fitting tavern, his hands tumbling down to her waist, his tongue touching the soft hide of her lips. The image both excites and embarrasses her. "The future is fair," the weatherman likes to say, "no matter how stormy the past." He's folksy but also a smart aleck. Helen likes to invent new lines for him. "Weather is the forbidden frontier," she would have him say. "What we do about the weather defines us." She knows the actual man who appears on her television is a jerk. She saw him once in a bar sitting with one woman and staring at another. His real life is of no interest to Helen.

In the fantasy world she daily creates, the forces that battle over the weather have volition: they are gods. The mortal things—humans and trees, buildings, sewers, and homes—both serve the gods and struggle against them, until they fall weather-beaten to the hoary screech of crane, the thunder of wrecking ball, or the insidious algebra of cancer. Each morning she searches the city for signs of change in the struggle, and each evening she listens to the weatherman predict tomorrow's skirmish. Her secret life has no other plot. It is not so much a narrative as an embellishment. An insanely elaborate construct, but Helen Swann knows she is not insane. Merely intelligent, alone, and gravely bored. In her private world, actions have meaning, and the trivial torment of daily life is transformed into a grand struggle.

"You should get professional help," her mother said when Helen described her attachment to the weatherman. They were on the phone. Helen had grown tired of the silences and revealed too much. "And I don't mean one of those TV psychics," her mother added to make the conversation lighter.

"I should go to a real psychic?"

Her mother offered a polite laugh. Helen wanted to tell her that the weatherman was something like a psychic, an oracle who forecasts the future, details the past, and ascertains from the incalculable morass of existence the high temp for the upcoming day and the low for the night.

"He's pretty," Helen said at last. "Like an antelope."

"Like an antelope on *television*," her mother said. "Get yourself a real antelope. You're still an attractive woman."

That had made Helen ready to hang up.

"I suppose that means I'm *ancient*," she said and changed the subject without letting her mother reply.

Helen had booked a final flight to Arizona, but her mother died the weekend before. Helen canceled the trip. She did not want to see the emaciated body, and there was no one there with whom to mourn. Her father had left them when she was an infant, and her mother had destroyed every photograph of him. But she had kept the name Swann.

"It's the only thing he ever gave me that he didn't later take back," her mother explained.

Helen had thought, *What about me?*

For years Helen tried to conjure from memory the image of her father. She found family albums among the things in the shed. One eight-by-ten showed baby Helen standing on tiptoes between her mother and a man, but the man's face and body were covered by a picture of a swan clipped from a magazine—her mother's idea of a joke. Helen pulled the clipping away carefully, but glue had damaged the photo, erasing most of him. Her father was tall, she could determine, with narrow shoulders. Either he wore a hat or he had a pointed head. Helen slipped the photo into a cheap frame and it hangs in the storage shed, the incomplete shape of her father drawing the eye away from the smiling woman and pretty little girl. She has not made much progress emptying the unit. She gave her mother's clothing to Goodwill and threw away the porcelain figurines that were broken in shipping. Her mother had collected the figurines for decades, but Helen did not feel obliged to glue together their hollow bodies. She never understood the attachment.

A motorcyclist slips through the gap between the bus and the curb, the blank space needed for the colossus to make a turn. A contemptible red motorcycle, like a fire ant. A car pulls in behind it, a pieced-together creature, the front half a Mustang and the rear of something cheaper, like a Cavalier. Auto titles and death certificates are handled with equal aplomb by Helen's new software program. One format for all public records. If she clicks on "Marriage License," certain boxes are highlighted and the cursor moves to them automatically. If she clicks on "Death Certificate," some of the same boxes but also different ones are illuminated. It will simplify her work once she feels comfortable with it. She doesn't look forward to her elementary job becoming even more rote, but neither does she wish to be slow to learn it.

"Out," Outis calls, and the herd do as they're told. They are at the corner of Laurel and Main, halfway through her daily odyssey. A man takes the seat in front of her, although there are plenty of empties—a newcomer, a stranger to their customs. His long coat is made of camel's hair or ermine or the pelt of some more exotic creature. He turns sideways in the seat to face her. He speaks her name.

"Don't tell me," he says. "Your car broke down, too. These things tend to happen in bunches."

It is Henry Alt, who also works at City Hall.

"I always ride the bus to work," Helen replies. "Better for the planet, saves wear and tear on my car."

"Really?" Henry Alt says. "I guess. Although you know what they say—something there is that doesn't like a bus."

He doesn't smile but *grins* at her. He is likely forty-five and the hair at the front of his head is scarce, but the women at the Hall think of him as handsome. Helen has never participated in the speculation as to why he lives alone. The consensus is that he drinks too much.

His eyes patiently roam her face, which embarrasses her. She studies her lap and thinks about the software, the mistakes she made the day before. She needs a new computer, one that can run the program as quickly as she can type, but she dreads learning the quirks of a new machine.

"Does the bus go left on Olive?" Henry Alt asks her.

Helen nods.

"You've seen him then?" He leans in closer. His shirt is made of yellow silk, the shade of old leaves. "The fellow who works that corner?"

Fellow, she thinks. Who says *fellow* anymore?

"I'm not sure," she says. "Who do you mean?"

"I always drive by—look at that!" He aims a finger out the window.

A snowman stands on the steps to the library, a gold crown on his head, something peculiar for a nose, an open book jabbed into his frozen abdomen as if he's reading. Charcoal briquettes serve as eyes, but one has fallen out. Henry Alt laughs heartily. The snowman's nose, Helen sees, is the toe of an old shoe. Either the shoe has been cut in half, or the remainder of it is packed inside the snowy head.

"My god, when I was a boy," Henry Alt says, shaking his head happily, "how I loved *snow.* Snowmen, snow angels, sledding, sliding, rolling down that hill in Penny Park, you know the one?"

"No," Helen says. "I didn't grow up here."

"Neither did I," he says. "Upstate New York. You ever been there?"

"No," she says again.

He *is* handsome, she decides. There had been a meeting last fall when he sat beside her. He made a joke about the mayor and everyone laughed. His breath had smelled of wine, but it was right after lunch. People often have wine with lunch. He wears a suit every day, and a laundered shirt. He has an array of ties. Evidently he has income from sources besides the city. Or he has family money. She cannot recall the kind of car he drives.

"I spent a few winters here as a boy," he says. "I guess that's why I live here now, those winters. Little islands of happiness."

"Out," Outis calls.

They're stopped at the intersection of Laurel and Sacker. The bus takes in a few additional people. Henry Alt seems to be musing over his youth, his lips pursed in memory. He has been passed over for promotion, Helen knows. One of the men in his office is ambitious and clever, and has skipped ahead of Henry Alt, who seems naive about such things. His tie today is made of alternating diamonds of black and gold. It, too, is made of silk. She doubts that he needs the job at City Hall. She considers telling him that it is her birthday. What would such a man do with this information? He would feel obliged to do something, she thinks. Take her to lunch, perhaps. Or, at a minimum, burst into song.

The rear tire of the bus rides up over the curb as they make the turn. Henry Alt's eyes widen comically, and he lifts himself from the seat to examine the street corner.

"Hope we didn't flatten any feet."

"The bus always does that," Helen tells him.

Does he really need to be told? It has to be obvious that nothing so large can change directions easily. Something has fallen against her shoes—his briefcase. She gives it a kick to push it back beneath the seat.

"It's coming up," Henry says. "You must have noticed the guy on the corner. He showed up a few weeks ago, with one of those signs. *Vietnam Veteran. Stranded.* That was all. Then he modified it: *Vietnam Veteran. Need Ticket Home. God Bless You.*" Henry Alt laughs once more. "Do you remember when suddenly every homeless guy had a sign saying *Will Work for Food*? I always wondered how such a thing could sweep the nation. Do they have an underground network? 'Hey, guys, put the words *God* and *Home* in your sign and you'll get more money. Pass it on.' That sort of thing?" The wrinkles by his eyes are deep. He continues smiling as he speaks. "So last week, I'm at that corner and the guy now has a *dog.*" He says *dog* as if the word is inherently funny. "And the following day, he has a bowl with the dog's name on it: *Sarah.* Can you imagine? A dog named Sarah." *Sarah* has become an even funnier word than *dog.* "Now his sign says *Spare Change for Dog Food Appreciated.*"

Helen nods and smiles at appropriate moments. She is perfectly competent at social interaction. The last time she and her mother spoke, her mother had said, "Take a husband. Buy a house. Become a slave to your mortgage. Let the children climb all over you."

Helen had laughed into the phone. "You make it sound awful."

"Make mistakes," her mother insisted. "Go ahead. Live."

It had made Helen think of her father and the mistake her mother had made.

Henry Alt is still talking. The neighborhood where he boarded the bus is full of old and dignified homes. She imagines his house, can see him walking about in a grand place, shifting from window to window, a hearth fire providing light, wineglass in his hand, wine dark curtains framing him. He touches the curtains and then waves to someone across the street. Helen's imagination glides across the pavement, where she finds herself, ensconced in her storage shed and waving back.

"What have we got here?" Henry Alt asks. The bus has come to a stop in traffic. He lifts himself again and stares through the windshield. "No accident," he says. "Just roadwork. There are those cones all around a manhole. What a job that must be."

Helen rises in her seat to look. Gloved hands lift a great coin from the street and reveal the round cavity beneath.

"Can you picture it?" Henry Alt asks her. "Spending your days down there? Living under the city?"

We all live under the weather, she thinks.

"Just what kind of network is there beneath us?" he asks. "Sewers and power lines, sure. Catacombs, do you think? Not likely, but there could be. An underground universe."

Why is this man so happy and handsome, but also frivolous and without ambition? Helen wonders but has no answer. He's attractive, and yet he is alone. He's intelligent, and yet he has a dead-end career. He clearly has money, but here he is riding the city bus with Helen to the same place of employment. Henry Alt annoys her. She thinks again of the software program. She entered the wrong information first for several days, misunderstanding the error messages. In some cases, her entry told the computer that she was recording birth certificates, when she had been attempting to record deeds of sale, marriages, deaths. She has to recall the mistakes, delete them, and begin over. The prospect of it tires her, although it is really no different from entering them in the first place, no more difficult or complicated. She will be working eight hours today filing one thing or another. Why should the prospect of redoing these files be more fatiguing than entering new records? A better computer would make her work go faster, but, following this reasoning, she understands it will make it no easier. She will be there eight hours a day, either way. There will never be an end of things to record and file.

There is, however, no record of her secret life. If she fails to imagine it, it disappears. Thinking this pleases her. Her world is hers alone.

The bus staggers forward, and Henry Alt's briefcase slides against her feet once more. When she and the boy ran off, they did not even pack a suitcase. Failed to think of clothing. The boy could have avoided doing time if he had agreed to stay away from her. A romantic, stupid child. She had hardly known him, really, and cannot say what has become of him. She never saw him after the motel, never spoke with him, although she heard things from time to time—the news of his release from prison, the report of a broken rib following a fight in a bar. But for years now, nothing. No word. As far as she knows, he never tried to reach her after he got out. A condition of his parole, no doubt.

She had not loved him, but she had loved the flight. All vehicles for human transportation are divine in the world she creates. Nothing unmoving is immortal. The weatherman alone mediates between the mortals and the gods, and only Helen is witness to it all. The people around her look at the same world, but they don't see what she sees.

She reaches down for the offending briefcase, a tan box, pliant to the touch, as if it were covered with skin. She passes it over the seat to Henry Alt. What would he say if she explained to him that to endure her life she has to imagine this bus as a minor deity? Would he think her deranged?

The truth, she believes, is the opposite. Her secret life permits her to hold tight to her sanity.

Henry Alt thanks her for the briefcase. "I'm lucky it didn't scoot all the way to the back of the bus," he says, tapping its leather hide. "I would've hopped off and not realized I'd forgotten it until lunchtime." He laughs at himself, and then lowers his voice. "Not one paper in here. Sack lunch and a bottle of vino for my secretary. I owe her. A bet."

Helen understands she is supposed to ask about the bet, but she declines to do it. Her breath on the window is turning to frost. Traffic has let up, but there are still two more turns and another three stops before they reach the Hall. She is eager to be through with this trip, and beginning to be angry with the weatherman for the cold. *A warming trend,* he had said. She feels foolish in shirtsleeves and hopes Henry Alt's car is already at a garage being repaired. What is the point of such a man? What good is his handsome face? What's the advantage of a big house if he lives alone? What's the value of his money if he works at a job no better than hers?

"It's easier to watch my weight if I make my own lunch," he says, patting the briefcase again. He is almost as thin as Helen. "I'm lucky—" The bus stops and he leaps from the seat, the briefcase clattering to the floor as he trots up the aisle. "Here we are," he calls out.

They are not at their stop. She thinks to tell him, but he has already run to the front of the bus. They are not at any stop but waiting at a traffic light. Henry Alt says something to Outis, who shakes his squat head. Henry Alt continues speaking, gesturing with his arms, the coat spreading wide as if the man within it were expanding. He must know the enchanted words, Helen thinks as the mechanical doors open.

Henry Alt hops down the stairs and sprints around the bus. She follows the top of his head as he runs to the concrete island. She shifts in her seat, rising to track him. "Hey," he yells, loudly enough for her to hear. For an instant, she thinks he is calling to her. "I haven't forgotten you," he says.

Sitting on the island is a bearded man with a dog. The dog bowl reads *Sarah.* The cardboard sign says:

Robert Boswell

Veteran and Family
Stuck Here
Can't Get Home
God Bless

The transparent manipulation of *Family* for a man and a dog insults Helen. Static invades the air, as if the window providing her view were a television losing its signal. It's snowing, she realizes. The man's face has about it the roughness of hard living and the swollen scarlet features of a drunk. He wears a woolen hat with an incongruous ball of thread at the top. Henry Alt hands him a few bills. They exchange words, a shake of hands, then Henry strides away into the street. The red-faced man examines the cash. Helen sees then that a woman is with him. She had been invisible. It occurs to Helen that this is all it takes—add one person and you become a family.

A cold draft from the open door initiates the trembling. She will freeze today without a coat. The weatherman has betrayed her. The woman on the traffic island lifts her arm high above her head as she calls out to Henry Alt. Helen sees that she is wearing one of her mother's dresses. Helen gave them to Goodwill, and now this woman begging at an intersection is wearing one. A tattered, quilted coat covers the top of it, but the pattern on the dress is clear and familiar. Helen cannot hear the woman's words but watches her dark hair as it is lifted by the wind of a passing vehicle. Her mother's hair was not quite so dark. The man joins her. Helen imagines that this man is her father. He is about the right age, the right height. He puts his arm around the woman's waist, and it seems to Helen that the twelve years she spent recording the events of other people's lives did not really happen. The memory of that time is like the memory of a movie: she witnessed it, but it did not happen to her.

Henry Alt leaps up the steps onto the bus, thanking the driver, who nods and yanks the shiny handle to shut the doors. On the floor, by Helen's feet, wine bleeds darkly from the fallen briefcase, discoloring the leather and sweetening the air. The leviathan lurches and then gently rocks as it resumes its movement forward. Helen

152

feels the pitch inside her, startled at the motion, coming after such a long stall. Henry Alt spreads his feet to steady himself in the aisle. The stained briefcase slides beneath her seat and disappears, leaving a dusky, elliptical trail.

Henry Alt is the *hero*, Helen thinks. He was drawn to this city to be near her. He has kept at his meaningless job for years with the vague faith that his future will announce itself. She is that future. She can see the work of gods in their union. As Henry Alt comes down the aisle, she understands the weatherman's lie about the cold. It was all done for her. The gods work in mysterious ways.

Henry Alt walks carefully, his hands lighting on the metal rails that top the seats, one and then another. He removes his coat as he approaches. He is going to present it to her. The offering bears epaulets of fresh fallen snow.

It's my birthday, she thinks. The words bloom on her tongue.

GUESTS

Bobby Bell's fingers numbered four to a hand. His thumb and pointer were identical to God's, but the others were just fleshy stubs, stunted and fused, and only two, on each slender paw. He was a dumb kid, besides, if progress in school is a fair measure. He sized me up my first week in town, came by my locker to demand a fight, the fall of 1967.

We'd moved to New Mexico from Illinois because my father was sick. How the change was supposed to help, I didn't know. When I asked, my father removed his glasses as if the problem were with the black-rimmed lenses. His head tipped slightly on its thin scaffold of bone. I felt a corresponding tilt in my senses.

"I'm host to a disease," he said. A smile flickered across his lips.

I began to tremble.

He continued, "You could say it's a landlord and tenant affair." When he focused on my expression, his attitude shifted. He slipped the glasses on again, which made his eyes the wrong size for his face. "You're worried." His hand lighted like a butterfly upon my head. "All right. I'm host but there are no tenants, just uninvited guests, too small to see." His lips crinkled, a modest grin. "Too small," he assured me, "to even imagine." His head tilted once more. "You won't worry, all right?"

I promised.

I had inherited my father's slight build, which must have cheered

Bobby Bell, to think he'd found a frame, at last, more flimsy than his own. I colored easily, as well, which provided him a hope even he knew to leave unsaid: blood that surged so close to the surface would wet his wrinkled shirt, spatter his shoes, and saturate the dirt where they paced. From the moment I met him, even before he required a fight, I understood that his world was neatly cleaved into those who could beat him and those he could enslave. The division, extravagantly uneven, presented him his quest—to find someone over whom he could have dominion—all of this written upon his face, as the truth of my father's condition was written upon mine. Which might have been why Bobby Bell thought he had an edge, as I was taller and only barely thinner. Why would he think my eyes were asking to be blackened but for a father frail as a child's pledge?

During that time, my mother came to my bed every night to take from me whatever book I was reading and point to the ticking clock above my head. She'd sit on the mattress and tell me how well my father was doing, how this move could make all the difference.

"Friends will come," she said the night before the fray, meaning that I would make some eventually, that perspective was the larger test—we were here to save a life, to protect him from the guests that lived within.

What a good boy I was, wanting to believe and then, after I no longer could, willing to pretend. When she left, shutting the door and light, the room drifted away in a darkness that knew no end, which I would close my eyes against, and wait for the smaller dark of sleep.

Later that night I woke and stumbled into the hall—disoriented, still in Illinois. Light at the far end of the house drew me. My mother knelt by the easy chair to fit a pillow beneath my father's sleeping head. He wore the top to his striped pajamas, the dark hair on his thin legs exaggerated like the carbon filaments I moved with a magnet to whisker a cartoon face. Mother's gown rose up her legs as they straightened, covering her to the hips, the tan of her legs ending abruptly in the buttocks' white exclamation. I retreated to the hall, watching her float a flowered bedsheet over him, then touch her lips to his temple, her solemn nakedness like a holy garment—in itself a kind of prayer.

How distant I lived from Bobby Bell.

The fight I remember with a clarity that defies time, as if I had more than lived it, as if it had not yet happened. We met at the bus stop, two stupid savage children, enveloped by a crowd of onlookers I sensed more than saw. Bobby Bell pointed at my narrow chest.

"Fairy," he accused, a rage in his throat, an evil passion in his eyes.

I had no decent reply, but spoke what first popped into my mouth.

"Pixie," I said, wanting to laugh, but the finger, that deformed hand thrown out at me, seemed a kind of reminder, like the mechanical voice in the underground that reminds you you're on a train, like my father's dry cough even on a morning following a rain, the sky pristine with sunlight and the cleansing smell of creosote.

We wrestled on a patch of ground made bare by children's shoes, exhaust from the school bus lingering in the air. We lunged and grappled like things less than human. A friend of Bobby Bell's invented a jeer.

"You fucking Mr. Happy," he yelled, his breath close and bitter, as if he might not be well.

Did my mother choose my father for his weakness, as Bobby Bell had chosen me? Is it cruel to suggest that she loved him most when he was his weakest? What of the girl, a few years later, who claimed to be drawn to my silence? Was she Bobby Bell in feminine guise, her white thighs holding me with such gentleness that I wept? What of the women I later met, who picked me less as a man than as a mission, and whom I treated like guests who'd overstayed their welcome? I don't understand the first thing about love, especially that first thing, when passion inhabits your body before you're aware, a passion you come to detect by the symptoms that endure.

As it turned out, I was weaker than Bobby Bell could suppose, and quicker, too, throwing him to the dirt, shoving his nose against the hardened ground, the blood that colored his shirt, his own. I can still hear his single cry, as I bent his arm beneath my knee. His skull I tethered by his hair to my fist, and I might have gouged a hole with it, but his arm escaped. I had to make a dive.

Shall I attempt to describe the feel of that inhuman hand in mine?

"You've made your point," another boy said, as if it were a debate I'd won.

I climbed off Bobby Bell and backed away, studying the crowd to see who might be pleased I'd won and who might jump me if I turned. That act of accidental compassion—my world, like Bobby Bell's, cleaved—caused in me a peculiar response. I could see Bobby Bell, his body in a twisted sprawl, but I could not see the others. As if my vision had grown too small, I could not hold them in a single frame.

"That don't make no never mind," consoled his friend, touching the place on Bobby Bell where my knee had pinned his knobby spine.

The others huddled—or hovered—about the fallen boy, but they were impossible to take in, the many guests, witnesses to that unfortunate accomplishment.

To be truthful, I've never had trouble imagining the small. I pictured the microscopic company my father kept with a clarity that was almost scientific. And I could see how, in Bobby Bell's eyes, each thing claimed only the value of its use to him: a tool, or not a tool. Viewed in this fashion, all of creation could be made minuscule. How unlike Bobby Bell was my father, who always saw the other side even in his own slipping away.

"Such beauty," my father said to me, gripping the rail of the bed. "I might have missed it otherwise."

We're fifty-three now, Bobby Bell and I, wherever he lives, whatever small place he now calls his. We have our own uneasy children. And still, I can't retreat far enough to see them all, those bodies assembled about the fallen one. How, precisely, do they gather? How, exactly, do they stand? I think it matters. Are they stooped or standing erect? Has one covered her ears, another closed his eyes? Does that head swivel to miss the farce? Or is she laughing, giant that she has become, at the grappling of such silly and malignant boys? I carry them all with me—a fist that rises in what might be fear, shoulders that turn in what might be submission, hands that rest on what might be knees.

He told me what threatened him was too small to imagine, as if, given this, I could be spared the rest, but it wasn't the microbes that troubled me after his death. He had it wrong, my father and his tiny beings. The guests that stubbornly remain haunt us because they're larger than visible things.

ALMOST NOT BEAUTIFUL

After lunch that day, Lisa's sister drank too much.

"Saying I drink like a fish doesn't make sense," she argued. "It's like saying I read like a word."

Lisa could only stare blankly in response. Being with her family was both cruel and unusual, a barbarous act that no decent society should permit. She stood in damp grass on the wide green lawn behind their mother's house. Lisa and her sister were in their thirties, and neither liked coming home.

"Who said you drink like a fish?" Lisa asked. "Mom just said you shouldn't drive."

"I don't think of myself as a fish," Amanda said. "I think of you as a fish."

"I'm ignoring that," Lisa replied.

Amanda had settled herself on the rope swing that hung from the mulberry tree whose trunk held the girls' initials, carved one preadolescent day when they believed they would be not just sisters but best friends all their lives. The pine board on the rope swing was barely wide enough to hold an adult, although Amanda, like Lisa, was bone thin. The rain had turned the bare ground beneath the swing into a bog. A gin bottle rested in the muck at a festive angle, with neither its cap nor its label. Amanda peeled labels. She chewed nails, ate the caps of pens, picked scabs. Twice she had tried to kill herself. Scraps of the label littered her white satin dress.

Lisa decided to find their initials on the mulberry. Nostalgia might be the best they could hope for this weekend.

"Here we are," she said, keeping her shoes on the grass and out of the mud. The trunk's widening girth had gnarled the letters, and erased whatever sense they had once made. The marks looked like a cubist face. The dot on the *i* in Lisa's name had become a ghastly hollowed eye, while the *m* in Amanda resembled a pair of tortured lips, puckering up to report something it couldn't quite say. "Never mind." She did not know how to be with her sister, but these tree-distorted words weren't going to help.

Amanda took a slug of gin out of a Big Gulp mug.

"Want some?" she asked.

Lisa liked the idea but didn't want to venture into the swamp. Her sister's running shoes were caked in mud.

"You're too hard to get to," she said.

Amanda pat-patted the mud with her feet, making a sloshing sound.

"Don't be a haddock," she said, smiling at her own cleverness. "You've always been a haddock."

"And you've always been a charmer when you drink," Lisa said. "Why are you wearing running shoes with that dress?"

Amanda laughed as she swallowed. Gin flew out of her nostrils. Instead of replying, she gave herself a push. Mud flew from her feet, forcing Lisa to back off.

"Whee," Amanda called out. "Tweet, tweet."

At least she didn't drink gin through a straw, Lisa thought. At least she isn't out here naked, clucking like a chicken. Lisa liked to look on the bright side, but she was often too perceptive to find one. Invented bright-sides encouraged creativity, she liked to think.

On the downswing, Amanda's foot tapped the neck of the gin bottle and it began to spill. Neither woman made a move to grab it.

"Now nothing will ever grow there," Amanda said sadly.

Like any reasonable person, Lisa hated to see good liquor go to waste. But there was no way to save it without getting muddy and likely kicked in the head.

"You may have invented a new drink," she said. "Beefeaters and Mud."

"A Muddy Mary on the rocks, please," Amanda said. "Garçon, bring me a turbid toddy, *por favor*. A *murk*arita, no salt. A bourbon and bilge water, if you please." She set her feet against the silt to stop the swing, splashing her dress. "Come on, Sis. You can come up with something, can't you?"

"Sydney's making margaritas for happy hour."

Amanda glared at her, as if the comment were a rebuke. "I have a memory."

"Of course, you have a memory," Lisa said, her voice light and false. "No one could get by without a memory."

Amanda took another swallow from the Big Gulp. "That's not what I mean."

Lisa knew what she meant, but didn't want to hear about her sister's wretched past. They were only two years apart, and Lisa could not see how her childhood had been more or less ordinary, while her little sister's had been made up of nothing but anxiety and pain. Amanda had a grudge that she could neither release nor satisfy, and Lisa was weary of it.

"Okay," said Lisa. "I'll bite. What is it you're talking about?"

Amanda shook her head. "Lost your chance." She bent low to retrieve the bottle, and almost fell from the swing. She dipped the mouth of the bottle to let muddy water roll in. "A mucktail, *s'il vous plaît*." She held the bottle up to the sunlight and studied the brown swirls. She took a drink. Almost immediately, she spat it out. "Let's have ourselves a cognac," she said. "Cognac is the proper drink for dusk."

Lisa crossed her arms against the whole display.

"The sun won't set for another three hours."

"Head start," Amanda said. "With a head start anything is possible. You of all people should know that."

As she climbed from the swing she dropped the bottle into the mud. It landed upright, and she kicked it over as she sloshed her way to the damp grass.

Pelicans can fly three thousand miles without stopping. The pelican skims the surface of the ocean at speeds equal to a commuter train. In the purse of its whopping beak, the pelican is capable of carrying a newborn hippo. During the Second World War, pelicans were used to transport supplies to troops trapped behind enemy lines. Sexual intercourse between pelicans and humans has never been documented, despite persistent rumors to the contrary.

Lisa had dressed like a trout—a new but shabby silver dress with a glossy diaphanous exoskeleton, and everyone else at the dinner party was in jeans. It wasn't the kind of mistake Lisa often made. In fact, she had never before purchased such a dress, a thing of such formal ugliness that one could not help but think the wearer slightly deranged, lost either to nostalgia, stupidity, or mild brain trauma. She recognized this but thought she could pull off "ironic yet funky." Optimism, once again, did her in.

To make things worse, the dinner party was an excuse to introduce her to a single heterosexual male who had just started working with one of the hosts. There was also a new couple in the neighborhood there for filler. The hosts, Max and Roberto, had become Lisa's best friends, and they hated to see her without a man. "No one should be without one," Max liked to say. He directed local commercials and had invited a new cameraman, who arrived at the house in a T-shirt, shorts, and flip-flops, his chin as square as Clark Kent's. Heterosexual, employed, and possessing a chin: he seemed too good to be true.

Max and Roberto had a gift for decor. Their house had little details that made it stand out, such as the chrome molding along the floors and ceilings. Lisa had predicted the chrome would look ridiculous, but instead it reflected the glitter of the chandelier Roberto had found at a garage sale and lent the room definition and dignity. Something about this chrome experiment had led Lisa to buy the trout dress. It was really their fault.

Max sized her up the second he answered the door. "This is a cry for help," he said. "Do you want a cap? Then no one could mistake your intent to look foolish."

She waited on the doorstep while he retrieved a Dodgers cap, which she wore backward. The single man, whose name she has mercifully forgotten, flinched when he saw her, literally flinched. She thought he might fall down and break something.

"I usually dress normal," she said. "Utterly average dresser on most occasions."

Max and Roberto backed up this claim. The new neighborhood couple decided the best way to be polite about the dress was to make endless inquiries about its purchase, a technique Lisa recognized as a way to seem complimentary and yet remain virtually honest. They would begin laughing as soon as their car doors shut. They'd be up a good part of the night laughing in bed, and then they'd make riotous love. Lisa understood the advantage of having a stooge at a dinner party. She just didn't relish the role for herself.

She drank too much. Around midnight she was carried to the couch. Max and Roberto pulled up chairs and chatted with her once the other guests were gone.

"How'd I do?" she asked. "Sweep him off his flip-flops?"

Cheerfulness in the face of utter humiliation seemed to Lisa a noble form of self-deprecation.

"He seemed to enjoy carrying you," Roberto noted.

In the morning, hungover and still in the stupid dress, Lisa joined Max and Roberto in their kitchen for breakfast. They had just had a dinner party the night before, yet the room was so clean it hurt her eyes.

"I'm going to be alone the rest of my life," she announced.

"Get a pet," Roberto suggested. "Take up golf."

"Go see your family," Max said. Lisa had told him about her mother's invitation. "And come back feeling sane in comparison to the others who share your genetic curse."

"Hear! Hear!" Roberto said, and the decision was made.

Lisa found her mother—her given name was Ophelia—sprinkling white powder on a window ledge.

"Ant poison," she explained. "Don't let your sister sniff it up her nose."

The house was old and stately, but, as their father had liked to say, the foundation held more cracks than hard places. Ophelia lifted the rugs and salted every crack with the poison. "They wish to eat me," she went on. "I shall not be eaten just yet." Their mother liked to strike an imperial pose now and again, usually during happy hour. She spoke as if she were accustomed to being waited on by maids and menservants when in fact she had worked all her adult life as a postal employee and had retired only two years earlier. When Ophelia and the girls' father bought the house in the early 1960s, it had possessed a kind of majesty. The girls' father—everyone had called him Snookie—had come into a modest inheritance and put it all into the purchase of the house. He'd had no siblings with whom to share his parents' wealth. When Snookie died, the paternal line ended.

"We've had ants before, but never like this," Ophelia said, lifting a couch cushion and shaking powder onto the covered springs.

Sydney, their mother's lover, stirred a tall pitcher of margaritas, his free hand in his pocket "counting his cock," an expression for male self-fondling Lisa and Amanda had used when they were teenagers. One of their uncles constantly played with himself, but their mother insisted he was counting the change in his pocket. Amanda had come up with "counting his cock," and did impersonations of him for their friends.

"One," she would say, her hand working her pocket. "No, no, *one*," she'd say. "Let's see . . . *one*."

Sydney wore no shirt and whistled "Oh, Susannah" while he stirred. Lisa wished that she and Amanda could be friends again; at the same time, she didn't really want to put up with the bother. Her sister was a mess and seemed at her worst around the family. Three times she had taken "vacations" in places now called therapeutic health centers. Her letters, a requirement of the first institution, eviscerated her binmates with such comic clarity that their mother had argued she must be ready to come home.

"Where is our young one?" Ophelia asked now.

Why one drink made her into Queen Victoria and three drinks took her out of it, Lisa could not guess, although she had the same kind of reaction to men: one date made her imagine what their kids would look like, and three dates had her wondering about the machinations of restraining orders.

"She's sleeping off the morning," Lisa said.

Sydney spoke up. "I made the margaritas in her honor. I was under the impression she loved margaritas. What on earth will we do with all these margaritas?" Sydney possessed no redeeming qualities that Lisa could see. He had a fat, fleshy head with gray sidewalls and a habit of going shirtless. His bare stomach revolted her. The freckled folds of aging skin reminded her of the disintegrating dishrag she used to clean up after the cat. "Margaritas don't keep well," he said. "That's a fact that most people don't understand about margaritas. Mixed drinks should be consumed quickly, especially margaritas."

"What's that a pitcher of?" Lisa asked.

"Margaritas," Sydney said.

Her mother gave her a disapproving look. "Go retrieve your sister," she commanded, accepting a festive glass from Sydney as she spoke, the rim heavily frosted with salt. Her other hand still held the shaker of poison.

Don't confuse them, Lisa thought.

Upon climbing the stairs, she found Amanda passed out on the hallway's Turkish rug. She lay on her side, stinking of gin, her legs bent, dress askew and spattered with mud. A line of ants marched over her satin dress, disappearing into its folds. Were they attracted to the gin? Did ants have noses? There were things in the world, often the simplest of things, that Lisa did not know. Did ants like alcohol? Shouldn't one know this? She bent down to swat them away. Her sister stirred, rolled over onto her back. The ants were actually marching through a fold of the dress to the hem and then crawling in under it.

Lisa lifted the dress. A black mass of ants swarmed on her sister's panties, so dense that Lisa's first thought was that Amanda wore no underwear. Her pubis was alive.

The ant not only has a nose between its black oracular eyes, but also one in the pit of each appendage. The ant is attracted to the genitals of all mammals, female and male. Autopsies have revealed colonies of ants living in the bowels of many humans. The scrotum of a drone is so small that close to one million would fit on the tip of a ballpoint pen. While the individual ant has the IQ of an insect, a colony of ants acting in unison has an IQ exceeding that of most U.S. senators.

Through a downpour of rain, Max drove Lisa to the airport in his convertible, water slinking through the wretched top he rarely put up. The windshield wipers, in their mechanical squeegee rhythm, made Lisa think of bad sex.

"Maybe we could have a teeny crash in this storm in this stupid car that doesn't even have a roof," she suggested, "and I could stay here in a hospital and not have to see my mother and sister."

"It's not a stupid car," Max said.

"Are you dry? I'm not dry. What good is a car that won't even keep you dry?" She reached between her legs for her huge dung-colored purse and pulled out a bottle of beer. "I don't suppose you have an opener."

"In my pocket, but there's a law against open containers in automobiles," Max said. "Even if you don't respect my car, we must respect the law."

"There's a law against sodomy, but I don't see you calling the cops to your house every morning."

She opened the glove box, put the points of the bottle cap against the glove box door, and hammered down against the bottle.

"You are *breaking* my car," said Max. "Please stop."

She hammered again and the top popped off, landing on the dash.

"Flying makes me nervous. Seeing my family makes me nervous.

I *need* to drink. It's what we do in my family. I'll have more to drink this weekend than I've had in the past six months."

"I'm not certain that's humanly possible." Max gave her a droll look.

"A person gets carried to a couch one time and suddenly she's a lush." She took a long slug of beer, then leaned over and kissed Max on the cheek. "You know I'm just being a twat. I don't hate you, but at times I'm compelled to act like I do."

He shrugged. "I hate *you*. A significant percentage of adorable men waste their lives on women like you."

"I wish one would waste his on me," she said.

"That has a country-and-western flavor to it."

She took another drink, emptying the bottle. Was it possible that she had drunk an entire beer in two gulps?

"It would be a lot easier going home if I could take someone with me as a shield." She had pleaded with Max to accompany her. "Did I mention how I'd pay the shield's airfare? Buy the shield's meals and shield wax?"

He rolled his eyes and signaled their turn.

Lisa lowered her window, the rain pelting her face, and tossed the bottle into the bushes that lined the road. She raised the window and took another beer from her purse.

Max grabbed her arm to stop her. He lifted his butt from the seat, worked his hand into his pocket, and produced a pocketknife.

"I don't want the door to my glove box to be tilty," he said. "Better we should both go to prison."

"Am I really so not pretty anymore that no one will ever want me?" Lisa asked.

"You're hardly not pretty at all," Max said. "You're almost not beautiful."

"I haven't had sex in seven months." She popped the bottle cap for emphasis. "And then it was Captain Mike. Remember him?"

"You pick the worst losers to screw," he said. Even the car swerved a bit.

She took a drink of cold, delicious beer.

"I was lonely. Drunk, one might say. The moon was full. Mist was in the gutter. A lonesome dog yowled in the distance."

"I get the picture," he said. "Where did you do it? The bathroom of some bar?"

"Please, Max." She tried to think of an exotic place. She hated to say it was absolutely dull sex on Captain Mike's underfilled water bed. She hadn't come, and he had made waves all night. Why did she even want a man? "Let's change the subject entirely."

"Drink up," Max said. "In moments you will fly."

She lifted the beer, the rim of the bottle's mouth touching her bottom lip as she spoke, as if she were addressing it.

"Shield me," she pleaded.

It took all three of them to get Amanda across the bathroom tile. Ants tumbled from her body like the fabled bread crumbs, making a trail behind them. Lisa spun the tub faucet, insisting that Sydney and their mother leave.

"I'll get her in," she said. "Just go."

Her sister's head bounced against the tile while Lisa pulled off the satin dress. Ants swarmed her hands when she removed the panties, and her anxious flicking pinched the skin on Amanda's thighs. When she discovered Amanda's bra was wet, she instinctively jerked her fingers away, snapping the bra against her sister's back, which elicited a moan. The bra had wicked up a load of gin. Could one get loaded from simply bathing in liquor? Was drinking even required? She should have known that getting her naked sister, all dead weight, into the high old-fashioned tub, complete with lion paws for feet, would be all but impossible.

She lifted her sister's legs over the tub's ledge, then hefted her by the elbows, the top of Amanda's head knocking lightly against the floor, but Lisa would have to be seven feet tall to get her in that way. She lowered her grip and lifted, but one leg slipped free of the tub. Ultimately she had to get on her knees to wrestle her sister's ass into the water, shoving up against the fleshy cheeks until they pressed against her own facial cheeks.

Her sister tumbled in face-first and came up spitting. She became instantly alert and sober, reaching for the shampoo bottle as if she had stepped into the tub on her own. The recovery was too fast. Lisa understood that her sister had been acting. But there was no way to call her bluff. Lisa's heart started to do strange things inside her chest. Ants floated up to the water's surface. Some were alive. Most had been killed by the heat of the water or they'd drowned or been crushed, or maybe they, too, were pretending.

She gathered up Amanda's clothing, on which living ants still roamed.

"I'm going to toss these in the washer," she said.

Amanda was rubbing up a big lather in an armpit and did not reply, the water coloring with mud and stippled with the bodies of ants.

Lisa did not examine her sister's panties until she was in the laundry room. They were covered with honey. She tossed them into the washer. The satin dress she took outside. When she shook it, ants flew up into the air, vanishing before they hit the ground.

The honeybee has nearly one thousand minuscule eyes and an equal number of brain stems. To think of it as a single organism is akin to thinking of quadruplets as a single entity. The thousand brains send out their thousand signals in response to the thousand visions of the thousand eyes, and the single body responds in rapid and consecutive order, which accounts for the bee's famed circuitry of flight. Contrary to popular belief, the bee does not die after losing its stinger; however, other bees do not care to associate with it. The stingerless bee becomes an outcast and must leave the hive. It has to make its way in the world alone. Stripped of its stinger, a bee is nothing more than a raisin with wings.

No one was at the airport to pick her up and her cell got no signal. Lisa waited at baggage for twenty minutes before going to a pay phone. On impulse she got out her phone card and dialed long distance to retrieve messages. The first was from Max.

"I'm back from dropping you off, and as I'm sure you'll be calling yourself soon, I thought I'd provide you with a happy voice.

You've only been a teeny shit. We all still think of you with moderate affection. What's that? Roberto wants his two cents. Not merely 'moderate affection,' he says, but a 'somewhat more than temperate fondness.' Now go face your family. Quit hiding."

The second message began with her mother's cough. "We won't be able to meet you at the airport, sweetheart. I have a beauty appointment, and your sister has made herself unable to drive." The time stamp indicated that the message had arrived while Lisa was somewhere high over the Midwest sipping on a weensy bottle of vodka.

It might have been a passing overweight, badly dressed tourist that inspired her to call her high school boyfriend and ask for a ride. She had dumped him years ago just before leaving for college. While she had gone on to earn a monetarily useless degree and to utterly flunk out in the romance department, he had skipped college and taken several major emotional strides. He had two divorces under his belt, a daughter living in another state, and monthly alimony obligations. He'd had it all, while she had accumulated nothing but a history of semicasual sex with incompetents, short-term affairs with fools, earnest-like confessions from married men, and one bad case of the clap.

"It's me," she said, the first of several tests she planned to give him.

"Lisa!" Timmy said. "You in town?"

Recognition of voice after two words: A+

"Just barely. I'm at the airport and I don't want to take a taxi."

"I'm not doing anything important. I'll come get you."

Ability to take a hint: A+

"It's great to hear your voice," she said. "You sound great."

"Is Amanda in town, too?"

Repartee: F

Lisa and Timmy had been a couple for three years by the time she evaluated herself "ready for something/one new." Why go to college among a sea of men and have a boy back home you would eventually have to betray anyway? True, she hadn't wanted to spoil the summer and had waited until the very end to break up. Actually, she hadn't given him a clue until her suitcase and stereo were packed in the family car. Her mother began honking the horn during her dismissal of him.

Tacky, she admitted, but ancient history.

Within a week of her departure for college, Amanda seduced him. This became what Amanda called "a boner of contention" between them. Amanda argued that she had done nothing wrong, but Lisa refused to speak to her for two years. After an even longer period of snubbing Timmy, she sent him a congratulations card when he got married the second time, and then another when he racked up his second divorce. He had called after that one, and they became phone friends.

Timmy had not aged well and his car stank. He had zero hair on the top of his head, a roll of lard about his waist, and he had taken to wearing loafers. His car—red, boxy, dirty—smelled of stickiness, like a lollipop left in the sun. He drove well, though, signaling before turns, slowing when lights turned yellow, and he was happy to see her.

"You look wonderful," he said. "You haven't changed at all."

She thanked him.

"I've put on a few pounds," he acknowledged with a shake of his head. "You still seeing that guy Colonel Mike?"

"*Captain* Mike, and god no. I don't remember telling you about him."

She crossed her arms, ready to be annoyed. A hard rain had ended minutes before Timmy picked her up, and the buildings shone wet and clean, but the city looked very little like the one she had abandoned years before. Instead, it looked like every other damn place in the country.

"I hate water beds, too," Timmy said.

"Let's forget whatever details I may have told you in a moment or several moments of weakness."

"Oh, *that*," he said and laughed.

She didn't dare ask. The steeple of the Infant Jesus Baptist Church was the first marker that indicated this really was her hometown. She had never set foot in it, but the steeple had been the metaphor of choice for "penis" with Amanda, which had led to an elaborate symbology used to baffle adults and strangers. Her sister might say, "That guy Craig is about as Baptist as you get," and Lisa would agree. "Church boy" took on a whole new meaning in Amanda's mouth. Timmy, alas, had lost much of his steeple appeal.

"How about you?" she asked him. "Seeing anyone?"

"Kind of," he said.

"How can you 'kind of' see someone? You make love with your eyes shut?"

"She's married." He ran a hand over his neck. "Really very extremely married."

His lover, he revealed, had taken her first breath eighteen years before he took his, had been married twenty-three years now, had two children at Ivy League schools, and was friends with Lisa's mother.

"*Her?*" Lisa said. "You're fucking *her?*" The woman had the scrawny good looks that screamed of the labor it took to achieve it—her body thin but dimpled with exertion and age.

Timmy shrugged. "Weird, no? I would have told you earlier, but I thought you'd react exactly as you have."

"*Her?*"

"I'd marry her if I could." He offered a sad smile. "But no can do."

She could see that he was in love, and the love was a multiply forbidden one. He had probably told no one else in the world of this secret love. She took a deep breath, but it did no good.

"I can't believe you're seeing *her.*"

Amanda said this: "The best time in my life was when I got out of the cage the second time, and I had a job with that shrink scheduling the weirdest kind of nimrods, and I was in love with Ernie, who you never met but who was really sweet, and I had a little place with yellow curtains on the window above the kitchen sink, and I could see the tops of the trees in the park when I parted the curtains." She had spoken to the windshield, but now she turned to Lisa. "You know what ruined it?"

Lisa couldn't remember ever hearing of any Ernie. They idled in the car on a city street, escaping their mother and Sydney. They had decided to see Timmy, but Amanda made Lisa pull over right on the darkest stretch of road. She wanted to explain something.

"What ruined it, whatever *it* is—peace, sanity, ordifuckinary life. What ruined it was *art*." She stopped and studied Lisa, as if she should somehow respond.

Lisa nodded self-consciously and said, "Art."

This seemed to satisfy Amanda. "I started reading novels again and going to museums. Ernie encouraged me. He was a big art guy. Not that he did any himself, but he was into it. Liked to gawk at paintings, et cetera. He read a lot. You never heard of these guys he liked to read."

"Have you ever noticed that this town has no streetlights that work?" Lisa said. "I'm sorry. It just bugs me that it's so dark here."

"Drive the fucking car somewhere else then," Amanda said. She had changed into jeans and a T-shirt that advertised a performance artist who called herself "Slippery Whenever." She crossed her arms over the ad and said nothing more.

"Go on," Lisa said. "You were talking about art fucking up your life."

"You don't give a shit. Let's just go see Timmy."

"I do. I care. I'm sorry. I just can't concentrate on this dark street." She shifted the car into drive and headed in the direction of Timmy's house.

Amanda sighed. "I wish I had a cigarette. And a bottle of gin. Do you even know what I'm doing anymore?"

"You mean for a living?" Lisa ransacked her head. There was hardly anything in the "Current Amanda" section to ransack. "Aren't you still doing the delivery thing?"

"Close," she said. "I only quit that three years ago. I manage a band. I work at a warehouse on the dock, too, one of those they-need-to-hire-a-woman jobs. I check in loads of produce. It's complicated but not interesting, although the people are good to me. Six months ago I started managing this band. I write some of their songs."

"Have I ever heard of them?"

"Have you heard of any decent band of the last five years?"

The old bile surged, but Lisa didn't feel up to it.

"Let's don't," she said.

Amanda put her hands to her head, as if it were about to fall off. She nodded. Lisa drove through the quiet neighborhood, one house like another, boxy and dull. If not for their father's legacy, they would have grown up in a house like one of these. Which one would their young mother and young father have chosen? How much different would they be, Lisa and Amanda, if they'd been raised in one of these stucco cartons? Timmy's home looked like a toy house, square with an overhanging roof, as if it were built of plastic connecting bricks.

Lisa opened the car door on her side, but her sister wasn't moving.

"What?"

"It's like this," Amanda said. "I needed to do some kind of art. I could see what it was I wanted to show. It was in my head, and in there it was beautiful. I just couldn't find a way to get at it. I tried photography and painting and sculpture, but I'm no good with anything but words and acting—or sort of acting. I tried writing poetry, which sucked, and a long, boring memoir. Finally, I got the courage up to be a monologist."

"Is that like a comic?" Lisa said, grateful to find a decent question to ask. She leaned lower to see her sister in the car. "A stand-up comedian?"

"Performance stuff," Amanda said. "I had a show about people and animals. I'd tell stories about my, you know, *life*. And then I had these facts about animals that I invented. One thing played off the other. It ended with me stripping while I talked, and when I had nothing on but a skirt, I'd pull its string, and they'd see the swarm of ants where they expected to see my cunt."

She sniffed the air, or it might have been that she was upset. Lisa couldn't tell. What was she supposed to do with this information?

She said, "I could tell you were faking today."

"That act. I did it in maybe a dozen clubs. It was the closest I ever came to getting at it. You know? I was good, I had an effect on people, but I couldn't get it quite right. It wasn't enough. Finally, I couldn't stand it and cut myself up. Ernie, I think, heard me, really heard me, but there were a lot of people who didn't. It was so frustrating. I kept pushing it, thinking someone out there must see what I'm after, someone understands. But no matter what I tried, none of it was *it*, none of it matched what I saw in my head. You understand what I mean? Please can you figure out what I'm talking about?"

Lisa had listened to every syllable, but she remained unsure what she had heard. She said, "I guess I do. I mean, I have this idea of the kind of man I want to have, but the clowns I meet are never anywhere close."

Amanda was out of the car and down the walk before Lisa could stop her.

Electricity is actually a living thing. A fungus. Microscopic and endemic, its ideal environment is the alkaline battery, which it seeks out the way its cousin jock itch seeks out the sweating genitals of young men. Humans, such as these young scratching men, are viral in nature. All mammalian life can be traced back to the River Ebo in equatorial Africa where, millions of years ago, a virus developed in the stew of murky water. Evolution and mutations led to the development of an enormous variety of creatures, but most died out before reproducing. Reproduction didn't interest beasts until, through a freak of nature, an animal was born with her vagina directly adjacent to her anus. Everybody wanted a piece of her. *Sex is no fun unless it's dirty.*

Max met her return flight bearing yellow, vinelike flowers molded by invisible wire into the shape of a horseshoe. He spread his arms wide upon spotting her.

"Flicka," he called tenderly. "You managed to show."

The horseshoe fit over Lisa's neck nicely.

Too drunk to follow the racing jokes that Max had practiced all week, she laughed whenever there was a syntactical gap in his gab— quips about jockeys, being in the running versus getting scratched, needing to place, betting the house.

"We're trying to change your image after the dress fiasco," he explained.

The flowers' lurid odor nauseated her.

"Stop in the bar?" she said.

"Love to," Max said. "Roberto just happens to be meeting us there. Neither of us can wait to hear about your hideous family."

"I love airport bars," she said. "Just one sec." She floundered about in her purse and withdrew her cell phone. The first message was from Max. "You look ridiculous in that stupid horseshoe," the recorded voice said. She pivoted and gave him a look, mouthing, "Very funny." He mouthed, "I'm hysterical" back to her. Except for the smell, she liked the horseshoe. It gave support to her neck, which made it easier to keep her head upright. It was like a life jacket. The second message was from her employer, some crap about this and that—good news, basically, as it meant she had not been fired. The third message began with Amanda saying, "This won't be short. If you're in a hurry, save it for later." Lisa punched the number three, and a mechanical voice informed her that the message would be saved.

"Why don't I get interesting calls?" she demanded.

Max slipped his arm around her waist to improve her equilibrium.

"My message was fascinating, you nasty, ungrateful pony. There's Roberto."

He had saved them a table in a corner. The booth appeared to be made of real wood that had once been part of an actual tree. This struck Lisa as remarkable. Drinks sweated on the table, making their obligatory rings. *Work, work, work,* she thought.

"Had to park in the remote lot," Roberto said. "It's slightly closer than our house."

"Couldn't one of you give me a big, sloppy kiss?" she said.

"Roberto ordered a big drink for you," Max said, dusting her forehead with his lips. "Feel free to be sloppy with it."

"She may not have a choice," Roberto said. "Aren't you going to take that off now?" He gestured to the horseshoe.

Lisa shook her head while drinking, the cool gin doing sweet things to her throat.

"Is there anything sadder," Max asked, "than embracing as art that which was offered as a joke?"

"I can think of a few things," Roberto said. "How about mistaking for crapola that which is offered as art?" To Lisa he added, "Inhaling gin is bad for the lungs."

She set the glass on the table harder than she intended. "I had the absolute worst time without you guys."

"Oh, good," Max said. "Regale us with the sorrow of being without us."

"My sister," she began, "and my mom—not to mention fucking Sydney." She shook her head, as if she had explained something.

"We may need to assist in the narrative," Roberto said.

Max agreed. "Let's begin optimistically. Any arrests?"

"I yam an optimist," she said. "Good stuff's supposed to be right around the dealy."

"She means dealy-bob," Max explained.

"But no such luck. It only brings me heartache." In her drunken state, she didn't pronounce the *h*. It came out "artache," which reminded her. "My sister says art ruined her life." She nodded in agreement with herself. "We did a nasty thing to each other."

"Finally!" Max said, but Lisa had already begun her characteristic lid drooping that meant she would soon pass out.

Roberto said, "I think we're going to need a cart."

Timmy ordered two pizzas to be certain there was something the sisters would eat.

"Not that I expect you to eat much," he said. "I understand the grueling demands of staying thin, although I don't participate in them myself."

Lisa thought of the scrawny woman he loved. She probably talked about nothing but food. Made him eat things for her.

"Thinness is genetic," she said. "Like baldness."

"That's what keeps me thin," Amanda agreed. "That and starving myself." She ran her hand over Timmy's bare head. "You look okay like this, despite what she says."

She bent his head down and planted a kiss on it, leaving lipstick marks, more an O than the traditional ellipse, as if she had kissed him open mouthed, tonguing his pate.

Timmy's living room had a nostalgic look about it. The coarse weave of the material covering the couch, along with its green and orange colors, seemed an embodiment of the nonhippie sixties. Shades-of-yellow shag carpet went wall-to-wall in the room, and a reclining chair—brown like a bear—faced a console model television. Timmy set the pizza boxes on a coffee table with a clear glass top.

"How's Feather Lick?" he said to Amanda.

Feather Lick? What the hell was Feather Lick? Was her sister a lesbian?

"It's Big Longing now," Amanda said. "I got them a gig in Jersey."

"You know about the band?" Lisa said, catching up, indignant, and embarrassed at the same time.

"We talk," Timmy said. "Keep in touch."

"He visited me last year, and I even got him laid, didn't I?"

Timmy bit into his anchovy-and-onion slice, nodding and smiling. *A smiling bite,* Lisa thought.

"I hate anchovies," she said. "Do you have any *drinking* beverages here?"

"We used to eat anchovy-and-onion all the time," Timmy said.

"She's just being a bitch," Amanda told him. "Be entertained by it or she'll drive you crazy."

"A person's tastes can change," Lisa said.

"I'll say," Timmy said. "There's a whole bar in the kitchen."

Lisa headed for the kitchen to avoid punching someone. The "whole bar" turned out to be a freestanding black-lacquer-and-chrome thing holding a dozen bottles, each with a green plastic nozzle poked in its opening. A relic from a previous generation, Lisa thought, a gift from his girlfriend. *His old lady,* she thought cruelly. She made a gin and tonic while perusing the refrigerator. Dill pickle spears became her dinner. She might be a complete bitch, for all she knew, but Timmy had been her boyfriend first. Amanda had hardly dated him, just screwed him. She wondered if she had gotten him laid by spreading her own legs.

Her next thought: if Amanda had gotten Timmy laid, did it mean that she could get Lisa laid? She hated that kind of thinking, but she was losing every sense of her sexual self. Her eyes had begun to linger over those glossy ads for boob jobs. She didn't like all this fretting about it. She was not so bad looking—*almost not beautiful,* Max had said. She needed a man she could take for granted. Music started up in the other room, the Eagles, "Take It Easy." It would be no challenge to take Timmy for granted. She had already done it. *Taken him for a ride, too,* she thought with some nasty pleasure.

Two G&Ts later, she returned to find her sister performing, reciting something about bees. When she finished, she and Timmy both looked expectantly at Lisa.

"What?" Lisa said.

Amanda took a deep breath. "I'll do it again." She asked Timmy to make her a drink. Then she undid her skirt and stepped out of it. She pulled off her blouse.

In panties and bra, a sparkling alcoholic beverage in hand, Amanda started in again without the music. Lisa was determined to listen.

"My sister and I used to be like those famous monkeys of the St. Louis Zoo who shared a tail," Amanda began.

She thinks of me as a monkey, Lisa thought. Then, *What famous monkeys?*

"Hard to tell where one of us ended and the other began," Amanda continued. She lifted her skirt from the floor and whipped it around in her hands to roll it up like a rope. She asked Timmy for his shoestrings.

It all reminded Lisa of a magician's routine. *Nude magic,* she thought. This was definitely *not* what Amanda had done minutes earlier.

Amanda tied the skirt at either end, and let the skirt-rope rock back and forth in her hand like the ticker in a clock. A near-naked body was a distraction, Lisa thought. How could anyone argue otherwise? Was this swinging rope meant to be a giant cock?

Amanda whipped the rope behind her, bent forward, and tucked it in her underpants. When she removed her hands, it stayed there—a tail.

Lisa made a face. Was Amanda going to wear that skirt home now? What was she thinking?

"Here's my tale," Amanda said.

She launched into a story about monkeys in a cage who would let no one cut the tail they shared. "Tail" and "tale" were interchangeable. Lisa got it. Sharing a tail, sharing a tale. This proved she was paying attention, didn't it? Her sister's body showed no signs of inching past its prime. Lisa's own body was still just fine, more or less, slender but with a curve or two, her admittedly small breasts riding nice and high. But her sister's thinness was softer, less tense. Lisa understood that being the older sister was, for the first time, a disadvantage. And it would remain one.

Timmy had set his cheap bottle of gin on the coffee table. Lisa covered the ice in her glass with more gin. To hell with tonic.

The monkey story involved some steeple talk, and Amanda imitated a man counting his cock, her hand in an imaginary pocket rubbing an imaginary penis. Her routine revolved around bits of their old code—the hand signal that indicated someone was lying, the nostril flare that meant they were dealing with a loser, the hiccup that said, "Let's get the hell out of here." Lisa had forgotten that there were so many signs. Her sister's body dimpled with goose flesh, which changed its color, adding a silver hue. Could that be part of the act?

When Amanda began marking the scars on her wrists and arms with yellow highlighter, Lisa said she had to pee. Amanda just kept on tracing the scars. By this time, the monkeys had been surgically separated and a bunch of other stuff had transpired. "I'll hold it," Lisa announced, hoping she'd get some credit for staying, afraid she would be asked to do something. That was like a magic show, too, she realized. She had never enjoyed them, even as a child, for fear she would be singled out and made to do something—to step into a box and vanish, or lie on a gurney and be sawed in half. She remembered sitting beside Amanda in an auditorium watching a magician in a silver cape. When he sent his short-skirted assistant out into the crowd, Lisa made herself hiccup. Without a word, Amanda gathered up her things and they left.

Thinking about that exit, Lisa missed parts of Amanda's performance. Her glass was empty, besides, and Timmy had moved the bottle. She hoped Amanda could drive.

"When Snookie steered his car into a tree," Amanda said, "monkey one and monkey two dived into their magic bottles. One was transformed into a fish and the other, a bird. Neither could understand what the other was saying."

Lisa didn't like that their father's accident was in the routine. She lifted Timmy's gin fizz, pretending to be engrossed in her sister's routine. What a glorious thing was gin. Her father had not been drinking that night. What good did thinking about it do anyone? When she relayed all this to Max and Roberto, she would skip over this part, which would be easy, as she wasn't really keeping up.

At the end, Timmy applauded and Lisa joined in. Amanda, still wearing nothing but her undies and the tail, walked up to Lisa's chair.

"What do you think?" she asked.

"You're thinner than I am," Lisa said.

"Yeah," Amanda said, "I am."

She reached between her legs, took hold of the free end of the tail, and dabbed at Lisa's cheeks.

The carrier pigeon is not extinct and has given up its death wish. It no longer flies but slings a tulip bulb, plucked by its own sharp beak, over its gray wing. It fills this cup with the nectar, then toddles round the flat green island, dropping off parcels to the toads, who have no use for them; to the gecko, who threatens to nip at the bird's feathered neck; to the tortoise, who retreats into its shell at the sight of the fowl's approach; and to the grouper in the dingy lagoon, who eyes the particles of pollen that float about like lifeboats cast from a sinking liner. They speckle the sun's light and attract the tasty mosquitoes, which provide this grouper her life's sustenance. The carrier pigeon no longer longs for extinction, content to be worthless to all but one creature, an ugly beast who cannot give thanks for the improbable gift and whose mouth is turned in a never-ending frown.

SKIN DEEP

Claude returns from the coffeehouse to find his suitcase splayed across the motel bed and the manager's wife picking through his shirts and underwear.

"Is this a scam?" He sets the cup of bitter coffee on the television. "Your husband sends me across the street while you rip me off?"

She shakes her head. "Nothing that fancy." Crossing her arms, she grips her shoulders: white blouse, frayed jeans, bare feet. A decade younger than her husband and as thin as a prayer. "Wondered what I could tell about you from your things." Her tongue lingers in the dark aperture between the rows of teeth. The face she shows him is narrow, pale, lovely. "Don't tell Teddy. He has a temper." Not long ago she shaved her head, the down a filter through which she must be seen. "I haven't taken anything." She extends her arms, standing cruciform. "Search me."

"Not necessary," Claude says.

"Frisk me."

"Forget it."

"You'll feel better if you're certain." Then she adds, "Close the door first."

"I don't need to search you," he says and closes the door.

"I'll shut my eyes."

Her clothing is tight, her bones the bones of a bird. She couldn't hide a matchbook. Claude runs his hands along her ribs and down her thighs. She remains in the windmill position. He pats her back and buttocks. He presses against her small breasts. Finally he pushes her arms down, which causes her eyes to open, as if she were a mechanical doll.

"Satisfied?" she asks.

"What does my bag tell you about me?"

"You dress well. And you don't know yourself."

"I forgot to check here."

He slips a finger inside the waist of her jeans, the gap between the denim and her pale skin. He paces a circle around her, rimming her pants with his finger. When he stands in front of her again, he lifts her shirt: small breasts, nipples upturned, fruit plucked prematurely from the vine.

"I guess you're clean," he says.

"Certain?"

He unbuttons her jeans, tugs them down. Her panties slide along her thighs, slanting and rippled like a flag. Her pubis is shaved to a narrow strip. His hand slides between her legs. "You don't appear to be hiding anything."

She grips the hand and begins rocking her pelvis.

"I can come like this," she says.

A drop of sweat forms beneath her fine hair, the scalp turning pink.

After, she says, "Watch me walk." She shuffles with her pants down to the bathroom. "You have to do yourself," she calls. "I'm a married woman." Her laughter is round, complicated, lovely to hear. She reappears, buttoning the jeans. "We have rules about what I should and shouldn't do."

"You should gain some weight," Claude says.

A veil descends. "I like myself this way." She slams the door twice before the latch clicks.

Claude slides the chain into its slot. He takes the paper cup from the television, the coffee still warm, still bitter and burnt, but easier to swallow.

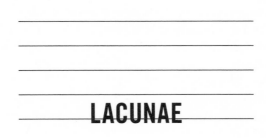

LACUNAE

Paul Lann's window on the silent world was narrow, but no one else had any view
at all. The hospital sat on a sandy mesa that overlooked an irrigated
valley. As a boy, Paul's paper route had taken him through this valley, and he had always gotten lost. The view from the seventh story
revealed the underlying grid, a finger pattern on either side of a
curving irrigation canal. Beyond the trees, the desert resumed, blond
and fierce and holding tenaciously to the sun as it receded beneath
the horizon. A hazy, persistent light lingered among the rooftops,
burnishing a satellite dish so that it shone like a spoon. Dusk in the
desert was a reluctant phenomenon. It required encouragement, expected coddling. Case in point: it was almost 10:00 p.m.

The waiting room, nothing more than a wide spot in the hallway,
had only the one window, where Paul pressed his forehead against
the slender strip of glass. Directly below, Paul's car, a disintegrating
old Mercury, suddenly rolled forward. He had set the brake when
he parked it, but as soon as he shut the door the car had inched
along the curb. "That's better," a security guard had said. He spoke
as if Paul had made the car move by remote control. "This is loading and unloading only," the guard added, as he did every time Paul
parked in the gray zone. "Picking up your old man?"

Paul had nodded and patted the Mercury's fender. "She won't be
any trouble." He had driven two hundred miles across the Arizona

desert to take his father across town from the hospital. Now, an hour after arriving and a single floor below his destination, he stalled. He made his living designing and building furniture. He had recently quit the *Tucson Morning Star* to work with wood full-time, which put him at the beginning of what might be a risky artistic endeavor—or merely a tedious business venture. He wished he could ask his father for advice. To succeed financially, he needed to make dozens of identical chairs, tables, desks, and dressers. To thrive artistically, he needed to build what the wood demanded—precise, one-of-a-kind pieces. At present, he compromised, constructing high-quality examples of everyday furnishings. A few boutiques carried his work, and he eked by. *The worst of both worlds,* his father might have said, but what the old man would have suggested Paul didn't know.

The window radiated heat, and his warm forehead felt like a symptom. "Don't come this time until they release him," his mother had said over the phone. Her husband's strokes had become routine for her. "I know how to sit alone in a hospital," she'd added. "I could use you later to get him out of my hair." Below, the Mercury slipped forward again just as a lamppost came on, light winking off the car's tilting hood.

Paul winked back. He was thirty-five, divorced and living alone, a reasonably intelligent man who smelled this evening of lacquer and body odor—a surprisingly inoffensive combination. He did his best work when he obeyed the wood. Something in the grain and texture guided him. He could get lost in it. He once spent eight consecutive hours on a commemorative paddle for a retiring vice principal.

The black vinyl roof of his car, sun-bleached and peeling, changed appearance under the direction of an evening breeze. A pattern emerged, an oval with irregular features. Paul could not transform the image into a face or a symbol he recognized, and yet his skin began to ring. Headlights flashed in the dim lot. Brake lights followed. Vertigo made his knees weak. The landscape, shifting with the fading light, seemed to gather itself just beyond the window, as if the glass were a divide.

The waiting room itself held three bulky chairs and a matching couch. A television guarded one end, while immense vending machines watched over the other. One machine had made Paul's coffee, a drink mahogany in color and with the almost satisfactory flavor of aged dung. The television entertained a family of visitors, a genetic grouping of broad bodies topped by chunk heads and orange hair. They huddled silently on the couch while a jingle recommended candlelight and cola, mechanized voices singing, "Romance is changing." As if in response, one of the vending machines flashed a digital green message: "Exact change only."

Paul tossed his coffee cup into a squat barrel lined with brown hospital plastic. The liner was not entirely open. The cup landed right side up and was held aloft, as if floating, a curl of coffee lolling obscenely in its mouth. He was tired, he told himself, and likely dehydrated. His father's condition encouraged morbid, idiotic thinking. The plastic liner in the wastebasket emitted a mild shriek as the Styrofoam cup exerted enough weight to force the bag open. The cup slid down and the dark liner closed over it.

This was not a revelatory vision, Paul told himself. Static electricity, inertia, gravity—the usual suspects up to their usual sport. After one of the strokes, his father had tried to say "Styrofoam" and substituted "Chappaquiddick." Yet Paul had understood. He and his father had been unusually close. *Woe unto the gaps,* Paul's college roommate had said upon their parting, and Paul had never seen him again. What was that guy's name?

At the threshold to his father's room, Paul could see most of his father's body, which was still in hospital garb, lying on the bed, pale arms folded over his chest. He did not look ready to come home. *West Wing* played soundlessly on the ceiling mount. Paul's mother sat across the tile floor, against the far wall, wrapped in the plaid of an institutional chair. An identical chair gaped beside her. His mother's magazine showed images of kitchens and living rooms. Her hands flipped through the pages quickly, as if she were shuffling cards, her extravagant hair shuddering. She dyed it black but left long strands of gray. The last time Paul had come home he had dropped her off at the beauty shop and returned for her too early. Her head had been plastered with dye but banded sprouts of gray hair erupted like dandelions gone to seed. "You can't see me like this," she had said evenly. "It spoils the magic."

Paul's father spoke. "We'll have to bury you in that thing." Mr. Lann was not in the bed, but standing at a window, fully dressed and looking out at the Mercury. There were two beds in the room. Paul had mistaken a stranger's body for his father's. "It looks worse than I do," his father went on, his voice soft and a little sad. This was the voice that Paul had grown up with, and it pleased him to hear it.

"The car's twenty-five years old," Paul said. "Cut it some slack."

His father was talking and making sense. He didn't look like a man who'd had a stroke a few days earlier.

"I'm seventy-two," his father went on, "and I'm in better shape than it is."

"You're seventy-*seven*," Paul's mother put in. She opened her arms to her son.

The man in the bed looked nothing like his father. He was closer to Paul's age. A purple scar divided the pale skin of his shaved head, traversing his skull from ear to ear, as if doctors had removed his brain.

"The Mercury is twenty-five in human years," Paul said as he hugged his mother. "That's a hundred in car years."

His father grunted. His face clouded. "Get me out of this damn place." He said this in his other voice. His *bad* voice. It had come into being after his second stroke, an urgent, expulsive vehicle, deeper in tone than any normal voice, darker in texture. "His angry voice," Paul's mother called it. But *angry* did not seem adequate. It was coarse and lurking. An *unclean* voice. "A residual of the lacunar infarction," a young neurologist had explained. "It may go away. Or at least get less creepy." And it did go away, only to return after the third stroke. A new, even younger, neurologist tried to explain it. "Damage to gray matter produces mysterious results." He described a patient who could not recognize parts of his body. "I came in when he was eating and he said, 'They're feeding me.' He was talking about his hands."

Paul's father's strokes came in almost regular intervals, like a relentless chorus to a monotonous song. Yet there were times when Edmund Lann could seem like the man he had been most of his life—gentle and ironic, a soft touch when it came to favors or money, a man who liked to laugh. More often he seemed hardly a man at all—a husk, a shell, a *thing*. It pained Paul to think of his father this way.

"Let go," his father commanded, and Paul broke his embrace with his mother. "Get me out of this . . ." He stuttered over a consonant, finally coming to *"damp."*

This dump, Paul translated, or possibly *this damn place.*

His mother offered an expressive and vaguely theatrical sigh. "It comes and goes," she told Paul, "like a haunting." She had been an actress when she and Edmund met. Their romance had taken place in Chicago. Edmund, a graduate student in business school, had attended an absurdist stage production called *Shelf Life,* in which his future wife played a chest of drawers. Much of the humor was built on double entendres about her chest. In the playbill, she altered her name to make it distinctive, changing "Catherine" to "Caddy." Edmund never called her anything else—until the bad voice emerged.

Lazy bitch, the voice would say. *Lardass.*

Paul knelt to place his father's feet on the footplates of the wheelchair. He believed the bad voice had lived inside his father all along, but he had worked to contain it. Now he could contain nothing. It slipped out by means of the little gaps—the lacunae. Paul knew this word from his own work. One of his teachers had used the term to describe the tiny holes in inferior wood.

"Have we left anything?" his mother asked. She flounced about the room gathering their possessions, her heroic tresses sweeping behind her. She insisted on taking everything for which the hospital charged them: the plastic water pitcher, razor, and toothbrush; the paper slippers and disposable dinner utensils; a translucent shower cap; slender bars of soap. "Our car is at home," she said, stuffing the booty into a wide-mouthed bag. "Helen and Laura gave me a ride over."

Laura was Paul's ex-wife, and Helen, his former mother-in-law. "They came here?" he asked.

"And the child," his mother said.

"That boy looks just like you," Edmund put in.

Paul didn't know whether to reply to his father's comment, which antagonized him, or his tone of voice, which had softened and sounded like the man Paul loved. His shoes pinched his feet, and he stepped in place stupidly.

"I guess we'll all have to ride in the Mercury," he said. After a moment, he added, "He's not my son, that boy."

"We know that," Caddy said.

"Out of the pokey, at last," his father announced happily as they wheeled him away. "That kid is the spitting mmm . . . mmm . . ." When the word finally emerged, it sounded like *mirage*.

The Mercury was all that remained of Paul's marriage. The house had slipped away—mortgage payments omitted during the drama. They'd both had affairs. Each had known and given permission. They had thought they were bored. Paul had proposed the experiment to celebrate their sophistication. He had covered local sports for the newspaper, and one of the photographers wanted to seduce him. The idea hadn't really been avant-garde, merely opportunistic.

It turned ugly quickly and ended one night when Laura didn't come home. Paul packed a few things into the trunk of the Mercury and drove off. He spent a month attempting to love the photographer. He built a chair to the precise dimensions of her bottom, the contours of which he measured repeatedly with his palms.

One night after interviewing a victorious high school football coach who said, "We *literally* knocked their heads off," Paul became discouraged with his job. He ran into Laura in a bar they used to frequent together. When he joined her table, her friends one by one departed. An argument ensued. They left the place together but got no farther than the Mercury. They had sex in the backseat without ever leaving the parking lot.

She had been living with a stockbroker and was about to move with him to Denver.

"This was just a slip," she said, buttoning her blouse. "A meaningless blip on the screen."

A year passed before Paul heard from her again. She called late one night. The telephone seemed to burn his palm and he dropped the receiver.

"Just wanted to see how you are," she said apologetically.

"I'm building things again."

"What are you wearing?" she asked. "Describe your haircut."

She was moving once more, abandoning Colorado and the stockbroker for their hometown in the desert.

"I'll live with my mother at first," she said. "How often do you get back to see your folks?"

They picked a rendezvous date.

That she was pregnant, she did not mention. Eight months along, her belly a mountain where there had once been a plain. She let the plan slip to her mother, who told Caddy the pair might reconcile. Joy mangled his mother's voice on the telephone, and it occurred to Paul that she probably was never a very subtle actress. She hadn't known to keep the weighty secret. She thought so much of him for not letting the mountain get in the way.

Paul canceled the trip without a call. His machine took Laura's inquiries, her apologies and explanations, her bitter dismissal. Paul did not return home until his father's first stroke. During his visits, he drove his father all around town—one of the few activities Edmund still enjoyed—but Paul never encountered his ex-wife on these excursions. He never dropped in on her. Eight strokes had followed the first, and still Paul had not seen Laura or her child.

He heard about them, though. His mother provided updates by telephone about Edmund's health and Laura's son. "He's walking now," she would say, and Paul would have to guess whether she meant his recovering father or his ex-wife's toddler. The boy could not possibly be his. The final time he made love to Laura—the Mercury's suspension groaning along with them—was more than a year before the birth.

Which meant Paul had nothing left from his marriage but the Mercury. If it had been in perfect shape, it still wouldn't have been a collector's item. A product of the late seventies, the Mercury was the automotive equivalent of clingy polyester shirts with giant lapels. A big sandbox of a car. Everyone complained about it. But it had been good to him, almost no trouble as long as he was willing to put up with its moods and mild deformities—the occasional sputter at intersections, the unsteady acceleration and tremulous lights, the threadbare interior and snarling hood, the front seat's tendency to come unmoored, the windows that would not close, the doors that would not open, and the loose front bumper, which rocked up and down at intersections as if muttering.

"You should really get rid of this thing," his mother suggested on the drive home from the hospital. She rode in the backseat, which was grimy with sawdust. "Don't you need a truck for your business?"

"Lardass doesn't like anything *old*," his father put in.

"Call her Caddy, please," Paul replied. He found his mother in the rearview. "The trunk's enormous. All of creation would fit in that thing."

He had no intention of selling the Mercury. Always in friends, there were little traits one had to excuse.

Paul's only job was to take Edmund on afternoon drives. Caddy needed an hour of uninterrupted silence, which didn't seem like much to ask, but an hour had never seemed so long. Thinking his mother's Corolla was at fault, he switched to the Mercury, which his father came to prefer because Paul let him smoke in it.

Edmund Lann tapped the car window with his wedding ring. "This damn thing will die," he said. The gold ring caught the sun. It didn't blind Paul, but he couldn't see past it and braked. "Right there," the bad voice insisted. The ring struck the window again. Beyond the sidewalk, in a lush yard, water flowed from the end of an elevated garden hose, soaking a leafy plant. There had to be a person holding the hose, but all Paul could see was a canvas glove gripping the nozzle.

"Remember this street," his father said. "Can you manage that?"

"It's Calgary Street," Paul said.

"Unless you're an idiot, you don't water leaves in this kind of heat," his father said. "It sucks the life out of them." As if to underscore the words, the air conditioner belt squealed. The rush of air through its vents became audible, a strained quality to the sound, as if the car could not catch its breath.

"I don't see how water can make a plant dry up," Paul replied.

Edmund waved his hand at the window, which meant they should move on. Paul pressed the accelerator. The engine revved but the car resisted for a moment before heaving forward.

"Where to?" Paul asked.

Edmund gripped the exposed foam of the armrest. "Anywhere, *dope.*"

The bad voice was never deeply submerged. It lurked below conversations, ready to show its scaly head. In the past, it had disappeared after a few days. But Paul had been in town a week, and the voice still dominated his father.

"Keep this heap moving," it said.

The territory damaged by a stroke determines the nature of the human consequences. His father's strokes resulted in general diminishment rather than the paralysis that selects one side of the body over the other. Why his blood vessels deteriorated in a single region of the brain, doctors could not explain. One specialist, pointing with a red laser at a cranial map, made a little circle at the back of the skull. "It's as if it has a mind of its own," he said, seeing no irony in the comment. The whirling laser had created the image of a target.

The car grew sluggish and slowed. Paul signaled and turned onto a side street to disguise the trouble. He was tired of people complaining about his car. After a moment, the Mercury recovered. It always did.

"Isn't there a Negro spiritual about Calgary Street?" his father pondered, his voice seeming to soften. But it immediately changed back. "I *knew* you'd turn here."

"You said 'anywhere.' I don't care where we go."

"You can't keep away from it."

"Am I to supposed to think that makes sense?"

Paul had learned to remain calm during Edmund's tirades, but it wasn't easy. The first stroke had sent his father plummeting from a kitchen chair. His fork had spun through the air and then caught in the carpet's weave, which made it stand on its tines. Paul hadn't been there, but his mother had described it repeatedly, as it were a historic event. She never neglected the detail of the tumbling fork. "We were using the good silver," she liked to note.

"There, buster," his father croaked. He poked his finger at the car window.

An expanse of grass came into view beyond the passenger window, walled off by the stucco face of a stubbornly ugly house. The Mercury took them past it and to the end of the block before Paul realized it was the former and current residence of his ex-wife.

"I didn't even notice we were on her street," Paul said.

A pickup flew past, tossing a rock against the windshield.

"You don't notice every day," his father replied.

Had he been hoping to catch a glance of Laura? He didn't think so. He had just been driving. The Mercury coughed as they rounded the corner. The air conditioner belt whined every time the car slowed. Paul needed to get back to his work. Hardwood from South America was already on its way to his converted garage. He had done his duty to his parents. It was time to go home.

His father's ring again tapped the passenger window, this time to refer to the automobile itself.

"It's like me," he said. He leaned forward to touch the tiny chip in the windshield made by the rock. "Not long for this world."

The Mercury lurched. Paul steered it toward the desert.

"We'll get out of the city," he said.

Edmund did not reply, slipping at last into the silence he would eventually find during each of their drives. Paul wondered whether he was brooding or simply separated from language altogether, wordless among the million things he daily encountered. Marooned in a sea of unnameable objects. The desert sprang up just beyond the city. Ears of giant prickly pear wobbled with each passing car, and Edmund stirred to life. He lit a cigarette and asked Paul about his job.

"I quit the paper. Did Mom tell you?"

"She doesn't tell me a goddamn thing." The cigarette raged crimson in his mouth. "But she did tell me that."

"I make furniture full-time."

"You always liked wood," he said. The hand that held the cigarette motioned to the windshield. The chip in the glass had already turned into a crack.

In high school, Paul had built a complex receptacle that still covered one wall of his parents' living room, holding a television and stereo, potted plants, books, videotapes, the swollen pile of mail no one could face. His mother had recently added a collage of photographs—Laura and Paul in their wedding clothes, Caddy as a girl in west Texas, and Edmund Lann wearing the face he wore before the lacunae formed in his brain.

"Wood can't be forced," Paul had told Laura when they were children and tormenting each other with their bodies. He had taken her home to show her his wall of shelves. "You have to discover the form within it." He had heard someone say this about marble.

She had not been impressed. "You found a tree that wanted to be an entertainment center?"

If he could relive that moment—as he had in his head a thousand times—he would tell her the passions of wood were every bit as mysterious and furtive as the passions of people. And then, before she could ridicule him, he would kiss her.

His father's ring tap demanded his attention. "Wheat," he said. The green field waved at them, wind blundering over its surface, a movement oceanic, peaceful, friendly. At this distance from his last nap, his father grew incapable of sentences. "Saguaro," he said of the giant cactus. His voice had begun to accumulate the slats of sleep. "Ruined," he decreed a ramshackle hut. He must have thought it abandoned despite laundry flapping on a line—a child's pink pajamas walking in the wind.

"Fire," Edmund said.

On the road's shoulder, a car blazed. Flames rose up from the underside and licked the deep blue doors. A man sat cross-legged, like an insect, before it. He waved them off when Paul slowed the car. He wanted no company.

"Damn," Paul said.

His father roused himself, looking about, expecting, perhaps, an artificial reservoir. The rearview mirror showed the flames for a long while and then a black question mark of smoke. Ahead, heat lifting from the asphalt made the road ripple and writhe, like the long black spine of a reptile.

He had to carry his father inside, an awkward package, but Paul negotiated the doorway and deposited his father in the recliner. His mother came in to watch.

"You've worn him out," she said approvingly. Her hands methodically worked a dish towel. "Cards?"

They played honeymoon bridge. She relayed news about the neighborhood: fresh tan paint on a house down the street had dried to a pumpkin shade, the limbs of a pine tree on Lavender were growing crooked to skirt a peaked roof, a new driveway another street over cracked the week it was poured but the fractures miraculously disappeared.

"Concrete is different now," she said.

Paul discerned the direction of her conversation, a sequential geographical journey that would take them to Laura's house. Subtlety in some people proceeds at such a deliberate pace and with such a logical stride that one cannot help running ahead and opening the door.

"How's Laura doing?" he asked.

"She still thinks of us as family. Coming to the hospital and all."

"Nice of her to make an appearance."

His mother's great hair trembled, and Paul changed the subject.

"I don't know how you can stand it," he said. "Every day with him. He's so rude . . . he's not even—"

"Your father's always been a little mean," she said, dealing their hands. "Now he has no other resource. I could hardly wish to deny him the one thing he can still feel."

"I don't remember *any* meanness in him."

"That's good," she said. "I'm glad you feel that way." She was the type of cardplayer who plucked and rearranged her cards, as if they were constantly shifting allegiances. "I don't have that kind of hole in my memory. We all have meanness in us."

This sounded like an accusation, but he let it pass.

She won every hand. Cards spilled from her grip in a natural procession, like the movements of a symphony, the acts of a play, the events of an orderly life.

In the other room, the television came alive, meaning that Edmund's nap had ended.

"You should see the child," she said. Before Paul could protest, she added, "I know he's not your son, but she *was* your wife. And that child does bear a startling resemblance to you." Her hands leapt up to keep him from interrupting, and the cards escaped, dropping to the table. "I don't need to hear about the yearlong gap. I believe that he's not your boy. You should still go see them."

"Give me one good reason."

"You love her." She scooped up the cards. "Lie to yourself if you have to, but don't lie to me."

She began dealing a hand of solitaire.

The Mercury had come from the factory white, but now its paint was gray and pitted like unhealthy skin. The interior was worse: dashboard gutted, radio gone, idiot lights dead, even the glove box—door and all—vanished, leaving only a gaping metal sneer. The add-on air conditioner sagged beneath the skeletal dash and beside a toggle switch for the headlights, which hung loose in the air from an awkward gathering of wires. A red wool blanket that had once covered Paul's childhood bed camouflaged the front seat. The engine idled nervously before the house where Laura lived. The shudder of the headlights suggested the flicker of flashback in movies, but Paul resisted memory. The air conditioner belt began to slip, and the engine died. Heat swept in and slid its dry hand over his mouth. Before he swung the car door fully open, Laura stepped from the corner of the house as if from the corner of a dream. She wore a sleeveless white blouse and yellow pants stretched tight over her hips. A garden hose gushed in her hand, while her bare feet crushed the grass. Paul hesitated on the Mercury's seat. The dome light decided to work and turned the windshield into a mirror. The crack had spread across the glass, separating the top of Paul's head from the bottom.

Laura watched him climb from the car, her brows rising as if she couldn't quite recall who he was. She carried the hose to the outdoor faucet and twisted the handle. The water slowed and stopped, yet she held on to the hose as she approached him, water rising and gagging out, as if from the mouth of a child who had almost drowned.

"Have you come to see me or him?" She dropped the hose and the spray hit his ankles. "Sorry," she added.

"You look like yourself," he said.

She offered her hand and he took it. They had once made love in a public park, beneath monkey bars, the night sky divided into neighborhoods by symmetrical metal tubes.

Her front door made a familiar rasp.

"My mom's not home," Laura said. "She's learning to throw pots." She guided him inside and to the couch. "I'm a teller." She named the bank that employed her. "It's only temporary. Mostly, I take care of Cliff."

Paul told her he did nothing anymore but make furniture.

"Eventually, the money might be good." He tried to articulate his dilemma, the split between art and commerce, but it sounded foolish to him. "I'm happier," he said, "being around lumber."

When the child tottered into the room, Paul's voice faltered. It was not in the boy's features, exactly, that they shared a resemblance. Not in the curl of his brown hair, although Paul's brown hair curled if he let it get long. Not in the shade of his eyes, despite the identical green. A thousand others in this town had the same eyes and hair, the same western slant of shoulders and shape of mouth. Rather, it was in the lope this boy had, the hesitation every other step, the slight turn of the body away from the direction set by the head.

"Cliff," Laura called and her son came to her. She had never changed her surname after the divorce. The boy's last name was Lann. She said, "I thought it would be too strange to send you pictures."

Paul asked the boy the only questions he could think of, the generic questions adults always asked. The thumb of Cliff's right hand held down the pinkie, the remaining three announcing his age. His school was called Paper Tigers. He told Paul that Laura's mother did not like to be called Grandma, a bevel of concern appearing on his forehead as he spoke the word. Then he announced that he had to go, his eyes veering anxiously in the direction of his room. Paul understood. The boy's things demanded his attention—the little plastic men and their resilient cars, the interlocking blocks and animals filled with down. They called for him, and he had to go.

"I had a fling," Laura said. "Right after I moved to Denver."

"It's none of my business," Paul said.

"The resemblance isn't entirely a coincidence. I think I picked someone who looked like you."

He nodded and waited while the urge to speak his heart passed. But then he had nothing to say.

"I'm still driving the Mercury."

"I noticed."

"My dad likes it because I let him smoke. He's a handful."

"Maybe you should move back here to help," she said.

I can ship my furniture from anywhere, he thought. But he didn't say it. Instead, he shook his head.

"I don't like being with him. He doesn't have anything to offer now. He isn't *him*. He looks like my father and occasionally sounds like my father, but he's just some . . ."

"I'm sorry you feel that way."

"It drains me. Even just driving him around."

She raised her hand and plucked a fleck of foam rubber from his hair.

"You know what I've missed?" she said. "That coffee table you made with the crazy legs."

"Not another like it in the world."

"That's not why I miss it."

Her son called from his room, and she got up. Paul followed her as far as the hall.

"I should probably go," he said.

She turned to face him. Her posture was perfect, hands at her side, her eyes open and blue.

She said, "You know how to find us."

On the drive home, the Mercury slowed down of its own will.

This car has no master, Paul thought.

The engine invented a new automotive emotion, a faint whispering weep. The wheels measured their revolution. The fluttering lids of the car sent its shaky light out over the neighborhood. The crack in the windshield made the houses at the far end of the street seem to lean forward. Tree boughs bent in the windless night. Blades of grass stood at alert. A tire swing twisted almost imperceptibly to reveal its startled O.

Paul gripped the dimpled steering wheel with both hands, and the seat slipped loose, nudging him forward. Windshield wipers that had not worked in a year began their metronomic sweep. In the dark of the desert evening, the residential street held its breath as the Mercury drifted to a standstill.

A wooden door on a shed opened with an interrogative creak, posing a question Paul could not articulate. The air conditioner suddenly came alive. A porch light practiced self-illumination. The crack in the windshield took the light and made colors on the glass. Paul looked for a person at the shed door or on the porch, but none appeared. The engine murmured and his heart raced. He perched on the edge of the seat, witness, he understood, to a break in a material join. A gap, a breach, a *lacuna.*

Beneath the window of the house, beside a swarm of orange hose, a large-leafed plant lit by the porch bulb revealed its drooping stalk and the brown movement of death that inhabited it. Paul had a moment to think of his father's wilting body before realizing it was the plant his father had pointed out. They were on Calgary Street.

He twisted the knob on the air conditioner until it stopped its racket. The car immediately began to roll forward. His seat slipped back into its groove. The Mercury eased him past the dark staring houses. These residences did not whisper to him. The parked cars did not sigh. The limbs of the mulberry did not break their ancient silence. The peaked window above an oak door, the painted flamingos on the wide lawn, the spires of picket, the timber of telephone pole, the long ramble of gutter, the red upturned wagon on a concrete drive—they did not speak to him. He heard them nonetheless.

The Mercury did not let him hurry. He chose not to question its wisdom. The windshield wipers continued their dry squeals of astonishment. If he felt his heart actually expand, what better explanation could there be for the long history of that venerable metaphor? *Hearts can swell,* he thought. One's father may speak the truth even as he settles into death. One's mother may see in a coincidence the opportunity for redemption. One's own child may have the blood and genes of another man. Reason may live in things that are not rational.

Passing the elementary school, an errant and joyous sprinkler sent a splash in the car's path. Even these windshield wipers, he thought, relentless in their obsession with clarity, have something to tell him. Something about seeing. About transparency. He knew he could not explain his vision—a million stars pricked the vast dark above his car—he could only experience it.

The Mercury died at the curb of his parents' house. The radiator offered an exhausted sigh. Was it possible to have compassion for one's father by means of compassion for one's car? He had no answer. How was he, measly and suddenly ecstatic creature that he had become, to answer questions that should be posed to a tumult of mountains or deferred to the deep expansive seas?

He did not thank the grass as he sprinted across it, but he stepped lightly. The door met his grasp, swinging slightly to his reaching palm. The room's icy atmosphere carried with it the air conditioner's solemn greeting. He stepped into the house in which he had been raised, whose carpet—even now—cushioned his every step.

"I've had a vision," Paul announced.

His father in his easy chair did not move. He was sleeping. The house, dark except for the muted television, held to a respectful silence. Paul knelt in the uncertain light beside the chair. He took Edmund Lann's hand. The carpet pile flexed beneath his knees. The wall of shelves began to squeak and bulge, its cubicles faintly changing shape. Beyond the room, out in the dark, a car horn sounded encouragement, and the great enduring nation of the wordless silently applauded.

Paul put his head next to his father's to whisper in his ear, but he did not know what to say. He could stay here and care for his father. He could help his mother. He could marry his wife and raise their son. He could build the things he needed to build. Is this what the world was telling him?

Finally, he said, "Father, what should I do?"

The man did not respond, but the recliner cooed as it fell gently back, unfurling until it lay flat and soft and ready, like a tongue.

THE HEYDAY OF
THE INSENSITIVE
BASTARDS

Assignment 1: Happier Time

As much as anything really happens, this really did.

It was late spring. I was in that drifting age between the end of college (sophomore year) and the beginning of settling down (the penitentiary), and I had taken to the mountains where my friend Clete said the air was so thin you could skip the huffing and absorb it directly through your pores. Clete was living out of a green VW van that had broken down at a scenic overlook a few miles outside the Colorado ski town of Apex. He had taken the tires off the van to keep it from being towed. Perched on the cliff, it looked primitive and vaguely prehistoric.

The Greyhound driver pulled over for me.

"Don't get too close to the ledge," he warned.

Evidently I hadn't concealed the fact that I was stoned.

Clete sat on the metal railing eating a combination of trail mix and Alpha-Bits from a plastic pouch. He was a big guy with brown hair in bangs across his forehead, a ponytail in the back. His body had an imposing quality, not just because of his size but owing to the confident way he moved through the world.

"I've got a kilo of shrooms," he said by way of greeting, leading me across the highway and up a muddy path.

In the shade of pines, he moved a fallen branch and dug up a bag of psychedelic mushrooms. He kept them separate from the van in case some law officer decided to search his home.

I spread my coat over the grass. The coat was blue and bulky but light—insulated by air—made of a petroleum product impossible to stain. It had so many pockets I'd forget about some for months at a time only to discover an old joint, a dime bag, a novel I was halfway through. The coat dated back to my last visit home. I got distracted on the way, a six-hour drive from the university, and arrived three months late. My parents still had my Christmas presents wrapped in elf-and-reindeer paper. The whole time I was there they complained about their lousy holiday. (As you know, I haven't seen them since. A person can only apologize so much.) The coat was one of my presents. A man could cross the Arctic in such a coat. It had become my organizing principle. And it was all the luggage I had.

Clete and I plopped our butts on it.

"I recommend this much," he said and passed me a handful of mushrooms.

It was a hot day, and we stretched out in the shade. Through the trees, we had a view of the highway, the beached van, and the green gorge beyond the railing. Clete and I have been friends for decades. We first met when we were seventh graders. My mother had grown tired of driving me to school when the bus stop was just down the street. Clete was on one knee when I arrived, his chin in his hand. "Spermatozoa are living creatures," he said, "and we make them." I did not know his name, and he didn't know mine. We'd seen each other at school, but we'd never spoken. "They swim, they wriggle, they *seek*."

"Is this where we catch the bus?" I said.

"That means we have some sense of God in us," Clete said. "I feel it." He put his hand over his crotch. "It's like a bright, tickling light."

We've been friends ever since.

"They're kind of gritty," I said, referring to the mushrooms.

Clete shrugged. He had spent the morning in a wildlife center watching a film on lions. "One." He counted with his fingers. "They sleep twenty hours a day. Two, the females do the hunting while the males snooze. Three, when pursuing prey, they attack the smallest and slowest in a herd—the baby wildebeest, retarded zebra, gimpy antelope. Given this evidence, what do you think the movie was called?"

I pointed to a couple of girls in short pants bicycling past the lookout point, but Clete couldn't be discouraged. When he got philosophical, there was no stopping him.

"*Lion, the Noble Beast.*" He paused to let the irony sink it. "Then I got to thinking how kings just lie around on their royal furniture and tax the peasants. Maybe lions *are* nobility after all." Clete had never been what anyone would call a good student, but he could be specific in ways most of us couldn't. "Take lime popsicles," he continued. "Do they taste anything like actual limes?"

"Have you been eating these all day?"

"I sampled while I was harvesting."

"You *picked* these?"

"They grow," he said. "Right out of the ground."

"Mushrooms can be poisonous, you know."

I studied the remaining mushrooms in my hand, torn between the idea of a bargain high and the possibility of dying.

"I took a library book with me," Clete assured me. "They're perfectly safe."

"So," I said, eating another but chewing more slowly, "you've got a library card."

"Everything we have, even the rain, comes from the earth," he replied. "Except for meteorites and certain toxic gases." He returned the bag to the hole and used the branch like a broom to disguise the topsoil. "I know where there's a party," he said.

We hiked down to the VW. The van had no side windows or seats in the back, just a long floorboard he had covered with foam rubber and shag carpet. I tossed in my coat, Clete locked up, and we headed toward town on foot.

"Where are the tires?" I asked.

"Hidden." He needed six hundred dollars to rebuild the engine. He didn't have a job but was saving money anyway. "Walking back and forth to town is good exercise," he said, "which saves on doctor bills and money that would have gone toward gas if the van was running."

"We're making a profit just walking along," I said.

"Picking mushrooms saves on drugs and groceries."

"How much actual cash do you have?"

He stuck his hand in his pocket and counted the small wad of bills, plus a few coins. "Twelve dollars and forty-eight cents, but this is a buffalo nickel. I'm saving it."

"Twelve forty-three then," I said.

I felt the most inside our friendship when we walked together as we did that afternoon, making plans and bumping shoulders, eating magic mushrooms from our fists, hoping we wouldn't get poisoned.

"I've got about fifty bucks," I told him. "I'd have more but I gave this woman a necklace when I broke up with her."

"The one with the parrot?"

"How was I supposed to know it wouldn't come when it's called?"

"Parrots don't know what they're saying," Clete said. "They just copy sounds. Humans are the same. We talk in the vague hope of finding out what we mean."

When we reached Apex, he showed me the library and a bakery that set out day-old pastries in the alley.

"Fires are good for forests," he said.

I smelled the smoke then. The flames were fifty miles away, but the box canyon that held the town had a roof of smoke. It had a purifying odor. I began to feel tall and rubbery and ready for the next thing. We walked a long distance. At some point, it turned out to be evening. Stars swelled from the dark center of the sky to the toothed ridges of the mountains. All the heat fled the air and I thought to ask, "Where we going?"

Clete pointed to a dark house up the hill. A girl named Val was dog sitting for a family spending the summer in Scotland. It was her party. The house had a peaked roof and plank porch. The windows showed a waffling brightness like the memory of actual light. Some kind of Mary Chapin Carpenter warbled inside, and I had a momentary fear of live music.

Clete didn't knock. The front room held maybe twenty candles. A boom box sat on a high table, its cord connected to an extension that trailed along the floor, out a window, and across the lawn to a neighbor's outlet. Clete ejected the tape, which drew applause from guys lounging on the furniture.

"I have *Texas Flood* in my coat," I said.

"You're not wearing your coat." Clete lifted tapes from the scatter on the table and held them next to a candle to read.

I wandered into the kitchen. A bone-thin woman, who turned out to be Val the dog sitter and hostess, was mixing a drink by flashlight.

"Thirsty?" She handed me the drink she was making. "Whiskey and ice is my specialty, and it's all we've got." She dipped into a plastic cooler for more ice. "These glasses are real crystal," she added, "but they're monogrammed. I'm afraid to sell them. It's a small town."

"I could sell them for you," I said. "Nobody knows me."

"That's so sweet." She'd spent the upkeep money the family had left on dope. Once the electricity was cut off, she sold the appliances. She was down to the blender and Toast-R-Oven. "I have to keep the phone on for when they call from Dundee," she said. She had trained the dogs to bark into the receiver. "I got screwed on the refrigerator." She had traded it to a guy at the bakery for a cooler of sandwiches. "Never do business when you're hungry," she advised. Her mouth was small and almost circular, like a split cantaloupe. She noticed me studying her mouth and kissed me. "Who are you anyway?"

I told her I was Clete's friend.

"Thank goodness," she said. "I need his help." She took another crystal tumbler from the cupboard and filled it with whiskey. "Clete doesn't take ice for some reason."

"He doesn't want to get spoiled," I explained.

She took the drink to Clete and grabbed his arm, leading us to a room with wood paneling, leather furniture, and no windows—a den. People sat around in candlelight studying a guy in a big chair who was staring out of eyes as distant and hollow as those tunnels that go under bodies of water. Val shone a flashlight on him. He didn't blink.

"What do we have here?" Clete asked. He knew the guy, whose name was Stu.

A bunch of them had snorted PCP, but Stu had done twice as much as anyone else. Now he wasn't moving.

"Someone egged him on," Val said.

She turned a nasty gaze on a guy sitting cross-legged on the couch. His head was narrow in the middle like a partially imploded can. He spoke.

"From now on he's not Stu, he's *Stewed*." His laugh was sniggering and ratchetlike.

Clete asked Val for the name of the laughing man as if he weren't right there. She answered with the single word "Barnett."

Clete leaned in next to me but spoke loud enough for everyone to hear. "We may have to teach that one a lesson."

Barnett quit laughing and drank from a tall glass of something green.

Clete addressed the entire room. "Who, if anyone, knows what PCP is?"

A guy with a headband said he thought the active ingredient had something to do with the manufacture of fluorocarbons.

None of us liked the sound of that.

Clete wanted the full list of Stu's symptoms.

"He's grown really quiet," the headband said. "*Pensive*, I'd say. And he doesn't move."

They all looked at Stu but didn't know what they were seeing, as if they had entered a cult and weren't permitted to understand what was staring them in the face: an unconscious man with his eyes open, sitting upright and rigid in an armchair.

Clete wanted to know how long he'd been like this.

Val checked her wrist. "Oh," she said, "can it really be ten p.m.?"

"It's ten to twelve," I said, showing her. She had confused the hands on her watch. A murmur made its way around the room. Several people counted with their fingers. Stu had been comatose for six to nine hours, depending on which of his fellow travelers you trusted.

Knowing the time earned me credibility in that crowd, but it made me wonder how long Clete and I had walked. I was certain the sun had been up when we started.

Then I asked, "Is there any of that stuff left?"

Barnett answered. "Stewed sucked up the last of it and licked the tray."

"He doesn't smell so good," Clete noted.

"Is there a hospital in this town?" I asked, adding, "I'm new."

"There's an on-call doctor," Val said. "He doesn't like this kind of thing, though."

Clete held a stubby candle right up to Stu's face, staring hard into the wanky eyes. Clete said, "Wilt thou be made whole?"

It got the ratchety laugh from Barnett, but Clete was dead serious. One time in Oregon he asked a highway patrolman who had pulled us over for driving without lights whether he didn't "relish the dark world." We spent what they called a cautionary night in jail, but everyone was very nice to us.

Stu made a sudden shuddering movement with the top half of his body. He raised one arm from the chair and held it aloft. Pointing to our hostess, he said, "V-V-V."

Val, as if to encourage him, tugged at her short skirt, wiggling her butt against her leather chair. The place had great furniture.

A tremor passed through Stu's arm and made his hand dance, as if he had discovered something miraculous or gotten electrocuted. His face contorted with the effort of speaking.

"V-V-*Val*," he said at last. His eyes settled on Clete. "Cl-Cl-Cl-*Clete*."

"Cluck like a chicken," Barnett yelled.

Clete turned to him. "You should get down on your knees."

A girl in a tube top and cutoffs called out, "You insensitive bastards!"

We waited for her to follow up, but she just crossed her arms and pulled her feet up onto the couch.

"She can't mean us," I said to Clete.

Stu's trembling finger indicated one person after another, moving around the room, naming the witnesses. He included the dogs, the big blond retriever, Ruff, and the yappy white terrier, Ready. When he came to me, who he didn't know from Adam, he said, "K-K-Keen."

That's how I got this name I still use. To call it an alias is only technically correct.

Eventually I went off to explore. The candlelit house had wild, watery shadows on its walls, a fickle stream of bouncing light and insistent waves of dark, like scales of light on an actual stream. A breeze would agitate the candles, and the walls would become the wide chopping sea. Human forms at the base of the wall, their heads upturned to watch the dreamy business, seemed to be praying. Some of them touched my shoulder or the soft places above my hips and said forgettable things about the brilliant, rocking light.

Later, I got hungry and found a jar of maraschino cherries in the cupboard. I filled my mouth, sweetness trickling down my throat. I thought I might hunt down a bed. In the stairway, I came across the body of a dead girl and swallowed one of the cherries whole. She lay on her back, her head higher than her feet, staring through an open skylight. There were no candles on the stairs. I had to let my eyes adjust. She was dressed in a green tube top and nothing else, but the body seemed innocent, her skin as soft as the cherries that pressed against my tongue.

The soles of her feet were black, and a trickle of blood ran over one pale thigh. I couldn't decide whether she had fallen down the stairs or given up on the climb and taken a seat, only to die in the process. Her face may have been in moonlight, as it was impossibly white. One thing was clear—she was not supposed to be looked at like this. I unbuttoned my shirt and draped it over her.

"Thanks," she said.

I jumped back and tumbled down the stairs to the landing, hitting the back of my head. When I came to, she was gone and Clete was kneeling beside me. Other people were stepping over my torso to go upstairs or come down.

"These creatures have strangely human qualities," Clete said, "like recuperating ghosts."

He lifted his eyes to follow their movement. Even in this situation, he and I thought of these house squatters with a combination of condescension and ironic pride, owing to the van and our independent living skills.

"How many people are at this shindig?" I asked.

Clete didn't answer. He waited for the landing to clear. Then he leaned close and whispered, "Wilt thou be made whole?"

It was time to go home.

Coming down from the mushrooms, I realized how high we had been and how long it would be before we were fully grounded. Along with that came the tedious desire to have never taken the stuff. With psychedelics, there was always a lingering descent, during which time you were not high but could not sleep or relax, like a hangover that begins while you're still drinking and spoils the whole evening. It comes with a bottoming-out feeling. The designs you'd imagined and the new light that you'd shed on your life grow dim and dull and disappear as you nose-dive. Your mind strains to retain some sense of what it was that had you smiling and optimistic, but you can't touch it. The dream of the high, as well as the high itself, vanishes, and the asphalt's cracks remind you that you're no kid and less young with every plodding step. Hallucinating has taken you no closer to understanding what it is you mean to do with your life.

Clete and I marched down the wide street to the heart of the little town, the bare streets and dark houses clucking disparagingly at us. In one window, beyond gauze curtains, an orange light licked at the dark world and dim figures crossed and recrossed the floor. A cold wind taunted the domestic bushes along the street and made my skin prickle and bump. I had lost my shirt to the approximately dead girl and longed for shelter, my nipples turning to squat little stones.

"I should have brought my coat," I said maybe a hundred times.

"We're at ten thousand feet," Clete said, removing his shirt and handing it to me. "The nights are always cold." He was wearing a wife-beater underneath.

I buttoned up the shirt, which was several sizes too large for me.

When we turned on Main to head out of town, the sleeves rippled like a swath of skin separating from my body.

Morning arrived. The sun should have heated me up, but my body held tenaciously to the cold. We stopped at a diner on the highway and ate eggs. Clete told me about the party, as if I hadn't been there. Stu had come around enough to have several drinks and pass out.

"His essential movement is to seek unconsciousness," Clete said.

Our booth had bad springs, which put our heads close to our eggs, a handy convenience this morning. A scrambled bit of egg escaped my mouth and hit the plate. Its brief contact with my palate had turned it an unnatural red, the color of maraschino cherries.

"Do I look funny?" I asked Clete.

Clete shrugged. "I've known you too long to say."

The food sated something in me deeper than hunger. Three walls of the diner were made of plate glass that needed cleaning, and we spent a long time watching a smeary light shift over the pines and aspen and wide stretches of high grass. The waitress had big eyes and narrow shoulders. Her name tag read "Kale." She knew Clete and would only talk in his ear, which made me a little paranoid.

"I'd introduce you," he said, "but she doesn't like talking to strangers."

"Is this really the right line of work for her?"

She went from table to table, listening and nodding, pointing to the menu. She'd whisper to one person, who'd speak to the others.

"Her legs are nice," I said.

"Every man in here is half or more in love with her," Clete said. He got her to scrape leftover eggs onto our plates.

"This guy's omelet has a weird spice," I said.

Clete forked a bite and savored it a moment.

"Cigarette ash," he said.

We stayed in the diner until the eggs and coffee had worn down my chill. Clete paid the shy waitress, and we hit the pavement again, happy for the heat of the sun. He carried a white paper bag bearing the diner's logo—a possibly cross-eyed elk. Inside were packets of salt, pepper, ketchup, mustard, and nondairy creamer.

Twenty minutes down the road, the peak of a tall black con-struction crane appeared. We watched it a long time before we got close enough to see the van. At the end of the crane's long metal wire was a big round magnet, which snapped onto the van's roof. Tireless and thoroughly defeated, the van rose up into the air. We joined the others—a crowd had gathered—in applause when it was set down on a flatbed truck. This was a terrible loss for us, but it was a great spectacle.

"We can kiss that one good-bye," Clete said.

"My worldly possession is in there," I said.

There was nothing to do but get the bag of mushrooms and hike back to Val's.

This series of events—losing my coat and the drugs and other secrets and luxuries of my life, along with being given a new name by someone mumbling out of a coma, and encountering the not-quite-naked-or-dead girl to whom I gave the shirt off my back—combined in an almost scientific way to make me swear off drugs. I was twenty-nine years old and wanted to change before I hit thirty. Clete and I developed a plan for me as we ambled back, a plan that would work all that summer and beyond. Even after I left the moun-tain, it stuck. The plan had four parts.

One: I would not get a job. There's always some guy with a goa-tee and great weed to turn you on during a break, or some friendly braless girl tired of washing dishes or mowing the graveyard or sweeping up the pencil shavings in Rosa Parks Elementary School who lights a joint or drops a line and offers to share. Work was a haven for drug users and I couldn't risk it.

Two: I'd use willpower and the help of friends who, even if high themselves, would discourage me from joining them.

Three: The mushrooms, being organic and free, didn't count.

Four: In order to be realistic and give the plan half a chance of working, I would stay drunk as much as possible.

A few people—including you and the therapist they assigned me when you had the flu—have since pointed out that as many people are done in by booze as by any drug or family of drugs. But Clete and I saw it differently. Being drunk was a momentary lapse into happiness, like drifting off while listening to a song about sex, whereas the drugs I craved were symphonies. They played at that low level just below the timbre of thought, a mattress of sound you could sleep on for days or a lifetime. Liquor relaxes the brain and lets the fool in you rise up, while the drugs I loved kept me still inside myself, permitting me to reside there in something like peace.

That's a hard thing to give up, and it's easier if you're drunk.

We moved in with Val and lived in the dog-sitting house three months. Without rehab or an arrest to keep me in line, I became Keen and did no drugs.

You asked for a happier time. That was it.

Assignment 2: Considering Others

A lot of people lived in the house that summer. It was hard to say who did and who didn't on any particular day. I had the boy's room, and almost nightly I had to kick strangers from my bed, which was made to look like a sports car.

Our regular lineup, however, included only a few of us.

Stu: Except for Val, Stu had lived in the house the longest. He had the teenage daughter's room and a job at the library, which lent out videos as well as books. He stole tapes he thought we might like. (The big-screen television was gone, but we had a portable hooked to the extension cord.) He had a nervous habit of chewing his toenails with his teeth, the indecent fragments littering the carpet like exactly what they were—little scraps of us we no longer needed. When I complained, he claimed I was jealous.

"Of what?" I was genuinely stumped.

"I can put both my feet all the way behind my head," he said.

I shrugged. "I can wiggle my ears."

This comment earned his contempt. "You can't pick up girls wiggling your ears."

The obvious question occurred to me, but I was shy about asking.

Stu went on, his voice dipping confidentially. "Your ears are not your best feature, Keen. You shouldn't draw attention to them."

Lila: She was the girl all the boys wanted to fuck. In any community of a certain size, there is always such a girl. I once worked in a landscaping crew, and we all wanted the foreman's wife. She wasn't beautiful or even particularly acceptable, but she was present and we liked the way she carried her tools.

Lila was pretty, but something about her life kept her discouraged and a little sour. She moped from room to room as if looking for her keys or purse, too preoccupied to respond to the typical direct address. Her body was bottle-shaped, but not Coke bottle. More like a flask. Yet every guy there wanted to get her square butt in bed. It might have been her slutty eyelids and the dark eyes they hid—eyes the color of bark but with a luster her attitude seemed to deny. I had a powerful sex drive in those days. My brain, bored without drugs, let my body have full rein, and it demanded Lila.

One day she told me that her first language was German, but she quit speaking it when she started kindergarten. Now she couldn't remember any of it—a whole language lost inside her. I thought maybe that was what she was looking for when she meandered about the house, the language she'd been born into.

After I'd lived there a month, and only then because she showed up in the green tube top, I realized Lila was the dead girl.

The dogs: Ruff, the golden retriever, was always happy to see you and generally optimistic about life, the way a dog ought to be. Ready, the terrier, reminded me of my third-grade teacher, who had her nose in our desks during recess, looking for something she could use to dim the day. Ready barked at the mailman. He barked at the neighbors. He barked at every single one of us who lived in the house. He barked at the sound of the toilet. A red hummingbird feeder in the backyard sent him into mad barking convulsions. Let in the house, he did laps around the kitchen, sniffing out disorder.

Ruff would wait by the tub when I got out of the shower and gently lick my legs, but Ready would sniff my toes, bark, and occasionally gnaw my Achilles tendon. Many evenings he would latch on to a pant leg and growl while whatever chump who got nabbed—often me—swung his leg back and forth, the little dog careening.

Val: A familiar kind of sweet-hearted addict who couldn't say no to anybody. She loved heroin because it let her remain kind. Her junk-sweet heart opened the house to any loser who came along.

Clete summed her up best: "Her dilemma is that she's alive."

One day she and I were in her room (the master bedroom, which seemed only fair), running a chisel around a window that wouldn't open. Without electricity, we relied heavily on breezes. After we got it loose and propped up a ski pole to keep it open, she told me she had learned the secret of masculine behavior.

It sounded like something I ought to know.

Her ex-boyfriend, a Mexican guy from Oklahoma, had told her that some nights he'd say anything to get a woman in bed and other nights he wouldn't fudge the truth at all. It could be the same woman, and he could be feeling the same desire.

"You're all bastards *and* saints," Val explained. "It's just a matter of luck which day matters—the one when you're being good or the one when you're bad."

I found out the Okie Mex confessed to this after breaking Val's nose in an argument over something stupid like who did the laundry last or what kind of vegetables are okay to feed a dog. The confession was his way of apologizing and letting himself off the hook.

When she finished her story, she went to the drawer in the nightstand where she kept her junk. She cooked the stuff in a glass tube over a Bunsen burner. (The boy had a chemistry set.)

"I'd offer you some," she said, "but Clete says I can't give you drugs."

"I don't shoot up anyway."

I'd only ever snorted heroin because I had a stubborn and wholly genuine fear of needles. Val listened while tying off with a paisley necktie from the closet, smirking only slightly and trying to hide it. I was touchy about this subject. As a teenager, I'd driven a hundred miles an hour in residential neighborhoods to prove I wasn't afraid of dying, just of needles.

I helped her slap her arm and hunt down a vein, but I couldn't watch the needle go in. She still wasn't convinced. Even when the rush hit her and she fell back on the floral bedspread, the look she gave me had near equal parts of ecstasy and doubt.

I told her about waiting in line at a county clinic to get a vaccination. I was maybe six and watched each kid ahead of me burst out crying. They give shots better now, but back then it was just swab and stab. When it was my turn, I lost it, kicking the doctor in the head and eyeglasses.

"I blacked out. My mother had to tell me what I'd done."

It had taken awhile to tell the story. Val had sunk into the lowest parts of her reclining body. She had to turn her head to make her lips work.

"It's not fear," she said. "Just weakness."

She meant it in a nice way, trying to defend me and doing such a lousy job of it that she pulled me on top of her and let me screw her.

While we were fucking I thought about how this junkie friend of mine from high school had died shooting pool. He fell onto the table after making the three ball. I think he was dead a couple of shots earlier, but his body kept on eyeing the cue ball and following through. He hit face-first, breaking a tooth, which I found and stuck in my pocket. We took his body to his parents' house and left it in the yard. I memorized the address, put the tooth in an envelope, and mailed it to them.

That experience let me see how weakness (we'll call it that for now) can be strength. None of that crowd went to his funeral but me. The family tried to have me arrested. "He was a friend," I told the cop. I didn't mention that mainly I wanted to see that tooth, which, sure enough, they'd glued back on. I know that sounds cold, but I couldn't really see his death as a tragedy. Not for me, anyway. I did almost cry a little, but the sunlight on his coffin had a spunky kind of brilliance, which made me happy to be alive and weak and wearing a suit.

I didn't tell Val this story while we were screwing, but I may have been distracted because when she couldn't come and could barely, for that matter, stay awake, she said, "Just go ahead. Don't wait for me."

A few minutes later, the ski pole slipped loose and the window slammed down with a bang, and I came so suddenly I didn't manage to pull all the way out.

"Don't worry about it," she told me. "That was really great."

Clete: Some months before Clete moved to the mountains, he and I went to our ten-year high school reunion and found ourselves at a party in somebody's crowded house. Twelve framed photos lined the dinner table, one for each of the dead in our class—all from drugs, or driving stoned into the giant saguaro by the post office, or drowning in a bathtub (that was about drugs, too), or falling over face-first onto a pool table. These were people we thought of as friends or at least people who wouldn't screw us over when we were too high to know better. They were all dead and it was a dull party.

Someone called Clete's name and then mine. It was a guy who we'd named the *Flirge* in high school because he was a liar and he'd smoke your pot without ever bringing his own or offering to go in on some. His family had a swimming pool, so we put up with him but no one liked him. One time we were in the pool (on acid but that doesn't have anything to do with the story) and the Flirge starts in all nonchalant about raping a girl, like it was this thing he'd done and he wasn't going to lie about it.

Clete gave me a doubtful look, then said, "Where'd this happen?"

"A parking lot," the Flirge said. The girl had passed out. He leaned her over a hood and did it to her from behind.

"What kind of car was it?" Clete asked.

"Black Mercedes," the Flirge said.

"That has a hood ornament." Clete is the kind of person you can't slip much past. "You wouldn't bend her over a hood ornament."

"We were on the side by the driver's door."

"Too high," Clete said. "You'd have to fuck on your tiptoes, which is fatiguing."

My point is, the Flirge was the kind of guy who lied about whether he had raped a girl, and he didn't chip in for drugs. You know the type.

He found us in this crammed full room and said, "I've been looking for you guys."

I was thinking, *Let's flee,* and giving Clete *Let's flee* looks. But

Clete was thinking, *People can change,* and he gave me a look that said, *If even the Flirge can shape up . . .*

"I got married last night," the Flirge said. He wanted us to meet his wife. "Wait right here?"

Sure, we said. The Flirge knifed through the crowd, so excited to introduce us to his wife that I was willing to believe Clete was right. We started enjoying the party more. Clete and I talked to a girl who'd had a thing for me in high school. Her husband had just got a job with NASA, and their firstborn was walking but not talking except for "muh" and "duh" for "Mom" and "Dad," and she had another bun in the oven right now. All the time, I was recalling how crazy she'd been for me and how that baby could be calling me "duh" and how that could be my bun in her oven, and it seemed like somehow I'd even given up a chance to be an astronaut.

I was straining to figure out why I hadn't liked her back when, but then I realized she was still talking and I remembered: she had a big mouth.

Was it worth not walking on the moon to avoid this fat mouth for the rest of my life?

Without question.　·

But it was a sacrifice, too. It seemed like I'd given up some portion of the heavens in order to have integrity and look for true love and avoid endless small talk.

About then the Flirge reappeared. The woman with him wasn't beautiful, but she had on a sweater that fit in a certain way, short happy hair, and a face you'd always like to see. I could tell she wasn't a big mouth by the way she smiled at people and walked close to her husband, and I thought, *What a weird honeymoon.*

I was also thinking the Flirge had made out all right. He'd turned a corner and would never pretend he'd raped a woman again, even if maybe he might bring cheap wine when you invited him to dinner or make waitresses figure separate checks. What's the big deal about that? In my head, I was commending Clete for recognizing this and thinking what a rare friend he was and also how I'd like to screw the Flirge's bride. I wanted to marry her. You can tell sometimes.

Here's the unbelievable part: I was happy for the Flirge. I felt a wide-open kind of gratitude that rarely descends on a person. I've been that happy maybe three times in my life. It thrilled me that such a loser could turn it around.

He led her right to us, but at the last second he looked away. He bumped into us as if it were an accident. Right then, I knew. He was still the Flirge and about to prove it.

"Hey," he said. "I want you to meet my wife." He leaned in close to us, made a quizzical face, and said, "What's your names again?"

Without even a second to register this, Clete moved his head right past the Flirge to his wife. He said, "You've just made the biggest mistake of your life."

She smiled for less than a second, less time than it takes for the television to come on after the remote is punched—that's how fast the human brain is—and then her features made tiny complicated twists and small turns. We left them like that.

I could tell you about a thousand other nights like that one, but the point is always the same: Clete is the kind of person who knows what it is to be alive and the knowledge causes him no shame. How many people in your acquaintance can you say that about?

The others: Many other people did stints in the dog-sitting house. A guy we called Skins slept on the couch without a sheet for a month and turned it brown. When he left he stole Stu's boom box, a weedeater, and two decks of cards. One guy—I don't remember his name—pretended to be an opera singer and made voicey proclamations about art. Another one—we called him Heller, which might have been his name—tried to prove he could levitate by sitting on the bathroom scales and showing us how his weight diminished the longer he meditated. Clete saw through the act. "His butt is sliding off the feet marks," he told me, but we didn't say anything to Heller, who had only that one trick. Another guy who insisted we call him Hawk liked to argue about whether the world was flat. "What?" I said. "It's a big conspiracy?" He explained: "Put a level on a field and that shows it's flat. That's what flat is. Sure, the planet is round, but the earth is flat." There was a chunky girl I won't name who went down on every guy in the place during her weeklong stay. Some of us tried to like her, but she had her own agenda.

Assignment 3: Family

Most nights we sat on kitchen chairs in candlelight immersed in some form of inebriation, and talked. The roof over the back porch had a leak that should have been fixed, but we liked to sit on the softening planks and breathe in the odor of the rain-sweetened wood. The morning sun dried it out, and the afternoon rain softened it again. The porch was like a great dark lung that would, days before the end of our summer, collapse.

One night on the porch has stuck with me. Clete got us going. "This man has to raise a boy who isn't his own son but his brother's, and the brother died because of this boy in a boy-caused auto accident or house fire or poisoning incident that kills the parents but not the boy. The man who has to raise him one day gets the hiccups and to get rid of them he drinks water upside down."

"Standing on his head?" I asked. I wasn't sure what kind of story it was.

"Like this." Clete got a glass and demonstrated, bending at the waist and drinking from the opposite rim.

"That really does get rid of hiccups," Lila put in. Several of us were on the porch.

"The boy watches him drink this way. And you have to understand that the man hates the kid because he's ruining his life. He doesn't want some diaper-needs-changing kid hanging around. Also he blames the death of his brother on the kid. He doesn't act outright mean to the boy, but it slips out.

"He sees the kid drinking this way and he encourages him. 'That's the way to drink,' he says. The boy goes around all the time drinking upside down. The man thinks it's funny to see this kid drinking upside down. He takes a mean pleasure in it."

"Insensitive bastard," Lila said. Stu and Val and some others were there, too."But what this does," Clete said, "is give him an outlet for his anger. It lets him get to know the boy. He feels sad for his brother and for the boy. When the kid is old enough to go to school, the man tells him, 'I was only fooling about drinking that way. You don't have to drink that way.' But the boy says, 'I like to drink this way.' The man says, 'Kids will make fun of you if you drink that way.' The boy says, 'I know, but this is the way we drink.' He raises a glass of water in toast and they bend over and drink upside down together, and the screen goes black."

"This was a movie?" I said.

"He's kind of a smart kid for kindergarten," Lila pointed out.

"They could be in some remote place where school starts later," Clete said.

"It's a beautiful story," Val said. "It's perfect just the way it is."

"It *is* a good story," Lila agreed.

Lila's respect for the story made me want to tell one of my own. I was drunk enough to just start off and see where it would go, but right as I opened my mouth I remembered a girl named Eve I used to know. She was a pal's girlfriend—beautiful girl with hair so pale we used to say it was the color of spit, and who was diagnosed with brain cancer and given six months. I visited her in the hospital after her surgery and she asked me to be one of her pallbearers. It's a hell of a thing for a living person to ask, especially a pretty girl no older than you with bandages on her head.

"Sure," I told her. "Doesn't look like you weigh too much."

That got a laugh out of her.

But she didn't die. Instead, she dumped my friend and got together with a guy who robbed convenience stores. They put together some money from their various robberies, and when she finished chemotherapy they moved to Alaska. I saw her once long afterward at that same high school reunion. Her hair had never grown back and she wore a scarf over her head, but she was still beautiful and married to the robber, who sold cars now and they had a summer cabin on the Oregon coast.

"What a time we had for a while there, huh?" she said to me.

We wound up sitting in her car and somehow started kissing. We had never done that before. I pulled my head back just a millimeter or so and spoke softly.

"They said you were going to die."

"Disappointed?" she asked.

We kissed some more. Maybe she wanted me to take her to bed, but that didn't happen, which led to my story petering out in a non-dramatic fashion.

"I remember her," Clete said once he was sure I was through. "She never did die."

"That's a lovely story," Val said.

"That robber guy," said Lila. "He thought it was just an adventure with a dying girl. But it was his whole life."

Anybody can go to a bar and hear some character complain how the world has never lived up to his potential and his own nowhere life is everyone's fault but his own. All you have to do is sit on the wrong stool. To get to the good stories, you have to make an effort. You have to become a regular part of someone's life and keep mostly to yourself so when you offer a word or answer a question she can see you're giving up something to talk to her. She starts to trust you, even *owe* you. You can't just sit next to a woman and expect this stranger to unfold her life like a shirt she's asking you to wear.

What I'm saying is, this was the first moment I thought Lila might like me.

Stu started in on a dream he'd had about deep water, a dental assistant, and walls in a room that flapped like the loose vinyl roof of an old car. I have opinions about other people's dreams. They tend to be like paintings by surrealists who don't have any goddamn imagination.

The dream ended badly (by which I mean it was tedious). He tried to redeem the story by wrapping his feet behind his head, which reminded me that he wanted Lila as much as I did. He didn't even have to get up from his chair, and just sat like that.

In situations like this we relied on Val to have a kind word, but even she couldn't comment. She did save him, though.

"I had a boyfriend who could bend his thumb flat against his arm," she said. "Like this." She bent her thumb flat against her arm.

Lila touched her nose with her tongue, inserting the tip in either nostril. We had to hold a candle up close to see, and we must have singed her hair. There was that burnt hair smell.

I told them about my idea of what makes a tragedy and how there really weren't many. A death (you can't have a tragedy without a corpse) could qualify only if it didn't once make you think: *I'm glad it's him and not me.*

Val disagreed. "We're all tragedies," she said. The assertion made her stand up and cross the porch. She sat on the ice chest, right across from me, and patted my knee. "But you told it really beautifully."

Clete took it a step further. "The real question is, What would you kill for? What would it take for you to claim the life of another person?"

"I'd never kill anyone," Val said. "Not for anything."

"Then that's who you are," Clete said.

"I tried to strangle my boyfriend when he wouldn't quit whistling," Lila said.

"Well," Clete said.

"That *can* be irritating," I put in.

"You weren't really trying to kill him," Val said. "You were just upset."

"It felt like I was trying to kill him."

"Then that's who you are," Clete said.

Stu spoke. He was sitting normal again. "The guy I get dope from sticks a gun barrel in my mouth every time I buy. To remind me what he'd do if I rat on him."

"*Every* time?" I said.

Stu nodded. "Some people won't deal with him for that reason."

"Bad business practice," Clete said.

"It tastes like oil," Stu said.

Our conversations felt like more than talk, as if we had made ourselves into a crew held together by something greater than happenstance or geography or the luck of free housing. I had the feeling we mattered as a group. Only to us, I guess, but I was happy with that.

I was happy.

Assignment 4: Accepting Responsibility

I found a metal detector among the kid's toys. Since I couldn't work and needed booze to stay sober, we hit upon the idea of combing the run under the ski lift for coins. The first day Clete and I found over nine dollars and barely made headway up the mountain. The lift was running, taking summer tourists up for views. Some of them tossed change down to us. We actually got most of the cash that way. The remainder of the summer was defined by this mountain we had to sweep. It gave us a goal and a direction: *up.*

We came home that first day tired and exuberant, bearing a frozen pizza (the oven was gas and hadn't been sold) and a six-pack. Screaming started as soon as we entered. We found Lila towel-wrapped in the bathroom screeching at the tub. Ready was bouncing his long nails on the porcelain, yapping. The terrier had carried a mouse into the tub where it couldn't escape and then tortured it to death. A mouse head lay by the drain, and Ready's bloody paw prints made the tub a crime scene.

Clete got toilet tissue and picked up the rodent remains.

"Good boy," he said to the dog.

Lila was too grateful to complain about our ogling her thighs and a portion of her hip where the towel parted. She even agreed to watch a movie with us after her shower, one of the videos that Stu had stolen from the library. Clete went to hook up the extension cord, and I hunted for the tape. When I couldn't find it, I sought out Stu. He was sitting on the cooler on the back porch smoking a joint, wearing my old coat.

"Where'd you get that coat?" I asked him.

"The Goodwill store behind the fire station."

"Find any drugs in the pockets?"

He eyed me suspiciously and then began thrusting his hands all over.

I didn't want the coat back. It was an important part of the life I'd left behind. While he was searching, I asked him about the videotape.

"How did you know?"

He'd found one of my trademark blimp-shaped joints.

"Never mind," I said. "Where's the movie?"

"I took it back," he said proudly, still rummaging. "Sneaked it back in. They never knew it was gone."

I suppose I pursed my lips.

"You know how a library works at all?"

"There's a fucking book in here," he said, meaning the coat.

Lila suggested we go to a bar. We didn't have any cash left from our day of detecting, so I took the elaborate Mickey Mouse clock from my room—which didn't work anyway without electricity—and we headed down to the secondhand store and then on to the Blue Board Tavern—a splintering hardwood bar that used to be a laundromat and still had a wall of dead dryers in the back, each staring out with its one enormous eye. The clock brought seven dollars.

The tables in the Blue Board were the color of ballpoint ink. We claimed one and started talking.

"I moved to this town because it's too small for me to turn tricks in," Lila announced. "People would talk."

"A sensible plan," Clete said.

"I live in fear of becoming a whore."

"Everyone with any judgment does." He then described my plan for self-improvement. I could sense myself rising in her esteem, but she directed the conversation back to Clete. She wanted to know why he had come to this place.

"It's beautiful here," he said. "Haven't you noticed?"

She gave him a look and maybe I was giving him the same look because she seemed to think of me as an ally. She and I got up and marched out into the street. A shower had passed over while we were drinking. The streets were slippery and glistening. The air was fresh and free of smoke. Without any warning, she took my hand and we walked to the middle of the town's empty thoroughfare, our eyes on the mountains.

Her hand in mine opened a window in my head, and a damp wind blew right through it. Above the paltry row of buildings, a forest ascended the mountainside, the trees green and vibrant. At the open end of the box canyon, the sun had dropped out of sight, but sunlight spotted the high trees, lit a distant waterfall, and colored the rock faces. What had we been thinking? The sky was shot through with turquoise and the last yelps of sunlight like a gaudy stone on a gold band.

"He's got us on this one," Lila said softly.

She clung to my hand as we went back into the bar, aware that we had been mutually grazed by the speeding, startled sensation of what it was to be a living creature.

"We won't forget again," I said as we made our way to the table.

"If we ever fail to look at those mountains," Lila said, "without realizing they're there, we should have to cut off our arms and legs and gouge out our eyes."

"You'd have to change the order," Clete said. "The arms shouldn't go first."

He had the bag of mushrooms on the table, dividing them into three equal parts.

"Doing this in a public establishment doesn't trouble you?" I asked.

"I picked these this morning, while you two and the rest of the mortal world were asleep," Clete said. "Anyone watching will just think we're earthy types."

We ate mushrooms and washed down the grit with beer. Lila surprised us with money of her own and bought pitchers. It occurred to me that Clete couldn't be sleeping much, as early as he was getting up.

"I sleep inside myself while I'm awake," he explained.

That pretty much got him rolling. He declared and philosophized, his mouth full, his brain brimming with thoughts and theories, observations and sidebars. We all talked excitedly for a while and then settled down to our communal swallowing and a happy gulping silence. The conversation, even after it was over, kept a good feeling swinging among us like the movement of a rocking chair after the person is up and gone.

Then Clete began afresh. "People want you to believe you treat a disease by identifying it and then killing it off with the right poisons," he said. "That requires a belief that the sickness and the person are two wholly separate entities. That's like thinking the clouds don't belong to the sky but are just happenstance passing through."

We nodded or made appropriate grunts. Now and again I'd realize that Lila and I were still holding hands.

"People who think about the world aren't usually violent, which leads me to assume that violent people don't consider the world around them," Clete said. "I knew a woman who liked to pretend she was the star of her own television program to the extent that she wouldn't swear because there's no swearing on television. She'd only have sex with the lights out. Everything she did took her to the next episode, and she'd think about how the show should end, editing her day down to its hour format.

"My point is, she may have been sick but she wasn't violent. As long as she imagined an audience and the Nielsen ratings hinging on her actions, she had to behave. Is that sickness separate from who she is, or the product of who she is?"

I started in on this teacher I had in high school, a delicate young woman who spoke so softly you had to strain to hear any portion of her speech. It was work to catch a single word. She walked around the room while she talked, and every head would follow her. She was easily the best teacher I ever had. After the winter break, she came back with a microphone and a speaker that hooked to her belt. We didn't have to strain to hear her, and it didn't take but a couple of class periods to understand she was no better teacher than the others. It was the quality of our attention that had been different.

"I was in that class," Clete said. "We read *Macbeth* and *Catcher in the Rye* and watched that *Romeo and Juliet* where Juliet does partial nudity. Miss Axelrod. You sat directly in front of me, and one day you had a condom stuck in your hair."

"Was it a Mr. Microphone?" Lila asked. "I had one of those in middle school."

"Another one of our teachers used to confuse me for my father," Clete said. "He was old and I don't think he was ever very bright, and he had taught my father. Now and then he'd call on *Everett*, as if I had become my dad. Which makes me think about that feeling of being transported, and how the weirdest thing—a kid like me sitting at a desk—can transport you thirty years, back to when you were young and had a brain and most of the time a hard-on, likely as not, for some junior girl in a short skirt you were supposed to be teaching."

This reminded me of the girl I dated when I worked construction who liked to call me Daddy while we were in bed.

"I remember her," Clete said. "Her family raised minks."

"What's your real name?" Lila asked me. "It can't be Keen, can it?"

"What does 'real' mean?" I shot back.

"What does 'name' mean?" Clete put in.

"What does 'mean' mean . . . mean?" Lila said.

What a night that was! We swept out of the bar and up and down the lighted streets, our arms linked in Gene Kelly fashion, smiling and shuddering with the joy of being the people who got to inhabit our very own bodies. Nighttime rinsed the light out of the sky, and we found ourselves on the bank of the dark little river that cut through the side of town opposite our house.

"Fish know water," Clete said, and we entered into a somber and wondrous bout of nodding. Lila and I may have wept a little.

Then we one by one began to add to the river from our own churning stomachs.

"I had no idea I was getting sick," Lila marveled. That set the tone for our happy retching. "Don't worry about hurting my feelings," she said. "If I'm pissing you off with this puking, just say so."

Clete found a tree we had to look at, a big winding thing with branches and leaves and a miraculous balance.

"It just erupts out of the earth," Clete said. "It goes up. What it means to be a tree is to send limbs up and roots down." He dropped to his knees and touched the base of the tree. "This is the center, right here. Touch the tree's heart."

We got down and fondled the bark.

"I had a boyfriend," Lila said, "who had a dog-and-pony show with a guitar at this café on weeknights. Not real singing but funny-talking kinds of songs about getting a life into which some rain must fall or fixing your car with chewing gum and spit. I took him for granted so much he wrote a song about a girl who cuts off her own nose."

"To spite her face," I said.

She shook her head. "To make her breathing holes bigger so it's less work to inhale."

We followed a crooked path that ran along the river, which was a shallow and fast-moving affair that made a gorgeous noise. We began hearing things in the river's music, voices and shouts and engines running. The rush of water seemed to give off sparks, which meant we were hallucinating but it didn't feel that way. It seemed instead that the river must always spark into the night air but usually we fail to see it. We were witnessing the daily miracle of moving water on a planet that was moving itself, spinning through the dark marvel of space.

We came upon a sandy bank often used as a party spot, and an actual voice called to us.

"*Pussy*," the voice called. "Here, pussy, pussy." Ratcheting laughter followed, and Barnett stumbled onto the path. "You're all pussies," he said, "especially him." He tried to look over his shoulder and nearly fell.

Stu lay on the bank, flat on his back, either sleeping or passed out. He was wearing my coat, which made me feel oddly proud and responsible, a little jealous, possessive, and nostalgic. I was feeling a lot.

Clete stepped off the path to put his ear to Stu's chest, while Barnett did almost the same thing with Lila's breasts, thrusting his face against her chest and clacking his teeth. She pushed him away and I took a swing at his chin, smacking him on the side of his head. He collapsed in such a complete fashion, Lila and I burst out laughing.

"He respires," Clete said of Stu. "But we're going to have to carry him home."

"What about this one?" I pointed at Barnett.

Clete bent over him and slapped Barnett's cheek. Barnett didn't rouse. Lila gave him a sharp kick to the ribs. He jerked and moaned, but he didn't wake up.

"He's the one who kind of raped me," she said to Clete and at the same time took my arm. She was explaining why I had slugged him, as if I'd known all along and acted out of gallantry.

While we were contemplating what to do, a crescent moon appeared above the dark line of the mountainside, and a coyote loped by on the opposite bank of the river, pausing to stare at us while we stared back at it, and then it continued on.

"Was that a wolf?" I asked.

"Coyote," Lila said. "I used to see them by the side of the road every morning when I worked at a bakery down valley. I've never seen one this close to town."

"It might have been a dog," I said.

"Or a vision of god," Clete said.

"I got fired from that job for stealing éclairs," Lila said. Then: "Why would god stare at us like that?"

"To remind us we're human," Clete said. "And he's human." He nudged Barnett's face with the round toe of his boot. "We can't leave him to the elements."

"Sure we can," Lila said. "Especially if god's got his eye on him."

She didn't want to wait alone with Barnett for fear he might come to. She hefted Stu's feet. Clete gripped him under the arms. They carried him off. I stayed with the inert Barnett, watching the stream, listening as its noise receded and a deep quiet settled in, a silence like I had never heard before. I couldn't even hear the thoughts in my head.

Clete tapped my shoulder, waking me. It seemed like he had just left, and he had. Stu had woken up before they reached town.

"Lila's staying with him in case he doesn't remember where he's going," Clete said. "You think we could wake this one?"

Barnett's body sprawled unnaturally on the sand, one arm trapped beneath his back and the other crooked over his neck, his face as white as porcelain, his mouth spread wide, the tongue not pink but the red of hard candy.

"I've got an idea," I said.

I was inspired by the need to pee. I unzipped and pissed on Barnett's face. His head rocked to one side and he puckered his lips expressively, but he didn't come to. After a while, it got pretty redundant but I hadn't peed all night.

"You could damage your bladder holding it so long," Clete said.

"Now what?" I asked.

"You were on the right track," Clete said. "Just thinking too small."

He grabbed Barnett's hands and I took hold of his feet. We rocked him back and forth a few times to get some distance and hurled him into the river. He made a big splash. His body dipped below the surface, then bobbed back up.

But he didn't stand. The current pushed him downstream. The reflection of the moon played over his body.

Clete and I scrambled after him along the river's edge, and then we each waded out into the icy water after him.

Barnett eddied briefly near a wide spot, twirling facedown, but the water was deeper there and Clete and I each fell trying to reach him. By the time we were on our feet again, the current had reclaimed him. We tromped through the water, high stepping and flailing. Clete dived for him, but the river kept him just out of our reach.

I gave up at the footbridge, climbing up to watch his form slide away, shivering in the night air, not at all sure I had the strength or warmth to make it up the hill to the house.

Clete, though, kept on, ducking under the bridge and skipping down a little rapids, somehow remaining vertical. I heaved myself off the bridge and trotted along the river's edge, my legs aching and beginning to wobble.

At a bend in the river, Clete fell and when he got up the current knocked him down again. I went in after him and dragged him out. Barnett was out of sight.

"I don't feel so good about this," I said.

"It's some consolation that he was an asshole," Clete said, "but we really shouldn't have killed him."

That was the full extent of our eulogy for Barnett. How and

whether we were going to make it home was playing with our minds. We crawled along the riverbank, debating whether it might be warmer to remove our wet clothing.

"I don't see how it could be colder," I said.

"Point taken."

Clete laid himself flat on the high river grass to undo his belt and jeans. The river had taken his shoes and one sock. I had both my shoes but only one sock, which was puzzling.

"You're not a careful dresser," Clete said.

We left our clothes in a pile, and worked our way across town and home. A few people pointed. They were the only people on the streets. Fortunately, Lila was on the back porch with Val when we came in. We dried off and dressed and were standing beside the open and roaring kitchen oven by the time she realized we were home.

"Stu's fine." She offered me her hand and I took it. "Where's the jerk?"

"He slipped off," Clete said somberly, stepping away from us. He left the kitchen.

"Is something wrong?" she asked.

I kissed her and shut off the oven.

"I need to lie down," I said.

We kept kissing and holding each other, bumping through the house. It sounds heartless and insensitive to say I forgot about Barnett drowning and drifting downstream like a log, but kissing Lila combined with my own near-drowning incident to erase it from my head. I sank back into the night as it had been before we killed him. Lila and I rambled through the house holding hands so deliriously that we became one creature and stumbled together into the bathroom to pee.

Stu was on the toilet, wholly conscious and masturbating by candlelight.

"Don't you ever knock?" he said, turning the page of a comic book: *Daredevil*.

That was the last little push we needed. Lila followed me to my bedroom and climbed between the sheets of my car.

"Promise me . . . ," she said.

I waited for the rest of it a long while. Finally I just said, "I promise."

Assignment 5: Understanding Mistakes

The same night that Clete and I killed Barnett, Lila and I became lovers. The next day she retreated a little. I found her in the kitchen writing in a notebook—her diary. She glanced at me and went back to her penmanship. I said good morning in an overly jolly voice. She lifted a hand without looking up. When I went to the faucet to get a drink of water, she hunched over the journal. All I could read were the words *my right mind*.

Clete and I worked the slope that day with the metal detector, but he was not his usual self. We discussed what he called "the slaying" in undertones.

"Stu remembers almost nothing," Clete said.

"We should have told Lila."

I waved the metal detector, and Clete searched wherever it beeped.

Clete shook his head. "Then she'd be a party to it. She'd have to turn us in or accept a portion of the blame. I went this morning and got our clothes. They're on the back porch drying."

A couple on the ski lift called out to us and threw down coins. We waved to them and walked to the spot where the change had fallen.

"I went back to where we tossed him in," Clete said. "I wanted to look for footprints and so on, but people were camping there. They must have come in the middle of the night."

"My pee is there," I said. "Can they use that to convict me?"

Clete didn't think so. "I'm more concerned with what Lila will want to do once the body is found. She's the only one who can point a finger."

"She may be having second thoughts about being my girlfriend. She wasn't what I'd call affectionate this morning."

"She's not a morning person," he said. The detector beeped, and he fingered the grass. "The other thing is the coyote. We were given an omen, and we still screwed up."

"I guess I really shouldn't have pissed on his face."

"Look at this." Clete lifted a hotel key from the grass. "This is another sign."

"The guy just emptied his pocket," I said.

Clete straightened and held the key up above his head.

"We're being given another chance. We aren't lost yet."

We showed the key to the lift operator, and he let us ride to the top of the slope. It was not the top of the mountain but a ridge several hundred feet above the town. Clete spotted our couple standing at the overlook. I let him talk to them. I hadn't been up this high before and wanted to take in the view. I located our house and the library, the bakery, the hardware store, the diner, the piece of road where I'd first held Lila's hand, and the sandy spot by the river where we'd killed Barnett. It seemed to me that I was getting to know this place.

Clete took his time returning the key. For a terrible moment I thought he might be confessing. I decided to sweep the area near the lift's exit. I found a nickel right off. Then nothing for a long time. The platform was wooden and slatted, and I got a beep at the edge. It could have been a nail, but I got on my knees and worked my fingers between the slats. I came up with a gold band—a wedding ring.

Clete returned waving a twenty-dollar bill. "I told him good deeds were their own reward, but he tossed the bill on the ground. He goes, 'You scavenge for coins, don't you?' I figured he had me."

I showed him the gold ring.

"There's *your* omen," he said. "Figure out what to do with it."

That evening, Lila sat beside me at the kitchen table while we ate the frozen pizza that we had brought home the day before. It had thawed and it cooked funny, but we ate it. A fly fisherman had found Barnett's body two miles downstream. The news was all over town.

Lila asked us exactly what happened.

"Don't lie to me," she warned.

We told her the truth, although I left out the part about pissing on his face.

"How hard did you try to save him?" she demanded.

Clete led her outside where our ravaged clothes were draped across the porch railing.

"If Keen hadn't saved me, I would have wound up in a liquid grave myself."

"The current took him," I said. "We couldn't catch up."

She squinted thoughtfully. "He had the kind of body that looked like it would float."

I understood this was meant to corroborate our story.

"We couldn't just leave him there," I said.

She considered this calmly, which reminded me that she'd hated Barnett and had tried to kill her ex-boyfriend for whistling. But when we returned to kitchen table, she said, "Why didn't you just carry him up the hill?"

Clete and I sat on that one for a while.

Finally I said, "Given the advantage of hindsight, that does seem the better plan."

"There it is," Clete said sadly. "What it would take for us to kill a man. We didn't want to carry the little weasel up the hill."

Lila said, "He didn't have the kind of body that looked like it weighed much."

"We're guilty of something," Clete said.

"Something *ugly*." She stood abruptly, knocking over her chair. "Don't tell Stu," she said. "Or Val."

We agreed. She took my hand and led me up to my bed.

"Human life," she said.

I didn't know whether she was talking about us or Barnett dying. We crawled onto the single mattress together. We fucked and fucked and fucked.

I wish I could say Barnett's drowning was the end of our association with death. Clete would later argue that tossing him in the drink had pried open mortality's door. That's maybe why we both felt responsible a few days later when Val woke up dead. She let out an otherworldly grunt that somehow each of us heard—Clete on his mat in the hallway, and Lila and I in our narrow convertible. We all jumped up, me in nothing but a T-shirt and the morning erection, Lila in my boxer shorts, one of her pale arms across her breasts. Clete was fully dressed. We followed him to the master bedroom. The smell was identifiable and unpleasant—excrement on flesh. Val's mouth and eyes were open. I thought of the first night I met Lila, seeing her dead on the stairs, which made me unsure.

"Anything we can do?" I said.

Lila cried, "She's dead, you moron!"

Clete touched Val's cheek, and then said, "It's up to us to care for the dogs."

No one wanted to redeem the sheets. We wrapped her in them and toted her down the stairs and out to the porch, where we ran into Stu, who had been up all night smoking dope and watching the backyard. He was wearing my coat.

"Is that real?" he said, meaning the body.

"It's Val," Clete said. "Help us get her over the rail."

I wound up with Val's head. Stray hair sticking out from the wrap bothered me in a way I can't describe. Clete hefted her mid-section, seemingly oblivious to the damp, unhappy odor. Lila and Stu carried her legs and feet. When we stopped to rest, I tucked Val's curls inside the sheet, careful not to glimpse her face.

Clete guided us up a difficult makeshift path in the hazy light of dawn. We switchbacked through an aspen grove and found an actual trail, which guided us up above the trees. We left the path and scrambled to Clete's mushroom patch. He had a shovel stashed there, and while he retrieved it we set Val down carefully. It seemed almost inconceivable that this unpleasant-smelling lump was our friend.

We took our time picking a spot with a good view of town and the rim of mountains on the other side of the box canyon. Clete had each of us lie there to get a feel for it. We huddled together on the ground and stared at the cloudless sky, the entire world busily getting on with creation all about us.

Perhaps, here, I should mention that our burying Val without an official ceremony or license or even a coffin is a crime I have not, technically speaking, confessed to. I'm leaning on your (legally binding) pledge of confidentiality, and acting on your encouragement to be frank. The truth is, none of us even considered calling the authorities. A heroin overdose encourages questions and inquiries and search warrants, which would have opened our lives up to a form of scrutiny we did not covet.

The digging was hard. At one point, I threw the shovel back like an ax to swing it down against the unforgiving earth, and I hit Clete in the forehead. He staggered backward.

"Sister Christ," he said. A moment later, he added, "I'm all right."

I apologized and kept digging. The hole did not look like a grave. Its sides were jagged, the walls far from perpendicular. But Val's body was small and fit nicely. We filled in around the body and patted down the dirt. She didn't make much of a mound. We dug up some plugs of grass and tossed them on the grave to combat erosion.

"One of us should say a few words," Lila suggested.

The job fell to Clete. "Val," he began and hesitated. None of us knew her last name. He was bleeding. The shovel blade had opened a wound directly above his nose. Blood and black earth marked it. "Dog sitter, landlady to the lost, junkie, snorer, a former honor student. A woman who fed dogs. Who gave them their heartworm pills."

The list was long. Spread out beneath us lay one of the wealthiest small towns in America, peaked roofs covered in real shingles, rambling condominium compounds, satellite dishes, green lawns, and the shining windows of Main Street, which looked like forgotten pockets of brilliance, the spare change of some lazy god glistening in dawn's slanting light. Those windows radiated intelligence, a careless and irreplaceable genius among the ordinary stucco and frame. They made me think of the discontinuous luster of Clete's splendid brain.

"Lover of sadness," he was saying, "keeper of the damned."

I was so grateful to have him with us.

Thunder sounded, which seemed appropriate but didn't please

us. The rain began. We stalled, feeling we ought to say or do more and yet eager to make our way down the mountain. We were united in the essential embarrassment of needing to go on living.

"I can't believe this is happening," Lila said, weeping. "Who *dies?*"

The sky rippled with light and split open like a walnut.

A few weeks later, after a flood of guilt and worry and actual rain, I returned to Val's grave, which was now covered with mushrooms. I ate them. I'd consumed enough to know the ones to avoid. Sitting by her grave site, recalling her generosity with me from the moment I met her, I thought maybe I should have done a little better by Val. I felt sick about it, and then I understood that I was actually sick. I'd eaten poison mushrooms and was dying.

I lay down over the grave. We, Val and I, were neighbors again. I rocked against the moss and earth to get comfortable, the two of us together, lying as if in bunks, shipmates in the hold of a great vessel. My body would melt into this ground and sink down through the soil and through the bones of Val and on down to the rock, where it would pool and be reabsorbed into the planet. And it meant nothing. All we thought about and did, whether we behaved well or badly, the hard days when we could barely stand up straight and the good days when every sound and shade of light seemed a gift— none of it mattered. Val and I were the waste any kind of life leaves behind, the proof of imperfection that everywhere marks this world like the wounds on this very mountain left from the mining days. I had done not one thing with my life that had real consequence for anyone but the many people I'd disappointed and the one person I'd killed. I lay there, knowing that for a few minutes more I would see the sky, hear the minor havoc created by the breeze, smell my own rank and dying body, and the world would not take any notice. I meant nothing.

"Feeling morbid?"

Clete appeared above me, huge as the sky. He had that talent you can't teach—how to be wherever it is you're needed most. He'd come to harvest the mountainside but saved my life instead.

"I ate poisonous mushrooms," I told him.

He slipped his hand behind my neck and made me sit. He inserted his other hand in my mouth, which made me gag and vomit.

"You're fine now," he said, and he was right. I'd taken a short journey in the direction of death, and I'd come back.

Assignment 6: Mental Health

I ran into Barnett in a bar later that summer, a couple of weeks after his body had been mailed off to his miserable parents. He slouched on the next bar stool. I didn't know what to do.

I decided to ignore him and drink my beer. A tap on my arm made me turn. Barnett slugged me on the cheek. I was knocked back but didn't fall off my stool. Even in the afterlife, he wasn't what you'd call brawny. He kept pushing with his fist against my cheek. The drunk on the other side of me threw his arm out to catch me. For a moment, Barnett's fist pressed my head into the drunk's embrace and held it there.

The bartender nabbed Barnett by the collar. It was a working-man's bar, and they were quick to take action. Barnett was identified as the offender and hustled out the door.

"You know him?" the bartender asked, setting a free mug of beer before me.

"Kind of." I didn't want to reveal that I had recently killed him.

The man who'd caught me, a guy with tiny eyes like they'd been pecked in his face by a medium-size bird, said, "Maybe he doesn't like your face."

"That would explain it, I guess."

I understood at that moment why killers so often poke a hole in their best-laid plans by yapping about it in a bar. It isn't to unburden the soul but to prove your superior knowledge of the subject matter.

I finished my beer and hiked up toward the house, meeting Clete and Lila and Stu coming down. They were taking the dogs for a walk. Since Val had died, Clete had taken over their care. He conversed with them and had begun reading to them: the Bible, newspaper articles, a book on UFOs, and *Harry, the Dirty Dog*, which was their favorite. He had told them about the source of the water that came from the tap and now he wanted to take them on a hike to a high stream fed by a deep snowpack so they could see it.

"They should know this stuff," he said, inviting me to join them.

I didn't talk about my encounter with Barnett until we'd passed through town and started up the trail on the other side of the river.

They were understandably skeptical.

"He hardly had a personality," Stu pointed out. "No way he's a spirit."

"It was Barnett," I said, although having to put the story in actual words had made it sound unlikely even to me. My jaw hurt, though, which was comforting.

"Somebody or thing popped me in the jaw," I insisted, reminding them that I'd identified him as Barnett before he punched me. Why would a stranger hit me? What are the odds of that? Ghost seemed more probable.

"So you're the kind of person," Lila said, "who sees a creature from the beyond and just goes on and drinks his beer?"

We were on a trail that took us out of the city and into a mountain canyon. A stream bisected the canyon. It had been loud and fast earlier in the summer but was little more than a trickle now. Time was passing. The summer would end. The people who owned the house would come back, wondering where their house sitter and major appliances were. We'd have to move on.

Clete said, "Seeing Barnett is another sign. A major one. Could be you created it with your own brain, but it doesn't matter."

"My brain bruised my jaw?"

"The mind is a powerful instrument."

That set Stu off. "That's nothing. Someone's mom in Singapore or Taiwan City lifted a bus to get it off her kid. Her brain squat-lifted a bus."

"Other people in the bar saw Barnett," I said.

"Nobody ever lifted a *bus*," Lila said. "A taxi, maybe. Were there passengers?"

"I made a girl call out my name one time," Stu said, "just by using my mind and wishing her to do it."

"You were about to sit on a burning log," Lila said, turning to us. "He was warming himself at the fireplace and forgot."

"We ought to make a fire tonight," I said. "It's cold enough."

"I wasn't talking about *you*," Stu said to Lila. "You're not the only girl on the planet."

"If it was a real ghost . . . ," Clete began and paused to think.

Stu said, "Why would Barnett's ghost want to slug you, anyway?"

A conspicuous silence ensued. We all quit walking.

"Who are we to speculate on the motives of the newly dead and/ or undead?" Clete asked.

He reversed direction and began heading down the mountain. The dogs had got ahead of us on the trail, and we went back without them.

Assignment 7: Educational and Financial Plans

Stu wore my coat all the time, even in the warmth of daylight. Clete called him "the old you." As in, "I know you're ready to sell the dinette set, but what's the old you think?" Or "If I left it to you and the old you, the dogs would starve."

The old you got caught selling library books at the used bookstore and was fired.

"I've enrolled at Colorado State, anyway," Stu said. "I can get seven thousand dollars in student loans. Add that to my savings and I can be a student for a year."

We had a party to say good-bye. Each of us did an imitation of him coming out of his PCP blackout, performances that he loved. When we were out of his earshot, Clete argued that Stu was never the same after the coma.

"I didn't know him before," I said.

"He was different," Clete explained.

Otherwise, the party was pretty much an ordinary night. They smoked dope and drank; I drank. We listened to Stevie Ray Vaughan and the warbling female singer who had been on the boom box when Clete and I first entered the house. She was Lila's favorite, and we were a democratic crowd.

Six days after he left for college, Stu came back.

"Snafu," he said, taking off his shoes and socks in the living room to chew his toenails.

I wasn't quite sure whether he meant some mistake had forced him to drop out, or it was a mistake for him to even try college. I wondered and wanted to ask, but he had locked onto his big toe—the thumb toe—and the time didn't seem right.

"We kept your room just the way it was," Lila told him.

We were tougher on wayfarers than Val had been. Usually there were only the four of us, plus the dogs. Clete explained to the dogs the hazards of running off versus the rewards of travel, and then nightly he opened the door and shooed them out.

"They'll never learn otherwise," he said.

Ready continued torturing mice in the tub. Clete had determined that the dog climbed from the wicker basket next to the toilet, up onto the toilet seat, up to the tank, and then down into the tub. It was an impressive stunt with a mouse in your mouth.

One morning I found Lila on her hands and knees in the bathroom wearing white panties and the shirt I'd given her on the night we met when I thought she was dead. She was cleaning the tub with the dish sponge. We'd been lovers more than a month. I liked her butt a lot—the whole bottom half of her body. For that matter, everything from the neck down.

"That's the kitchen sponge," I pointed out.

She wasn't really getting up the blood, anyway. Ready had slung this one around decisively. He was a weird dog, and this had become his pathetic ritual of self-worth. We'd hear the frantic scrambling of the mouse and then hateful paws against the porcelain every third or forth night. Stu had commented, "The bathtub is always changing colors," but we were generally content to toss the dog out of the tub and let the blood wash down the drain while we showered.

Lila liked baths and was not content, but she wasn't really cleaning the tub, just moving the blood around.

"You need to run some water," I told her.

"There's an idea," she said, scrubbing no harder.

Since burying Val we'd had tension in our relationship. Lila would grip my arm in the night and say, "We should have called for an ambulance. What if she could have been revived? What if we buried her alive?" I didn't have a good answer. All I could do was remind her that Clete had been with us. "He was stoned," she said, "and he doesn't sleep." I didn't have an answer to that either, but it comforted me that Clete had been with us.

You really couldn't do a worse job with mouse blood in a white tub than what she was doing.

"That's my shirt, you know," I said.

Without facing me, she whipped it off, buttons pinging off the porcelain. She tossed the shirt in the tub and used it to direct the blood toward the drain. I was torn between the glancing view I had of her hanging breasts and wanting to plant my foot in her behind. We each reminded the other of what was completely wrong with us and couldn't be fixed. It made me hate the sight of her and also seek her out.

"You want to get married?" I asked right then. I still had the ring I'd found with the metal detector. It was in my pocket.

Her head swiveled around. A glare from the girl in the panties. She went back to the blood.

"I guess," she said.

Assignment 8: Emotional Support

The wedding obscured the fact that the dogs had gone out one night and not come back. Clete's faith in their intelligence kept him from worrying initially. Then we were busy setting up a ceremony. Lila, I discovered, got checks general delivery from her parents. She paid for the license and the justice of the peace, who did the official business, but I asked Clete to say some words.

"We are gathered here to unite in marriage Lila and Keen," Clete began. "Others may be seated." Stu and the justice of the peace sat down.

"Any time people gather to witness the joining of man and woman in wedlock," Clete said, "certain questions come to mind. A: What do we know about these people? B: Why have they decided to make this commitment of a lifetime? C: How in this age of divorce have they found the courage to make the leap of faith it takes to marry?"

He paused, as if to field answers. No one raised a hand.

"A: About the bride and groom, we know nothing. We may know details of their lives, but none of us knows what lies in their hearts. This marriage is a pledge of each to the other, that he or she will plumb the depths of her or his heart. We do not marry because we know the other. We marry because we desire to know the other.

"B: Also a mystery. Commitment is the function of marriage, not a prerequisite. Let's zero in twenty, thirty, or, health permitting, fifty years from now. These two will have discovered their answer. For the moment, theirs is not to wonder why but to answer the wild demands of their hearts and loins.

"C: More mystery. Consider that the bride didn't know the groom until two months ago. Consider that the groom's behavior over the summer has been less than ideal. Consider, too, that both the bride and groom are dropouts and unemployed. You might think it's an absolutely stupid time for them to marry."

He paused again.

"But the problem with 'why' is that love knows no why. Love knows only *yes*. Only *I must*. Only *this is and must continue to be*. Only *now*. If Romeo and Juliet had been willing to put things off a bit, they could have run off successfully. They were stupid not to. Yet their love wouldn't have been the great thing it was. Is it better to die for a great love than to live in a tepid one? Love—" He hesitated. The office door was open, and a couple of secretaries and one marshal had stopped to listen. He waved them in. They joined the ceremony. Clete picked up where he'd left off. "Love demands of us not sacrifice because nothing matters but the beloved. It demands of us not promises of fidelity regardless of health or wealth, because neither money nor physical suffering matters in the face of that love. Love demands only one thing: our stupid willingness to give over to it. It's a dumb thing to do, and it's the thing which, more than anything else, ennobles us.

"Do you, Lila, take Keen with all the stupid and hopeless love that you can offer?"

Lila said that she did.

"Do you, Keen, take Lila with that same dumb, blind love?"

"I do," I said.

"By the power vested in this man over here, who will speak presently, I afford to you all the rights and privileges and chores accorded to all brides and husbands, partners and lovers, sweethearts and pals."

Clete kissed first the bride on the lips and then the groom (me).

The JOP kept his part short, and we were out the door.

Assignment 9: Decision Making

We spent our wedding afternoon in the master bedroom, which we'd moved into after Val's passing. The honeymoon ended after ten minutes of sex and an hour nap. Clete stuck his head in and called my name. Sweat dotted his forehead. He had the dim, scared look of a survivor.

"What's with you?"

"We have to go to the dog pound," he said. "We need money."

Ruff and Ready had lost their collars long before Clete and I arrived at the house. The pound had already held them beyond the normal three days. Charges had accrued, one hundred thirty-five dollars each to free the dogs. If they weren't out by 5:00 p.m., they would be destroyed.

Even after the ceremony, Lila had a hundred and twelve dollars. Clete had spent his money on our wedding present (an antique ceramic sculpture of a Greek orgy). I'd spent my money on a haircut and a clean shirt. Stu had not properly registered at Colorado State. His student loan had been denied. He'd spent his savings on the trip over and back. He owed all of us money. We had enough to save only one dog.

"This is damnation territory," Clete said.

His words were like worms in my ears. I had to literally shake my head.

"Which one do we save?" I said this many times on the walk to the pound.

Clete wouldn't answer.

The pound guy's name tag read "Carl Dernl." He wouldn't budge.

"Some people shouldn't own dogs," he said.

Clete put his arms around me. He slid one hand down and stuffed the bills in my pants pocket.

"Pick one. Whichever choice you make, I'll support it."

He took a big breath and left me with the lolling, trusting tongue of Ruff on my palm, and the jittery nipping of Ready at Carl Dernl's institutional pant leg.

How I decided on my wedding day which dog would live and which would die I can't entirely explain until I admit that Barnett probably had redeeming characteristics that I had failed to evaluate or notice at all. Lila, I should add, often decided that someone had "kind of raped her," a way to forgive herself for crawling into bed with guys she didn't really know. Stu liked drugs, and it wasn't entirely Barnett's fault that Stu had no common sense and snorted so much PCP he toasted his brain. For that matter, Barnett never did anything to me or Clete. He wasn't a good person, but we should have been more careful with his mortal package.

"I've got a life," Carl Dernl said. "Make your decision."

The great eye of god saw into me. I felt whatever humanity I'd mustered trolling out and filling the room like a sacred and noxious gas. I breathed as much of it back in as I could. I hated Ready and loved Ruff. For that reason I felt I had to save Ready. Otherwise, the decision was too individual, which lacked respect for the size and weight of the decision.

I can't explain it any better than that. I took the miserable little dog home with me.

Assignment 10: What I've Learned

On the day the family whose house we had trashed, bartered, and partially destroyed called from the airport, Lila and I took Ready with us to the bus stop. Clete said we were obliged.

"If there's one dog here, they'll know the other is dead and they'll suffer. If they're both gone, they'll assume Val kidnapped them, and they'll just be angry."

Clete and Stu stayed on the mountain. I don't know how they avoided arrest. Maybe the authorities never looked for anyone but Val. The bus driver was the same one who dropped me at the lookout, but he didn't recognize me. Lila and I rode all the way to Las Cruces, New Mexico. Lila's sister lived there and had an extra room. I still didn't think I could risk working, but Lila got on at a florist shop. She likes flowers. We're still officially married, even now.

For a year, we got by. We heard reports about Clete, but we didn't have a way to reach him. About Stu, we didn't even hear rumors. One night Lila and I went to see a band called Sawed Off and Sewn Back Together at a bar in El Paso, Texas, forty-five miles away. Lila's sister was there, too, and went home with a Cuban medical student. We had to take Ready with us and leave him in the backseat. He barked if left alone, and the landlord had already given us a warning. I was the better drunk driver and took the old two-lane home to avoid the highway patrol. The road meandered by small towns and cut through a pecan grove. Lila was passed out in the backseat when I drove her sister's car into an abutment for an irrigation canal. It smashed the front end pretty good on the passenger side, but Lila and I were unhurt.

The accident only temporarily woke her up.

"I'm sorry," she said to me, "but I can't keep my eyes open."

She crawled out of the ruined car and trudged off into the pecan orchard to sleep. After sitting in the wrecked car long enough to count my legs and arms and other important features, I decided to join her. I had to climb over the seat and use the back door to get out. I found her lying beneath the limbs of a pecan tree. I laid my body beside hers. The stars in the river valley were as bright and numerous as they had been on the mountain, shining down on us without judgment or even interest.

I hadn't thought to see if Ready was hurt. He bled to death while Lila and I slept on the damp earth. That's how I wound up killing both of the dogs left in our care. But Ready had lived for a year with

Lila and me. How can you put a value on that? (Keep in mind that's seven people years.)

I had to deal with the sheriff the next morning, but I had sobered up and claimed a blown tire. He had totaled an El Dorado one time after a blowout and was sympathetic. The tire had actually blown *after* we hit the concrete, but I reversed the order. I caught some flack for my expired insurance, but the incident didn't get me into legal trouble. The abutment was not damaged in any way but the cosmetic, and how good does concrete have to look?

Lila and I got through the towing, the legal papers, and the pet burial. The wreck was an incident that could have been a disaster but wasn't. Lila's sister even found an old Isuzu pickup one of her friends wasn't using that we could drive. But Lila kept thinking about Ready bleeding to death while we slept. She was convinced if she'd stayed awake or I had a brain, we could have saved him. Before long she quit sleeping altogether, which affected her floral arranging. Then one day she told me she had to turn me in for Barnett's death.

"I'd really rather you didn't," I said.

"Not sleeping can make a person crazy."

I couldn't tell whether she meant she'd go crazy or that she already had and turning me in would be the proof of it.

"You keep killing people," she said.

Her list started with Barnett, of course, and included Val, which I had nothing directly to do with, and Ruff, who technically wasn't a person, and Ready, who wasn't even a good dog. Logic, however, had little weight in this argument. We talked for a long time. I made several good points, and she agreed to think it over a few days.

But she didn't sleep again that night and in the morning, an hour or so after she left for work, the same sheriff who had been nice to me in the groves knocked on the front door.

"I hate to bother you," he said, "but your wife came by and told me you'd murdered a man."

"I wouldn't call it murder," I said, which I realize now was a slip.

It was a friendly arrest but handcuffs are required in such proceedings, and I was pretty down about the whole episode. I plea-bargained my way into this cell for three years with good behavior, eligible for parole after nine months.

It's been eight months and counting.

It's an irony, I suppose, that Barnett is in this same prison. He's a jackal and you shouldn't give him parole, but he's the closest thing to a friend I have in here—and he's a dead man. He tells me things. Like that Stu moved to West Virginia after he left the mountain. He started a Mexican restaurant, got married to a kind woman, and they have a baby. This was Barnett's way of showing me I'd misjudged him. He'd kept up with Stu while I hadn't, even though I had the advantage of being alive.

When Clete visited, he arrived in the early morning, strolling down the concrete corridor with the rolling stride of a man familiar with confinement only in the abstract. His head was well above those of the guards who led him, and he sniffed at the prison air experimentally. Despite his years in the van, true confinement wasn't an odor he knew.

The white scar on his forehead, where I had hit him with the shovel blade, had taken the form of a crescent moon. His eyes were calm, his nostrils wide and pink. He stood straight and walked easily, not with the phony, inflated carriage of incarcerated men. There was no fear in his spine. He was tall and poised, a fully developed human male. Clete was an adult, and I suddenly understood that I had personally been acquainted with only a very few real adults in all my life.

"Even though this place is exactly as I was led to expect," he said, "it's also a lot worse. You must be miserable."

I told him that I was and at the same time it was okay.

We didn't talk about my keeping him out of prison. Clete is not his real name. I could have gotten less time by divulging it, but neither Lila nor I would do that.

Instead, he said, "You made the right decision saving Ready." He had told me this before. "You picked the hard road." I thanked him for that, and he moved to a different subject. "The man's family," he said, and I understood he was talking about Barnett, "has moved to Portland, Oregon. His mom and dad and one little sister. A ranch-style house with an unkempt lawn. I rented a mower and took care of it. I would have trimmed the hedges, but I couldn't find rental clippers."

I asked him about Lila.

"She's getting a lot of sun. Her skin is golden. She may move back in with her mother or maybe with me."

I know you can check the visitor roll and see that I haven't had any visitors whatsoever. I'm not trying to fool you. It's just that there's only so much you can feel, and the rest you have to pretend. I felt for the dogs and Val. To feel for the man, it helps me to have a messy lawn to think about and the presence of my friend.

Clete understands me. He would know that the darkness of this place and the terrifying movement of my life into it have bruised my marriage and maybe even my mind. I hear things through the open window: automobile engines claiming combustion, the human jingle of voices, the shattering of leaves on windy days.

Clete would look me over in these ridiculous overalls, my hair shaved short, and he'd nonetheless recognize me. He'd raise his arm and point.

"K-k-k-*Keen*," he'd say.

This is as close as I can come to saying what I've learned: you can't know whether what you're doing will have good consequences or bad. So there's nothing to do, I guess, but to obey the law and slough off the responsibility there.

There is one last thing I remember: all the dogs in town barked at us—at Clete and me—when we walked to the party that first night not knowing what we were getting into, that I would meet my wife and think her dead, that we would wind up killing both the pets, that Val would become our friend and die, that we would manslaughter Barnett, that I would get a new name and make a life for myself that I could survive—but it would lead to a drowning, an overdose, pet fatalities, an automotive crash, and incarceration. The dogs barked, and the windows showed their watery light, and we walked fearlessly up the hill and into the best and worst parts of our lives.

Which pretty much wraps things up. The decision is all yours now.

Am I a threat to society?

I await your decision.